CW00553807

£2·00

3/23

Josephine Hammond grew up in Africa from being an infant in Sudan, moving to Nigeria for most of her childhood and more recently living briefly in Kenya.

She taught French and Italian at University College London and after many years teaching turned to writing.

She has published three books *Battle in Iraq, Adelina Patti Queen of Song* and *Wilderness and Paradise. Africa in my Heart* is her first work of fiction.

To the wildlife of Africa and those protecting it.

Josephine Hammond

AFRICA IN MY HEART

AUSTIN MACAULEY PUBLISHERS™

LONDON * CAMBRIDGE * NEW YORK * SHARJAH

Copyright © Josephine Hammond 2022

The right of Josephine Hammond to be identified as author of this work has been asserted by the author in accordance with sections 77 and 78 of the Copyright, Designs and Patents Act 1988.

All rights reserved. No part of this publication may be reproduced, stored in a retrieval system, or transmitted in any form or by any means, electronic, mechanical, photocopying, recording, or otherwise, without the prior permission of the publishers.

Any person who commits any unauthorised act in relation to this publication may be liable to criminal prosecution and civil claims for damages.

This is a work of fiction. Names, characters, businesses, places, events, locales, and incidents are either the products of the author's imagination or used in a fictitious manner. Any resemblance to actual persons, living or dead, or actual events is purely coincidental.

A CIP catalogue record for this title is available from the British Library.

ISBN 9781398437524 (Paperback)
ISBN 9781398437531 (ePub e-book)

www.austinmacauley.com

First Published 2022
Austin Macauley Publishers Ltd®
1 Canada Square
Canary Wharf
London
E14 5AA

Chapter 1

In the beginning was the word and the word was Africa. It was where she had been born, in the large bed in the front bedroom overlooking the plains of Africa, the wide savannah with its dry grasses and flat-topped acacia trees. It was where she grew up, where she took her first steps, had her first pony ride, saw her first leopard. Africa was geckoes sticky-padded to walls, long tongues lashing out for flies. It was the Tanganyika trains trundling their long, plump, articulated bodies across the floor on their hundreds of legs like a football team walking crocodile fashion. Africa was the cry of the hyena in the dark of the night and the strident cicadas singing under the stars. The throaty cough of a lion. It was the harsh croak of frogs round pools in the moonlight under the clatter of palm leaves. It was the smell of heat, dust and dry grasses, of wood fires in the open and animals living side by side with people. Africa was her first love.

School was cold, misery, the ceaseless rain of the English West country and the lollipop flights taking her home for the holidays. Travelling hopefully on the way out but in a black cloud, deepening as the plane approached Heathrow, on the way back. London was work and now but home would always be Africa and the farm. Through dark, rainy days her head was full of the blue skies of Jaribuni, its palms, its white sands, its dust and its heat, her family and friends. She might have her feet on the pavements of London but her head and her heart were in Jaribuni. She looked at autumn leaves, skeletons muddled and speckled by the rain and they were snakes' skins, weed wide enough to fool the eye. In summer, visiting birds, egrets, house martins, wagtails and flycatchers were reminders of home to her.

Mid-morning on the main Mombasa Road, a car coming from the south, careers along the rough carriageway flying off the speed bumps and swerving violently all over the place. The car screeches to a halt in front of a police barrier, caltrops made up of vicious tyre-spearing spikes. Stopping millimetres away from sudden death the young woman driving flops over the steering wheel sobbing uncontrollably.

"Doctor Mwara? Hello, yes, this is an emergency. Can you come right away, please?"

Georgina put the phone down, her own words echoing in her head. An emergency, that's what it was. The poor girl was in such a bad way, shivering and shaking, cold in spite of the hot African sun. Her eyes were unnaturally large and round, staring out of the dark circles of their sockets. Her clothes were streaked with dirt and was that blood or red wine staining her skirt, wondered Georgina. She asked herself why the police had brought the girl to her for safe keeping, but then again, the local hospital with its bare concrete floors and iron bedsteads covered with only the thinnest of mattresses would hardly have helped to make her feel better. And as for the police station best not to even think about the discomfort she would have endured there. No, much better that she should be here with some measure of comfort to ease her distress. The police probably assumed that she knew the girl and certainly she recognised her face and knew whose daughter she was but the family lived on one of those farms beyond the edge of town – a dairy farm she thought.

She turned her attention to the girl sitting on her sofa.

"Now, my dear, you will have to remind me of your name. I know we met when you were a very little girl but we haven't seen each other since."

The girl mumbled her name through the curtain of thick, dark hair that was tumbling around her grey mascara-streaked face. It was the first time she had been capable of speaking for some hours.

"Jessica."

"Ah yes, I should have remembered that, it's a name from my favourite Shakespeare play 'The Merchant of Venice'. There is a love scene where Jessica and her lover, Lorenzo are talking and he says:

'In such a night
Stood Dido with a willow in her hand
Upon the wild sea banks, and waft her love
To come again to Carthage.'

"So romantic. But you don't want to hear me chattering on. I think you should have a good hot shower; it will warm you up and help you to relax. And the doctor is on his way. Meanwhile I will ask cook to make you some soup. You must be hungry; it's nearly lunchtime and I don't suppose you have eaten yet today."

"Thank you," said Jessica standing up. She felt an enormous wave of gratitude to Georgina not so much for taking her in but for not asking too many questions and for being so practical.

Georgina looked up at her, a tall willowy figure compared to her own five foot nothing. She could see the girl had no idea where she was or what she should do.

"Come on," she said, "this way."

And she led her by the hand through the open courtyard in the centre of the house to a bedroom where she gave her towels and soap and helped her to undress. She could see the girl was unhurt, just very dirty and smelling faintly of smoke. What on earth could have happened to put her in such a state of shock, could it have been drugs? Strange how you look at someone quite closely but all their thoughts and their experiences are locked inside them. The detail doesn't show on the outside, only powerful emotions can be seen.

Georgina could see that having helped the girl out of her clothes, that she would have to be led into the shower; she was incapable of making the smallest decision and was simply standing helpless and naked.

"I will find you a *kikoi* to wear so that you have something fresh and clean. I'm afraid you are too tall for anything else I might have. There, the shower is running now and it's warm. In you go."

Georgina left the girl standing under the shower while she went to the kitchen to ask her cook to prepare some chicken soup. Georgina was a great believer in the healing power of chicken soup. When she was a child during the Mau-Mau emergency when she and her family were too frightened to eat, it was chicken soup that their cook brought them. It both nourished and warmed them making them feel stronger, less afraid. Georgina heard a voice shouting from the front door amid the noise of her dogs barking. Dogs. Always better than a doorbell, she thought as she went to see who was there.

"Ah, Dr Mwara, come in. Jessica is just taking a shower and I have put her in the guest bedroom. Wait a moment, take a seat, and I will see if she is ready."

Jessica stood in the shower with the water pouring over her, silky, cleansing. Her mind was quietening down as the warm water soothed her. The jets of hot water on her skin were needles inoculating her from evil. She couldn't bring herself to turn it off. It was a protective curtain between her and the rest of the world where harm can happen. She closed her eyes and held her face up to the water feeling it run over her eyelids, nose and mouth and sliding through her hair. This moment should last forever, her mind drifting, her body feeling the sensuousness of the water, she could almost forget what had happened – but, no, she shuddered, she could never forget.

Georgina came in to tell her that the doctor was here, bringing Jessica back to reality. She turned the water off and stepped out of the shower to towel herself dry. Wrapping Georgina's *kikoi* around her she stared at her reflection in the mirror. How could she still be here worrying about keeping people waiting, how could she still be able to stand up, how could the world ever look the same again. Suddenly she felt that world spinning round her and her legs seemed to give way. She put out a hand to hold on to a nearby table. Georgina rushed to help her, "I think perhaps you had better lie down, my dear. I will bring the doctor to you."

Jessica lay back on the bed lulled by its many pillows and the clean, cool feel of its linen sheets. The mosquito nets draped at each corner gave it the appearance of a four-poster which was somehow reassuring, solid and protective. As she waited hearing the bass notes of the doctor's voice interspersed with Georgina's light tone, she let her fingers play with the loose fringes of the *kikoi,* its bright, gay colours contrasting with her mood. Only black could feel right, she thought. I must wear black, black, deepest black she kept thinking, as the doctor came into the room. He was so big and bulky that he blotted out all the light coming through the door but his face was kind and wrinkled with smiles.

She must have been saying 'black' aloud without realising it because Dr Mwara asked her, "What is that you are saying?"

Jessica stared at him and shook her head; it was beyond her to explain. Georgina sat beside her and held her hand while Mwara carried out his examination, blood pressure, pulse and temperature, all of which were normal.

"I can't find anything seriously wrong and you have no physical injuries but you have obviously been through some terrible shock or ordeal. Would you like to talk about it?"

Jessica looked at his broad face smiling gently at her and hesitated, but no she couldn't. She knew she would have to talk soon but not yet, please not yet. She shook her head vehemently. Mwara sighed, he liked to know all the gossip and was longing to discover what the matter was. Georgina had told him nothing beyond the fact that the police had brought the girl there.

"Well, Jessica, I shall prescribe you a sedative to help you sleep and calm you down. You will have to talk to the police tomorrow and if you are rested perhaps, you will feel more able. I have some Valium with me as I thought it might be needed. It's 3,000ks I'm afraid."

"I can pay. But I need my bag. I don't know where my bag is. Where is my bag? I must have dropped it somewhere." She could feel her hysteria rising.

"Don't worry," soothed Georgina. "I will pay and you can give it back to me later. Now I will see Doctor Mwara out and bring your soup and a glass of water for your medicine."

After she had finished her soup and taken the sedative prescribed, Jessica turned onto her side feeling pain deep inside that made her curl up and clutch her stomach but she soon fell into a deep, deep sleep. She woke briefly when the maid came in to close the curtains and the mosquito nets around the bed as well as clear away her empty soup bowl, but she soon fell fast asleep again.

It was only the following morning that she woke fully. Memory, that fickle and wayward companion, tweaked her mind immediately. She saw agonising pictures of her parents and the people that worked on the farm and in their house. She quickly got out of bed and began to move around the room hoping to dispel the thoughts that were pursuing her. She went downstairs still wearing Georgina's *kikoi* and went into the sitting room. Jessica looked around, everything in the room suggested peace, calm, and security; from the polished wooden floors to the solid mahogany furniture with its rich patina reflecting the ornaments: silver, native carvings and basketwork. Outside there were chairs with bright comfortable cushions to sink into but above all, the house was cool with gentle breezes blowing in from the creek whose blue waters rolled slowly by at the foot of the cliff.

She went out onto the veranda which was fragrant with the scent of the many flowers growing round it, frangipane, jasmine, bougainvillea and hibiscus. There she found the dogs and also Georgina with a table full of delicious looking fresh fruit.

"*Jambo*," Georgina called out, "Come and sit over here," she said patting a chair next to her, "and help yourself to some fruit. Coffee or tea?"

"*Jambo* and thank you," replied Jessica and realising she was hungry helped herself to a mango. Then before she sank her teeth into the fleshy fruit, "Coffee would be lovely." Georgina rang the little silver bell on the table and the maid came to find out what was required. "A pot of tea and of coffee."

"*Asante.*" *(*Thank you.*)*

"*Karibu,*" *(*You're Welcome), replied Nemeh. Georgina ran her house on old-fashioned colonial routines, but with kindness and respect on all sides. Then turning back to Jessica, "I'm a tea drinker, I'm afraid. I grew up on a tea plantation and I married a tea grower so it was inevitable. I do drink coffee after dinner sometimes, oh, and mid-morning but that's all. Now then, my dear, how are you feeling this morning. Did you sleep well."

"I did, thanks to Dr Mwara's sedatives," replied Jessica, "and I feel less tired but I can't say better. It's all been such a nightmare."

"You will probably not be surprised to hear that the gossip is spreading so I know now a little of what has happened. My dear, it is the kind of thing that no-one should have to suffer and if you don't want to talk about it, I quite understand. Words always fail and seem inadequate; perhaps it's because we are prone to exaggeration and use strong nouns and adjectives to talk about the most trivial events leaving us nothing with which to describe the truly tragic, extreme or outrageous things. Later, though the police are coming and you will have to speak to them. I can stay with if you like."

"Yes, thank you, I would like that. I am not sure how good my Swahili is these days. And if you don't mind, I will wait till then to talk. Just now I want to eat this nice breakfast and drink in the tranquillity of this lovely place, it's so very soothing."

As she sat over her coffee watching the fish eagle fly past and the vervet monkeys tumbling about their business she looked out at the tiny island in the middle of the creek. She wished she could be like that island impervious to change or harm. She said as much to Georgina who replied with some asperity.

"Don't you believe it. Once, that island was covered with mangroves but people came and pulled them up. It changes shape all the time now. In fact, the whole shore line keeps changing because of where the mangroves have been dug up. Their roots fix the soil in place and without them the sand and mud is washed away on every tide."

"Oh, I didn't know that. Just now, I feel raw and stripped bare, it's as if salt water were pouring into my wounds. So I am like that island after all."

"The police are coming at ten thirty, perhaps you would like to write down some of your story so as not to forget anything."

This struck Jessica as very sensible, "Good, yes, perhaps I should," and Georgina went off to find pen and paper. Jessica watched Georgina's slight figure as she disappeared into the house. She was so small and thin but somehow there was fine steel inside her. Jessica felt that she could rely utterly on her. Her cornflower blue eyes saw to the heart of everything and everyone looking out from a fine boned face framed by pure white hair which intensified the colour of her tan.

With pen and paper in front of her Jessica began to write, shaken every so often by sobs and heavy sighs. As she wrote the images kept returning as if burnt onto her retina. Flashback they call them, she thought, now I know what that means.

"I was at a party with friends in Goshi, the Zinj Safari Camp," she wrote, "and stayed the night so as not to be driving home late when you can't see the speed bumps in the road or those vicious police barriers that can rip your tyres. Also I wanted to be able to have a drink or two."

Her mind slid away from what she was writing and began writhing and turning through many questions. Is this really relevant? Does anything matter anymore. I can't bear it, how am I ever going to talk to anyone again about anything? But I must keep going. If only I had been there.

"OK Start again."

"So I drove home yesterday morning. I left Goshi about 9am. I drove up the track that leads to our farm at about 10am and as I drove, I saw smoke. Not just a bonfire, lots and lots of smoke, billowing and blowing all over. As I got closer I could smell burning and what to me seemed like cooking, you know a barbecue or something which I thought was strange so early in the morning. Then I passed the big baobab tree and rounded the bend and I could see the whole farmhouse was smoking, burnt to the ground. I braked hard and jumped out of the car screaming, I couldn't take the car too close because of sparks and the heat. I didn't know what I was doing. Panicking I guess.

"I ran to the yard, the smoke was making me choke and I was so hot and sweating. I found our houseboy first. His throat had been cut."

Jessica paused with a sharp intake of breath. My God it seems so inadequate to say that. Plain words that carry such terrible information, she thought.

"I knelt by his body and touched his shoulder as though to see if he were really dead but how could he not be with that ghastly, gaping wound and his head nearly falling off. Then I thought about my parents. "Mum, Dad, where are you?" I called. There was only the sound of the smoke hissing and sputtering on the wind. I stood up and looked around. Not much further away I found my father. He had been shot in the head. And then I saw my mother."

I can't go on. This is too terrible to write, she thought as she drooped over the table feeling a deep ache inside her, a physical pain that stabbed and stabbed and stabbed again.

Georgina came up behind her and put an arm around her. "If you need to, take a break from it, I phoned my friend Rosie who has a teenage daughter about your size, she has brought over some clothes for you to borrow. Go and try them on and choose a dress or whatever to wear, then later we can go to the 'bend-down' boutiques near the market to buy you some things of your own. Hardly what you are used to, but better than nothing until we can go shopping properly in Mombasa. We're not very smart in this little backwater anyway so nobody takes much notice of clothes. And you would be surprised, a lot of designer clothes end up in those 'bend-downs' thanks to the international charities."

Jessica got up with some relief and went to do as she was told. Upstairs in the bedroom she stood in someone else's clothes and looked at herself in the mirror. I have lost everything. I am all alone. Where do I go from here? I don't even look like me anymore.

As she returned to her writing Georgina asked "Have you much more to write?"

"I don't think so. I am not putting in too much detail. I suppose they will want that from me when they question me."

"Yes, I'm afraid so, but at least if you have the main facts written down it will help you to speak to them more coherently."

Jessica read through what she had already written. Then mumbling to herself "Oh Mum, my poor, poor Mum," she continued to write.

"I found my mother's body. She was naked, torn, battered and bloodied, her face frozen in the horror of what was done to her. Her body marked by every hand that mauled her. I hope that my father had died first so he didn't see what happened to his wife, my poor, poor mother. After that I don't remember much. I stumbled around for a while, there were other bodies – our farm workers and more of the house staff too, our *askari*. I think the cow sheds had burned as well, that would explain the smell of barbecuing. The horses too were burned and the bodies of the dogs lay in front of the veranda where they had died. Poisoned. I couldn't think what to do, who to phone, I was frightened that the people who did this horrible thing were still around so I ran away. I ran back to the car and drove towards town when I was stopped by one of the police road checks. And they brought me here to Mrs Hamilton."

Jessica went back to the veranda and sat thinking. Her eyes were glazed and staring towards the creek but she saw again the burnt-out farmhouse, her mother's body, those of her father and their workers. Just now in Syria and Iraq people are suffering similar traumas, she thought, but that is war. Perhaps in one of those places there is a girl like me who is also sitting contemplating the loss of all her family. But here all is peaceful, how can such a thing happen here? I don't understand. Is it more terrible when it happens as a unique thing, an incident out of the blue? Is there comfort in not being alone in misfortune? When you live in constant fear of death and injury does that make it easier when they do occur? So much beauty here and yet so much ugliness.

Voices crashed into her thoughts. Georgina was showing a policeman onto the veranda. It was the same one that had brought her to Georgina's house the day before. He was tall and kindly looking, young but with a face as old as time, full of understanding and sorrow at the misdeeds of the world.

"Jessica, this is Inspector Mona, he has come to question you."

"Good morning, Jessica."

"Good morning, Inspector. What has happened to my car? Has anyone found my handbag?"

"We have your car at the police station and we have brought your handbag and your overnight bag. Sergeant Wanjiku, will you fetch them from our car. I know how you English ladies depend on having your handbags with you always."

It seemed the Inspector spoke very good English after all. He had with him a young sergeant who took notes as they spoke.

"Now then, I realise that you have been through a dreadful ordeal and I am very sorry for your loss. "*Pole,*" as we say in Swahili." At this he gave slight

15

bow of the head looking at Jessica with sad eyes. "I have to ask you some questions however painful it might be for you. We'll start at the beginning; can you give me your full name and the name of your parents?"

"My name is Jessica Langley and my parents' names are Donald and Lydia."

"Address?"

"The farm is called Shamba ya Tembo, near Jaribuni."

"Where were you the night of the attack on your parents?"

"I was at a disco at Goshi, the bar on the beach, with friends, Cora and Hugo Patterson-Smythe. I stayed the night with them at their parents' house as it's very near the bar. We were at school together once upon a time."

"What time did you leave their house?"

"About nine o'clock. Look is this relevant, how will knowing that help you to catch whoever did this evil thing?"

"It won't but I am just trying to build up a picture of how events occurred, including you finding your parents bodies."

"Sorry, I guess I feel guilty that I wasn't there with them. I should have been there."

"I don't think that would have made any difference except that you would have met the same fate as your mother."

At this Jessica began to sob uncontrollably. Georgina went to comfort her and called for a glass of water for her while Inspector Mona sat looking down at his hands, very uncomfortable saying '*Pole*' over and over again. His sergeant shuffled from one foot to the other. After some moments and many sips of water Jessica became calmer. Mona apologised yet again for upsetting her. "Well, I suppose it is true, I would not have been able to stop any of it happening," admitted Jessica.

"No," agreed Mona, "you wouldn't. Now can you tell me what happened after you left your friends' house?"

"I drove home and..." Jessica, on the edge of collapse, drew several deep breaths before saying, "here you are, I have written some details down for you. Georgina and I thought it might help." She handed him the notes she had been making.

Inspector Mona read through them, "This is very helpful. Perhaps I don't need to ask you any more for the time being. Unfortunately, I do need to ask you to come with me to the farmhouse. I have to know if anything has been stolen, or if anything has been moved since you first arrived there yesterday morning. More importantly, I need some official identification of the bodies. Would you be able to come now?"

Jessica looked at Georgina with pleading eyes, "Do I have to?"

"I can come with you, if you like," said Georgina.

"There is no need," said the inspector, "I will look after her, but she must come. We can't leave it until tomorrow, we have closed the place off and set a guard over it so it won't be disturbed but there is the heat and the problem with flies and vultures."

"No, it's OK. I'll come now. It is better to get this over and done with."

In the car on the way to the farm Jessica sat in silence. The monotonous hum of the engine and the drumming of the wheels on the road lulled her mind into some kind of limbo. She seemed to be wake-sleeping through the journey. Only the babel of Swahili from the radio from time to time broke through her trance. Mona glanced at her every so often and saw that her teeth were clenched and her jaw tight, staring straight ahead of her, locked in her own private hell. He tried to talk but she seemed not to hear him so he gave up and they drove on in silence.

As they pulled up at the still smouldering ruins of the house Jessica drew a sharp breath through her clenched teeth. She got out of the car and squared her shoulders, head held high. "I must get through this," she thought.

"Are you OK?" enquired Mona.

Jessica nodded.

"Come on then, we will go over to look at the bodies first. I need some official identification. Follow me."

The bodies had all been left exactly as Jessica had found them only now they were surrounded by flies. The police guards had been vigilant in keeping away the buzzards, vultures and other carrion birds. She was able to tell the Inspector exactly who they all were. Sergeants Wanjiku and Mwangi were both busy supervising the removal of the bodies. They turned back the covering shrouds so that Jessica could identify her family and staff. First there was the houseboy whose throat had been cut, Emmanuel who had been with the family for twenty years. Then there was Joseph, the cook – he had been shot in the back. Jessica's old *ayah*, Rachel, who still helped out around the house was lying not far from Lydia, her mother, where she had been cut down with a *panga* while trying to defend Lydia. Near Rachel was the *askari*, Mingati,

17

perhaps he too had been trying to protect Lydia. The gardener, Samuel, too had been killed, his stomach split open and his innards trailing out onto the ground; ground that was soaked in blood. Joseph's blood, Emmanuel's blood, Rachel's blood, Samuel's blood and the blood of her parents, Lydia and Donald. All mixed together in death.

Jessica went and sat down on the low stone wall that edged the veranda. She put her head in her hands and wept. Inspector Mona, stood by waiting. Sergeant Wanjiku asked, "Mind if I smoke?"

"No, I think I will have one too if you can spare it. I don't smoke often but this..." His voice trailed off as his hand gestured towards the carnage. It all reminded him of what his parents had told him, their memory from when they were children, just little *totos*, of the *Mau-mau* coming through their village burning all the houses killing the men and children and raping the women before killing them too. His own grandfather had died that night, cut down with a *panga*.

Eventually Jessica held her head up searching in her bag for a tissue. Dabbing at her eyes and nose, she looked at the burnt shell of the house wondering how on earth they expected her to know whether anything had been stolen. Inspector Mona saw her looking up and went over to her, throwing away the stub of his now extinguished cigarette.

"OK?" he enquired. Jessica nodded. But she felt like those zebras who when a member of their herd is killed stand by the body, heads bowed, unmoving for hour after hour.

"Is everyone accounted for?"

"I think so, oh my God, no. Where is Jaba. He would have been here."

"Who is Jaba?"

"Our cattle man and odd job man. He joined the farm quite recently and looked in on the horses and cattle and then closed up the sheds for the night. He is not here; he must have escaped."

"Mmm," was Mona's reply. "You know the wives of Emmanuel and Joseph saw you here yesterday. They came looking for their men."

"I didn't see them. Were they hiding?"

"Not exactly. I think Durah had fallen in a faint. Zarifa was just fetching some water for her. Shall we go and look at what's left of the house?" he asked as he held out his hand to help her up. Mona said no more as he led her up to the house and she was grateful for his silence. But he was thinking that this

Jaba could have escaped or been kidnapped or had helped the gang who attacked.

The house was a charred wreck. The air all around left a taste of smoke in their mouths. The *makuti* roof had collapsed, the blackened beams fallen in, the thatch burnt completely away. The glass in the windows had shattered in the heat and, of the shutters that had once provided security, only the metal hinges remained, twisted and warped clinging desperately to the walls. The bodies of the dogs lay with their tongues lolling out, eyes rolled back in their heads, poisoned to stop them attacking or alerting anyone. As Jessica and the inspector walked around the house their feet crunched on broken glass, shattered china and charred springs from beds and chairs. Jessica flinched at every cracking and crunching sound. Nothing was left of the beautiful Persian carpets her parents had collected. Pictures and photographs had all been consumed by the flames leaving behind mangled and blackened frames. The antique silver which had been in the family for two or three generations, she couldn't remember how long, was now melted into strange shapes. Jessica's eyes were moving fast from one ghastly remnant to another and her blinking became more and more rapid as she tried to take everything in but was afraid to look. She pointed out that in her father's study the gun cupboard had been broken open and all his guns taken. "They must have done that before setting the fire," she murmured. "Did your parents keep any other valuables here?" asked Mona.

"There were mobile phones and laptops but they have gone, no sign of them, surely something would be left if they had been burnt. Then only my mother's jewellery, and she didn't have very much. A pearl necklace and earrings; maybe two or three rings. Mum never took off her wedding ring or her engagement ring – a large solitaire diamond. They didn't keep much money here; these days with debit cards and *Mpesa* there is less need for cash."

"I am afraid there was no sign of any rings on your mother's hands. *Pole.*"

Jessica sighed and stood for a moment silently twisting her hands together and turning her own rings round and round on her fingers, a habit that her mother had also had. "That ring was unique. My mother told me that when they became engaged Donald, my father, went to Johannesburg to buy the diamond and had it made up to his own design. It always seemed so – so – romantic..." Her voice trailed away and with another deep sobbing sigh, so deep that it seemed the whole world sighed with her, she went back outside.

Ambulances were there taking the bodies away. Jessica turned her face away and walked towards the outbuildings. Her parents' cars were carbonised skeletons in what was left of the garages but more distressing were the blackened bones of cattle which had been burned in their shed, all eighty of them. And the horses – Jessica couldn't bear it any more. She looked round for Inspector Mona but he was over by the ambulances making sure that all the bodies were safely and respectfully taken away. Seeing Jessica come out of the shed and stumble against the stone wall he quickly walked over to her to help her back to the car.

"It's all just black, black on the ground and black in my heart."

"I think you have had enough; I will take you back to Mama Hamilton's. Just sit for a moment in the shade and have some water." He handed her a bottle which she sipped from gratefully.

On the way home, they were again silent; Jessica was in a state of collapse, her breath coming in gasps. She thought back to breakfast time when there had been a brief respite, an oasis of calm, perhaps she had been pretending to herself that such things couldn't happen, hadn't happened, not here, to her home, not to her, to her family. She sat with head bowed twisting the silver rings she wore round and round her fingers until they were red and swollen. Tears stung her eyes and fell to her lap staining the dress she had borrowed. She felt as though she were weeping tears of blood. As she looked out at the world that was passing by the car windows everything seemed brighter, sharper edged, strange and she could hardly believe that life was going on just as though nothing had happened. Ragged children were running around the huts that they passed, chickens were scratching in the dirt. Women were lighting fires and pounding maize or chopping *sukuma*. Lorries, bicycles, *boda-boda* motor bikes, *tuk-tuks* and *matatus* were still fighting for possession of the road. The smell of cooking fires and dust that had always meant Africa to her, was now part of the horror.

For his part Mona was thinking about the investigation he would now have to carry out, where to start, how to ask this poor girl any more questions and above all why anyone would do something like this. For now he would deliver her back to Mama Hamilton and hope that she would be more able to talk over the next few days.

Back at Georgina's house Jessica felt safe and breathed a sigh of relief that Georgina didn't ask any questions. Georgina had taken one look at her face, ashen and drawn, shrunken, helpless. She made her sit on the shady veranda and got her a glass of wine. "Alcohol is the only thing that does any good at a time like this," she declared. As they sipped their drinks they heard the dogs barking excitedly. Cora and her brother Hugo walked out onto the veranda surrounded by the noisy canines; Jack Russells and Labradors of uncertain parentage. Cora rushed straight over to Jessica and wrapped her arms around her.

"Jessica, I just don't know what to say. I am so sorry about what has happened. We heard it from our staff first and didn't know if it was true. It's all so horrible and so unbelievable that such a thing could happen here in this little backwater."

Jessica began to cry softly once again and Cora wept in sympathy.

"We have been trying to ring you but you didn't answer your phone," said Hugo who was looking uncomfortable at being in the presence of such strong emotions.

"No," sniffed Jessica. "It was the last thing on my mind but anyway it was in my handbag and I think my charging cable was in my overnight bag, they both got left in my car when the police stopped me and brought me here. So it was out of reach and out of battery."

Georgina invited them both to sit and have a drink. "A Tusker, for me, please," said Hugo looking as though he was relieved to be back on a normal conversational level. Cora asked for a glass of white wine. While Georgina bustled off to fetch the drinks Cora and Hugo sat talking with Jessica.

"You must be feeling dreadful," began Cora.

"Obviously. Sorry I don't mean to be abrupt. I am no longer the person I was. You can't imagine the pain that something like this causes and I don't just mean mental anguish, it is physical too. My father's death was quick it seems but every time I think about what happened to my mother I feel such agony, an ache deep inside my stomach."

"I'm not surprised, no-one can possibly cope with such an awful thing," said Cora.

"And then there are the flashbacks. You hear people with PTSD talk about them but it is hard to understand the reality of them until it happens to you. It is as though the image of what you have seen or endured has been burnt onto your retina. It comes up before you, like being haunted except that it is all too real."

"Oh, Jess, it must be awful."

Hugo, trying to be the practical one, now spoke, "Well, Jess, you had better come back to our house and we will try to help you forget your troubles."

"No, no, no. I will never forget. Time may make it less painful to think about, but I will never forget. Also, I was at your house when all this happened, I am not sure I could bear to be there just now. I will stay here, if Georgina doesn't mind. There are things I must do. I am now in charge of what is left of the farm and responsible for the workers who died, for their families. I have lost everything not one scrap of my childhood is left. No photographs, no letters, no paperwork of any kind, no posters; small things like the certificate that I got when as a baby I had my very first haircut that Mother framed and put in the loo. All my clothes are gone except for what was in my overnight bag, what I am wearing now is a borrowed dress. I have lost everything, the one thing I can hang onto is my integrity otherwise I am nobody. I must speak to the families of the dead; I must organise funerals and memorial services and I must decide what to do with the farm."

Georgina handed the drinks to Cora and Hugo declaring that she was happy for Jessica to stay.

"Thank you so much," Jessica said to Georgina, then turning to her friends, "Don't worry, I will make sure that my mobile is up and running by this evening. We will keep in touch. Just now I need to be alone and quiet. I need to think."

Chapter 2

Jessica decided her first task was to contact the families of the staff who had been murdered and to arrange the funeral. The worry of it kept her mind busy, keeping more sinister thoughts at bay. Hugo and Cora kept turning up to see her or 'to cheer you up' as Hugo put it. They brought news from the outside world, or that is how it seemed to Jessica who felt she was living apart from normal life. They told her that the news had spread across Kenya and was even on the international news especially in the UK since her parents were originally British.

Television channels from KTN to the BBC and CNN, radio channels both local and from all over the world and newspapers began pestering her with requests for interviews. A journalist from The *East African Standard* was on the doorstep every day while the Reuters man was poised with pen and notebook to spread the word, any word to all the major newspapers internationally. The President, Uhuru Kenyatta himself, sent his condolences. Jessica shut her mind to all of them. Her grief was a private thing and she did not want to share it with the whole world. Let the police put out their statements if they wished but she did not want to become the object of fascination or prurient chatter that would last a month or two before dying and falling away from the headlines.

The nights were ghastly, she lay for hours listening to the cicadas chirping and the frogs croaking, her mind filled with the horror of what she had seen and grief at her devastating loss, curling up against the physical pain that she felt deep inside her stomach. How was she going to keep going? Just now she had the funeral to organise and the staffs' families to consider but what would she do afterwards? For two nights there was a huge moon so that her room was filled with an ethereal light as bright as day, painting everything an eerie silver, keeping her tossing and turning, sweating in the heat and unable to find any rest or peace of mind. Even so there were times when she fell asleep only to wake up in the dying throes of terrible dreams that frayed the edges of her mind.

During the day she had Georgina to talk to, she had business to see to. It kept her going. She had always been a practical and efficient person and needed activity, projects and ideas. "I must work through this. I must survive," she told herself. But there were nights when she paced up and down with no idea what her next step would be.

The funeral was her first priority, not an easy thing to arrange and delayed by police investigations but she was to discover that choices were so limited that it didn't take as long to organise as she feared. The families of the staff who had been killed opted to have a joint funeral for which Jessica was very grateful. The thought of attending four separate funerals as well as her parents one was a gloomy and harrowing prospect, this way it would all be over and done with in one go.

So her parents would go to their graves in the cemetery near the church accompanied by their loyal staff. It seemed right that as they died together, they should be buried together. There was only one type of coffin available and Jessica was sure that her parents would have been happy with the simplicity of everything. Georgina had offered her house to be used for the wake afterwards.

The funeral took place a week to the day after the terrible events on a clear, bright afternoon. The ceremony was simple with a congregation of all faiths and races though it was led by the C of E vicar. The imam from the local mosque and the Catholic priest were both there to support those who belonged to their churches. Both Africans and *mzungus (*white people), grieved together. Prayers were said and hymns sung but for Jessica the most moving moment came when the official ceremony was over and there was a group of friends and relations of the staff, mourners who gathered together by the graves and sang in quiet, deep tones that felt as though they came from the very depths of their souls and from the very deepest part of the earth. Afterwards she went to shake hands with all the family members saying how sorry she was and promising to come and see them, to help them.

"We saw you that day, Mama. Me and Durah. We were there to look for our men who had not come home that night."

"I am sorry, I didn't see you. I was so frightened and so deeply shocked."

"Yes, Mama, also us. We never see anything so horrible. We are sorry for you too, *pole*," said Durah.

"Do you know what happened to Jaba? Have you seen him?"

"No, Mama, he run away, we think," said Zarifa. "No one has seen him."

Later at Georgina's house she found that she couldn't spend long with any one person she drifted from one polite conversation to another listening to scraps overheard from others. One phrase kept being repeated, "It's like the Mau-Mau all over again." But she also began to be afraid that she had never really known her parents judging by the things others were saying about them. She felt they had been made unrecognisable. Who were these people that they could voice their opinions and so-called facts with such conviction? She didn't want to find herself arguing so drifting between conversations was the only safe thing to do. She couldn't bear to be told over and over again that time would make everything easier. She wasn't ready to let go of her emotions, forgetting would seem like a betrayal of her parents.

She overheard Leo, her father's snooker partner "…he loved his farm, never made much money but he was happy…" then as she moved on, her father's old school friend, "…they met in England when Donald was at agricultural college, Cirencester I think, so they were pretty much childhood sweethearts. She took to the life here like a duck to water." This was a surprise to Jessica whose mother had always told her not to get involved with any man too young. "Too young?" Jessica had queried "when is too young?"

"Oh before you are twenty-five," her mother had replied. I'm twenty-eight already and still haven't met the man of my dreams, thought Jessica. She thought of her current boyfriend, Daniel Parker who had found himself too busy to come to Kenya and support her. Her anguish and grief made his absence seem trivial, she had no room for fretting about him in her mind or heart and had stopped answering his text messages. She had even blocked his calls considering that he hadn't bothered to answer her call for help. She sighed, deciding that she must forget him. She moved on sipping at her wine, watching all the people chattering, eating and drinking. The more they drank the more they chattered, their voices rising to the wide, blue sky, deafening the birds. It seemed as though a funeral was more fun than a party, more enjoyable than a wedding.

The men were all saying "What a great guy Donald Langley was, did a lot for conservation, man. You know, worked on that KAP committee. He didn't deserve this, boy." All said with a shake of the head and grunts of agreement all round. The women were talking in their little groups too. Donald Langley –

I couldn't believe it when I heard. Such a super person. He worked so hard to protect the elephants and you know he supported that little school for the blind too out at Tiwi. As for poor Lydia… that is my worst nightmare.

"I think it is everyone's. That's why we have *askaris* and lock up as soon as it is dusk."

"That might make us feel better but any determined burglar can just take a hatchet to the doors."

"I don't know about you but we have an alarm system with BSafe Guards. Surely the Langley's did too. Perhaps they never got a chance to use it. It seems the dogs were poisoned and one of the dead was their *askari*. He was Maasai and the police took him back to his village for burial among his own people."

Jessica kept to herself walking around the edges of the party. Inspector Mona was hovering, looking quite serious, not talking to anyone either, not even to Sergeant Wanjiku or Mwangi who were with him. He was watching carefully with a grave expression on his face. "Thank you for coming," she told him.

"It's nothing, the least I can do, besides it is always interesting to see who turns up. Quite a number of these people are friends and associates of your father from the conservation programme, aren't they?"

Jessica looked around, most of the Africans had already gone home but she recognised one or two faces of people that she had met at her parents' house, being away at school and then university and having to find work in the UK she was out of touch with the people in the area. "I'm not sure," she replied. "I know he worked hard on the prevention of poaching for ivory. He loved elephants – gentle giants he always called them. He even called our farm after them."

Just then Hugo and Cora came up, "So this is where you are hiding," Hugo joked.

Jessica sighed, she knew he meant well but she wasn't in the mood, "Not hiding, just avoiding awkward conversations," she answered. "But I am glad to see you. Everyone is talking nineteen to the dozen about my parents, how they knew them, how they knew each other, it's as if they no longer belong to me. I think I need to talk about other things. Look there are the dogs, why don't we walk them down to the beach?"

The three friends discarded their glasses and strolled across the garden to the narrow cliff path that led to the beach calling to the dogs to follow. The way was vertiginously steep and wound round the three huge baobab trees that grew up from the cliff face. Their roots created a series of steps but the path with all its lumps and stones, twists and turns was not an easy walk so they were silent as they concentrated on the safest places to put their feet. The dogs leapt and jumped ahead of them. Then they walked through the mangrove trees that lined the shore coming out from under the trees and with a big jump landing on the beach. The sand was of a muddy brown colour close to the shore line and dotted with shoots of mangrove roots, but closer to the water it was pure white. Cora and Jessica kicked off their shoes to enjoy the feel of the hot wet sand oozing around their toes. As they walked along the edge of the water with the dogs darting in and out shaking great drops of water everywhere, heading towards the fishing boats beached near the edge of the village, Jessica's eye was caught by a movement among the mangroves at the base of the cliff. "Did you see that?" she asked the others. Cora had noticed nothing but Hugo said that he too had seen a movement among the trees. There had been a flash of blue, barely seen, and something had moved in the dark tangle of foliage. They both peered into the gloom of the thickly entwined mangroves and saw it again.

Running towards it, Hugo suddenly stopped and laughed with relief, "It was just a monitor lizard," he told Jessica.

"Oh," she breathed, sounding let down.

"Were you expecting something?"

"No, not exactly it's just that as I've been going out and about. I have sometimes had the feeling that someone is watching me. It's kind of spooky – unnerving."

They turned to climb back up the cliff; Jessica felt that she had to go back to say goodbye to her parent' friends and her relations.

At the house, waiting to say goodbye was Miriam, Jessica's great aunt on her father's side. She stood with her wrinkled sun-spotted face smiling kindly, her house boy beside her. Jessica had noticed earlier that she had her left arm in plaster and wondered how she had managed to drive herself the sixty or so miles from her house. Now she asked in an admiring tone how the feat had been achieved. Miriam waved her one good freckled arm in the direction of her houseboy, her skin hanging in thick folds like rhinoceros hide, saying it had been no problem as he had changed the gears for her while she steered and pressed the clutch. "You are always welcome to come and see me," she said, "Don't be a stranger, these are difficult times and I am the only family you have."

"That's very true Aunt Miriam, I promise I will visit soon."

"Good girl. Your father would have wanted that. He would also have wanted you to start again with the farm. Have you thought about that?"

"Not yet. It is too soon to make up my mind about anything but you are kind to be concerned. Goodbye Aunt." With a kiss and a final wave of the folds of skin hanging from her arms Miriam was gone.

People were now leaving all at once it seemed to Jessica. She felt like saying in her best teacher's voice, "Form an orderly queue now please," as they all surrounded her, kissing her and shaking her hand. James Denton the British Registrar patted her hand and suggested that she visit him for advice about registering the deaths both in Kenya and in the UK. "I need to speak to you on other matters too. Come as soon as you can."

In the muddle of saying goodbye all at once to so many, only a few faces stayed in her memory: David and Victoria who had been good friends of the family and had known her parents for forty years, the parents of Hugo and Cora who had been so kind and Derek for quite the opposite reason. In fact, Jessica was annoyed that he was there at all, but in such a small tight-knit community tolerance was essential. He had smarmed up to her, his bald head covered in liver spots and flaking skin making her feel slightly sick but she managed to offer her hand politely. He ignored her hand and putting his bony hands on her shoulders leaned forward to kiss her on both cheeks. She pulled away from him rather more sharply than was polite so that he gave her a long, quizzical stare before saying goodbye, his American twang contrasting strikingly with the cut-glass and African accents of everyone else but finally he left. Henry Randall was there too, very much an old school English gentleman who lived with a Masai girl. Aïsha was tall and slim in the way that her people are. Jessica thought her very beautiful but wasn't at all sure what Henry did for a living, something in Mombasa was all she knew. Last to go were Martin and Sarah, her parent's best friends. This was the saddest goodbye of all. They were grieving deeply and were still in shock at what had happened. "Don't be a stranger. Come and see us," they said. And Jessica knew at once that this was not just politeness talking but a genuine need to see her and keep in touch.

They clung to each other for several minutes not daring to speak in case words opened the floodgates of their emotions. Then Martin and Susan stepped away into the warm velvet of the African twilight.

Jessica wiped a tear from her eye and sighed deeply. In the kitchen Georgina was supervising her house staff who were cleaning up. Jessica strolled out onto the veranda away from the clatter of plates, tinkling of glasses, splashing water and especially from the chattering voices. Out on the veranda all was quiet except for the rustling of leaves in the gentle night breeze and the chirruping of the cicadas. The moon was up and the stars were already bright. Night fall comes quickly at the Equator and never varies more than half an hour from one end of the year to the next. The night was warm but cool compared to the harsh heat of the sun. As Jessica looked up at the sky she saw the stars of the Southern Cross, the constellation that was Africa in her heart. She remembered her mother telling her, when her beloved Jack Russell, Buddy, had died of a snakebite, that he had become a star in heaven. Now, it soothed her to think that her parents might be part of the Southern Cross.

Georgina came and joined her bringing a glass of chilled white wine.

"How are you, my dear?" she asked.

"I'm OK. It's been a difficult day – so much emotion it's been exhausting. It's hard enough to deal with my own grief but when you see other people's as well it becomes even more difficult to bear."

"Your friends Hugo and Cora seem to have been a great help."

"Yes, they have. Especially today, Hugo did a fine job making sure everyone was supplied with drink. I don't have many friends here now certainly not of my age. They have all had to leave to work and get careers going. Hugo and Cora are the lucky ones who have been able to stay working on their parents' farm and running the safari camp."

"You sound as though you want to come back."

"I do. That was something I was hoping to sort out on this trip. I came for Christmas of course, but I also wanted to use the time here to see if I could find a way of working and living here."

"Why not on the farm?"

"It isn't really big enough. It isn't a huge spread like Hugo's family farm and I am no farmer."

"The land now belongs to you I would guess?"

"Yes, such as it is now. The land is all that is left. I would have to start again from scratch. It took years, generations even to build it up. My father told me how his grandparents acquired it. They arrived in Mombasa by ship from England and even though great-grandma was pregnant they trekked up to Nairobi thinking that was where the opportunities and the money were. But they had liked what they saw of the coast – the white sands, the green of the palm trees and the Arab buildings of Mombasa and Malindi. Nairobi back then was like the Wild West, the railway was just being built, land was up for grabs and bars and casinos were all unregulated. Great-grandpa went gambling and won a farm near the Ngong Hills. The area now called Karen after the writer who had a farm there, of course you know of Karen Blixen. But he became overconfident of his playing at poker and lost it only a few months later. At least, he lost the livestock and his remaining cash. They had to sell the farm to survive but also remembered that the coast was less frenetic, less crowded so they trekked back and bought their farm from a village chief who was keen to buy cattle as a dowry to get a new wife. It has been in our family for three generations and now this."

Jessica sat biting her lip. Georgina took hold of her hand and squeezed it comfortingly.

"I too have known grief; you know when my beloved Harry died. We had been married for fifty years. You never get over the grief, but time lessens its intensity. Then John and I got together."

"But he's just a good friend surely?"

"Oh no, my dear. We may be in our eighties but he's my lover. And, when he comes back from his trip to England we are going to live here together."

"Oh," said Jessica, hiding a smile and trying not to let her astonishment show.

"When is he due back?"

"In a couple of days. But that doesn't mean you can't stay."

"Thank you, you have been so kind but I think I must move on. Hugo and Cora keep asking me to stay there, or I could try to find a small place to rent."

"Well, let's see how things go. I believe you are seeing Inspector Mona tomorrow. We'd better get to bed early so you are ready for what might be a very difficult interview."

The following day Jessica woke early. Sun was pouring into her room and she could hear the leaves of the palm trees clacking in the wind. For the first time since the dreadful events she didn't feel as though she was cut off from the world by a heavy dark veil. Breakfast on the veranda was as always, a pleasure. The air was as usual fragrant with the perfume of oleander, frangipane and jasmine but now she found she was beginning to appreciate it. It was cool in the shade of all the climbing plants as she sat sipping her coffee and watching the monkeys trapezing through the trees. Down on the water the dugout canoes known as *mtumbwi* lolloped by and their close relatives the *ngalawas* with their sails tight to the wind competed with the fish eagle for their prey.

Now that Jessica had her car back she was driving herself to town to see Mona in his office. She took it slowly trying to remember where all the speed bumps were. Some of them were so steep it felt as though you were climbing a mountain. She passed heavy rickety lorries with legends like 'God will save' written above the windscreen. The *matatus* full of passengers with their goats and chickens also entrusted themselves to God's keeping. The *tuk-tuks* buzzed along often carrying extraordinary quantities of building materials for such small vehicles. One, Jessica noticed, was even carrying a coffin on its roof, empty or occupied, it was impossible to tell. Dodging in and out of all these and the ordinary motor cars were bicycles and *boda-boda* motorbikes often carrying whole families but still fast and cheeky, taking spectacular risks to move through the traffic. The road snaked through lines of shops selling everything from timber to mobile phones, fruit, vegetables and meat. There were open stalls draped with their wares, bras and t-shirts, knickers and trousers, much of which were from charitable organisations; the West's leftovers. And hub caps – whole stalls selling nothing but hubcaps, there were others as well with great heaps of mangoes, pawpaw, oranges, lemons and vegetables, *sukuma* a kind of spinach, potatoes, carrots, avocados, peppers, onions and tomatoes. There were stalls of shoes, children's clothes, and toys. Business was brisk and there was laughter and shouting as bargains were negotiated and, sometimes, struck. Through this noisy chaos Jessica threaded her way arriving at the inspector's office hot and dusty and regretting that she wasn't still sitting on Georgina's cool calm veranda.

The police headquarters was a concrete block, squat and utilitarian, built in colonial days by what was once called the Public Works Department hence

31

PWD style. A three-foot strip of dark green paint decorated the bottom of the walls the remainder was light cream with a layer of reddish dust. Steps led up the outside of the building to where the inspector's office was. Uneven in size and depth, they sloped sideways each one in a different direction making them awkward to climb. Jessica could feel the spots of perspiration coming out on her upper lip even though she had only walked across the road from where she had parked the car.

"Welcome, welcome, *karibu*," Mona greeted her as she puffed her way into his office where a fan on his desk kept the temperature down to a tolerable level. The room smelled musty and there were papers and files everywhere even stacked on the floor. The large computer on his desk looked somewhat out-dated and did not inspire Jessica with any confidence in the outcome of his enquiries.

"Sit down, coffee?"

"Yes, please," replied Jessica sinking into a battered sagging armchair.

"*Kahawa mbili, tafadhali*," (two coffees, please) he said to the secretary hovering near his desk.

"Well, I see you managed to negotiate our steps safely."

"They are quite a challenge," said Jessica.

"One day we will build them properly but just now there is only me and a half dozen men to keep this service going on very little money. Until we got mobile phones we had to use the public phone box across the street as the governor kept forgetting to pay the bill for our phone line."

None of this reassured Jessica that her parents' murderers would be found. On the other hand Mona himself seemed very efficient and competent. Jessica heard the slap, slide and suck of the secretary's fat thighs rubbing together as she brought the coffees and placed them on the table. After a few sips and slurps Mona began to talk about the investigation.

"Obviously there is nothing much we can retrieve from the scene of the crime. No papers, no DNA in the house and buildings. Fire consumes everything. But we have taken some DNA samples from your mother's body so that we can identify conclusively the men who raped and killed her if we find them. All we can do is question the people close to your parents, the white community and the staff families. They might know something from their own community."

"But they're nothing to do with it," objected Jessica.

"No, but if we can find out who your father's associates were and what matters he was involved in we might see what enemies he made. The staff's families could know if there is anyone who holds a grudge against him, a dismissed worker or people chased off his land."

"I can soon give you a list of people he knew here. The white community is a very small community after all, as you well know. You already know who the staff's families are."

And Jessica gave him as full a list as she could, of all their contacts and acquaintances beginning with their closest friends, Martin and Sarah Davey. But she was unable to help him with her father's contacts in Nairobi. "I only know that he went there regularly for meetings with the anti-poaching organisation, I think it was called Kenya Against Poaching – KAP," she told Mona. "He kept up his membership of the Muthaiga Club so that he had somewhere to stay every month."

"That gives me something to go on. I shall start my investigations there and perhaps Wanjiku can make enquiries locally. You know, I just want to say that I am truly sorry for what has happened. And I want you to know that not all Africans are evil like this. Most of us are kind and caring, we love our families, we work hard to earn a living – just like *mzungus.*"

"I know," said Jessica, "and terrible things happen in other countries too. They say that America has a mass killing somewhere every day but no-one says on the news that you shouldn't go to America. I do understand what all the bad press is doing to this country; tourists not coming, hotels closing, leisure facilities closing, less money going into the safari parks and so less money to fight the poachers."

"Do you feel as strongly about that as your father did?"

"I do, definitely. Not only can I not bear the cruelty of taking elephant tusks or rhino horn, or animal skins of any kind but these wonderful creatures are a resource for the country. The more people come to see them, the more money flows into the economy of Kenya."

"That is good. I think you are a good person Jessica Langley. I shall pursue these men with great diligence."

"Do you know how many are involved?"

"We think five. We found five different footprints at the farm, your farm. One other thing that might help, I know that most white people have many ornaments to decorate their house, small items of silver or china. Is there any

33

way you could make a list of those things? One or other of the attackers may have picked one of these up and slipped it into his pocket to sell later. They could turn up on one of the market stalls which could give me a lead."

"I doubt if I can remember everything but I will try. Don't forget they also took my mother's engagement ring which was quite a valuable diamond."

"I had not forgotten. I know that this list will take a while, you need time to think but the sooner the better. OK?"

Jessica was impressed, she hadn't expected such a level of competence. This implied that the police were better organised than she had thought.

They said their goodbyes and Jessica picked her way down the lopsided steps. As she walked away from the building she saw a slight movement out of the corner of her eye. She turned to look but caught only a glimpse of someone slinking back into the darkness of the shade thrown by the Police building. She didn't have time to think about it as she was soon distracted by one of the regular beggars that worked that part of town. He was a pitiful sight with his simple expression and strange eyes, one of which seemed to have rolled back into his head. But she remembered him from her childhood, he had been on the street for many years. Her parents always told her that she should never give him money as it would only encourage him to carry on begging.

As she got into her car, she thought she saw someone watching her and taking a photo of her car on his mobile phone. But she shook her head and tossed back her hair to dispel such ideas. "I am becoming paranoid," she told herself. "I must get a grip and stop thinking the worst."

On arrival back at Georgina's house she discovered that John, Georgina's lover, as she had been told to think of him, had returned from England bringing with him his grandson. John was slim and broad shouldered but quite short for a man, about the same height as Jessica so that she found herself looking straight into the kindest, gentlest face topped by a shock of pure white hair. He too had spent his life in Kenya as had his parents. Born, brought up, married in Kenya, in his turn his children were similarly born and brought up. All now gone to pursue careers and lives in other places. His wife of fifty years had died of cancer at about the same time that Georgina's husband had also died. John and Georgina had known each other for years but it was grief that brought them together. Neither of them relished being alone after being used to married life for so long and they had always liked each other.

John held out his hand to Jessica saying *"Jambo, karibu."* And then quickly abandoning the Swahili language, "I am so sorry to hear what has happened. I knew your father a little, mainly through playing snooker. He was a fine man and a good farmer. His work against poachers was much to be praised."

"Thank you," replied Jessica, with a slight catch in her voice. She mostly had her emotions under control now but every so often something would touch her to the quick. John's unexpected praise did just that.

"I am afraid my grandson is not here to greet you. Young people are such light weights," John said with a laugh. "He and I have done exactly the same journey but he has had to take to his bed with exhaustion whereas I am here expecting lunch and enjoying a drink in the company of you and Georgina. You may have to wait until morning to meet him I think. Now what would you like to drink?"

"He will collapse into bed straight after lunch, just you wait and see," laughed Georgina, "he is not as tough as he would like to think."

"How are the police getting on with their enquiries?" asked John, pouring a glass of wine for Jessica.

"Oh, you know, not too well really. But they have worked out that there were five men involved. They seem to have found five different sets of footprints. That is progress of a sort I suppose."

"It is early days; you have to give them time to work on it. But that seems like a good sign," said John reassuringly. He was remembering his own experiences with the police. As a lawyer he often had cause to be disappointed in the information they had gathered and in the level of corruption.

Chapter 3

Jessica was still in bed when her phone rang the following morning. It was her parent's friends, Martin and Sarah Davey asking her to go back to their farm with them for a few days. "We are leaving tomorrow to go back up country. Come and stay, you will love the farm and it would do you good to get away from it all for a few days." Jessica was tempted but felt that she should stay in Jaribuni to stay in touch with the police and their investigation. She explained this to Sarah who was very understanding, "that's fine, my dear, but we would love to see you when you are ready to come."

"I will let you know as soon as I feel able to get away."

She had only just put the phone down when it rang again. This time it was David and Victoria Walker who were also friends of her parents but who lived on the outskirts of Jaribuni. They were the leading lights of the social scene, Victoria being a born organiser was behind the many tennis and bridge games. David wasn't an organiser, he did as he was told by his wife but he played his part in her schemes and parties and joined in all the snooker games that were going. They had a fishing boat so he often took part in fishing competitions, he was known to have caught the biggest tuna ever hooked on that part of the coast.

"Do come and see us, we are at home tomorrow. Bring your swimsuit. We can have a dip in the pool, nice and refreshing then lunch together. Come about 11.30. We need time to enjoy the pool before we retreat from the noonday sun and take shelter in the shade of our veranda."

Jessica had no chance to interrupt this flow of words issuing orders, so laughing silently she agreed that she would be there at 11.30 the following day.

Meanwhile, in his office, Mona sat back in his rickety plastic chair and stared blankly out of the window thinking about Jessica. This was the worst case he had ever encountered. He felt out of his depth emotionally and professionally. His heart was heavy with grief for Jessica and anguish at what he had seen. He thought back to when she had first been brought into the police station, pushed and bullied by the arresting officers. He had taken one look at her face and the burning embers of her eyes that smouldered behind the dirt and realised that this was no ordinary case of careless driving or attempting to get past the road block. So it had been his idea to take her to *Mama* Hamilton to be looked after. Then he had driven out to the farm. Now sitting alone with his head in his hands, he thought about where to go from here, with no traces, no fingerprints, there seemed nowhere to start. "I won't find anything out sitting here, I must go to town, there will be gossip, there will be suspicion and I have my informants," he said to himself. He called Wanjiku and told him to go and interview the families of the Langley's staff. "See if you can find this Jaba who has disappeared. We need to question him."

He eased himself out of his chair and putting on his sun glasses, made his way down into the street. The heat and noise set his head throbbing. Even though he was wearing dark glasses the glare from the sun was a searchlight being shone straight into his face. The streets were crowded with shoppers, snake-hipped young women wearing the tightest of Western style dresses and all in the brightest possible colours, others in more sombre dresses all very smartly turned out in tight fitting skirts, blouses and high heels. There were *bibis* in traditional African wraps or *kikois*, there were also women in *burkas,* hidden behind yards of heavy black cloth. The men too varied between traditional dress and Western clothes but also among them was the occasional Maasai in his distinctive red plaid cloak walking very tall and straight with a long stick, never hurrying or varying his pace. It seemed that everything was tolerated here, all shapes and sizes of humanity in all their glorious variety.

The noise of traffic, roaring motor bikes, humming cars, rumbling lorries and *matatus* as well as the light chugging of the *tuk-tuks* filled the air which was heavy with dust created by these vehicles. Loud clunking sounds and the crashing of gears joined the cacophony every time a car or truck went over one of the monster speed bumps built across the road. Cyclists and motor bikes simply went round them.

Mona walked past Saïd's store, with its metal shutters pulled tight down now that it was the lunch hour, past the Well Being Pharmacy and the Zain phone shop each with its coloured signs announcing their name and business, none of which were fixed straight, all of which were dusty and shabby with peeling paint. He turned into the road which was the nearest thing the town had to a boulevard, wide and lined with trees whose thick canopy gave welcome shade to those walking by. Beyond the line of trees were the market stalls for which he was heading.

In the first cluster of stalls were the fruit and vegetable sellers, their wares all piled high in colourful pyramids, mangoes, paw-paws, oranges, carrots, cabbages, tomatoes, onions and potatoes. The stalls were constructed of wavy, uneven poles holding up a shade cover of either plastic sheeting or the thatch-work known locally as *makuti* while the table top was a sloping, undulating plank of wood also covered with plastic sheeting. He didn't think these people would be able to help him. They were simple folk, women for the most part, who worked small plots of land or *shambas* outside the town and brought their produce in each day. He greeted them anyway and stopped to chat. The news was of course all over town causing as much shock and dismay as it had among the Langley's friends and neighbours. Mona left them saying if you hear anything, any small piece of gossip come and tell me but he was well aware that they were unlikely to dare to go anywhere near the police station voluntarily.

He moved on to where there were stalls selling all kinds of household equipment, toys and clothes as well as hub caps. He understood why people had taken to tying their hubcaps onto their cars with plastic ties. Not only did the vicious potholes and speed bumps shake them off but there were many light-fingered young men who could pull them off and turn a profit.

The *mtumba* stalls were doing good business. These were where the cast off clothes, some of them brand new, from the wealthy West, that ended up here to be recycled at knock-down prices to whoever wanted to buy them. Mona was always astonished at the number of *mzungus* he saw eagerly casting their eye over these clothes and sometimes buying them. They called them 'bend-down boutiques' because of the way much of the stock was spread out on the ground; shopping there could be quite back breaking. More often it was the local people who bought here so that you often saw young men walking around in Manchester United or Arsenal tops that were one or two years out of date. They didn't care. Nor did anyone care what it said on their T-shirts. For the most part they didn't understand the legends in the various foreign languages. You might see a lad who had obviously never been out of Kenya and who had never ever owned a vehicle in his life announcing to the world through his T-shirt '*Yo hice el camino de la muerte y Sigo vivo*' which roughly translates as 'I survived Death Road'. with a picture of a motor bike and a map of Bolivia showing the road. He often bought things there himself, after all a policeman's pay was not at all generous, but he took care to wear plain shirts with no compromising logo. It wouldn't do for him to be seen promoting violence or drugs however unintentional or inadvertent.

Mona felt that he was more likely to find something out from these people who were wheelers and dealers with connections everywhere and anywhere that they felt they could make a profit. Unlike his fellow policemen he could be confident of a pleasant reception, not exactly a welcome but he didn't inspire the fear, dislike and disrespect that people generally felt towards the police after years of being randomly asked to pay out money to be allowed to pass the road blocks without being incarcerated or beaten up. Mona had been fast tracked through the force after doing a degree in Nairobi and had been sent on a training placement in England where he had admired the way the British police worked without corruption, for the most part, and approaching the public with politeness in the first instant, the belief in the mantra 'innocent until proven guilty' being paramount.

Now he approached the first stall he came to, a clothing stall which was run by Mary, a woman of middle age well built, not to say stout, and with her hair corn-raked back into several thin plaits that were tied in a bunch at the nape of her neck. She had bright curious eyes, a ready laugh, and was known to be a person you could turn to for help. She was always smartly turned out having the pick of her own stock as it came in. Mary was a clever operator who spoke two or three of the local languages but was also fluent in English and Italian, these being the main foreign languages prevalent in the country. English was important because of the colonial legacy and its status as the international language of business and politics. Italians had settled along the coast in large numbers after the mafia clear out of the 1970s. Mona spoke to Mary in Swahili however. He knew her well and respected her astute business mind and the way she was paying for her children to go to secondary school by her own efforts with her *mtumba* stall.

"*Jambo,* Mary, *habari?*" Hello, how are things going?

"*Nsuri sana.*" Good, good, she replied.

Mona then began to ask her if she had heard anything that might help his investigation into the death of Donald and Lydia Langley.

"*Samahani*, sorry," she replied. "I would like to help, I knew them well. *Bwana* Langley was a fine man. He liked to help people and looked after the elephants. He lent me money to re-build my stall after it was knocked down in a rainstorm. A good man. And *Mama* Langley used to buy things from me, never tried too hard to make a bargain. If I hear anything I will tell you."

After giving Mary his mobile phone number, Mona moved away to talk to the next person, a man whom he didn't know, thin with a rodent-like face, small eyes, a sharp nose set in a slightly pointy face. His name it transpired was Charo. He sat under a *chandarua*, that sheltered him from the sun despite the canvas being worn thin and holed in places. The gold chains that he wore twinkled and jingled in the sunshine as he moved his hands around constantly re-positioning his stock which was mainly menswear and shoes. Mona could tell when he spoke to him that the man was uncomfortable in the company of a policeman so he did his best to put him at ease. He began by asking him if he was having a successful day.

"Some good, some bad," replied Charo, "Just now it is lunchtime. People are busy eating. If I sit still no-one comes at all but if I keep moving and changing things around it seems to attract customers. Here comes someone now. Excuse me."

Mona stood back to let him carry on his business, he watched fascinated as a bargain was struck for a pair of trainers that were large and coloured a day-glow greenish yellow. The most hideous shoes he had ever seen, he thought. The young Rastafarian buying them tried to argue the price down but Charo recognised the glint of desire in his eyes and stood his ground. In the end the young Rasta paid the full asking price but went away happy with his purchase, bouncing on his newly shod feet. Afterwards Mona could see how pleased Charo was with the deal he had struck; he seemed more relaxed. Mona took this as a good omen and began to question him about the murders of the Langleys and their staff. Charo took a step back and began to look anywhere but at Mona's face. He strenuously avoided eye contact.

"I know nothing," he kept saying. "It is not my business. I may wheel and deal and sometimes charge more than is honest but murder – no way, man," as he was talking, he was looking over his shoulder and all around, frightened of being thought to have given any information at all.

"Somebody in this market place knows something," thought Mona. Aloud, he said to Charo. "Well, if you think of anything, anything at all that might help this is my number," he said handing him his card. Mona moved on to the centre of the market, further away from the road where the meat and fish stalls were. He passed one stall piled high with pungent tiny dried shrimps surrounded by clouds of flies. He braved the flies and the smell crunching over shrimps that had fallen to the ground to talk to the stall holder who was tall and gaunt with a flat wide nose that seemed to spread across her face, very unlike the Somali or Ethiopian type of faces with their more aquiline noses. She also had the biggest, ugliest feet with hard, yellowing toenails that Mona had ever seen. Mona introduced himself and enquired what her name was.

"I am Nuru," she replied.

Mona couldn't help thinking that the name, which means 'light', was out of keeping with the woman's rough appearance. She too had heard the terrible news and unlike many others was prepared to venture an opinion.

"You want to talk to people like Charo over at the shoe stall. I am not saying he was involved but he knows some dangerous people."

After talking to a few more people in the town Mona made his way back to his office.

Once ensconced in his chair with a glass of cold water he mopped his sweating brow and considered what he knew. It didn't take long. He was no further on than he had been but he felt that someone among those he spoke to might come forward with information. It was probably time to talk to the *mzungus* who had known the family. He decided to wait until he heard what Wanjiku had found out from talking to the staff's families.

He thought about Mary, Charo and Nuru but also some of the others he had spoken to. He thought about the people selling wood carvings, salad bowls and servers decorated with figures of zebra, elephants, rhinos or giraffe. They sold wooden models, all kinds of animals and especially elephants, not just small ones, but large enough for an adult to sit on and giraffes as tall as a tall man. It seemed to be a harmless enough trade. He did wonder though how on earth the tourists got the larger things back on the aeroplane especially now that security was so tight. There were also some Giacometti-like statues of Maasai warriors. All were advertised as hand carved in native villages but he knew only too well that most of them were made in a factory or workshop. Next to them had been a seller of sea shells, giant clam shells, conch shells and to his dismay some turtle shells and others, many bleached white by sand and sun but some still glowing cream, rose and orange with spikes and convolutions and points. This crime that he was investigating seemed to him to have nothing to do with the sea and its creatures but at the same time those selling the shells were oblivious to the importance of conserving species. Elephants or marine creatures, all were vulnerable and all were important as attractions of the country.

His mind moved on to the ladies selling *kikapus*, the traditional native baskets that were now very popular with tourists but the locals had always found them useful. It seemed a most gentle thing – basket weaving. He couldn't believe that they could have anything to do with such a horrific crime. There were handbags of all varieties on sale, from shiny plastic to leather and animal hide. This year zebra seemed to be the design of choice. Could these sharp saleswomen know anything at all? Finally, there were the two youths selling hub caps some of which may have been honestly come by. It was a trade on the edge of legitimacy and so they could have some very dishonest contacts. They had been very reluctant to say anything but he felt sure that they knew something.

His thoughts were interrupted at that moment by the arrival of Wanjiku who slumped down in the chair opposite him with a loud 'ouf' of relief.

"Tired out are you? You are supposed to be young and fit."

"It's been a hard day," Wanjiku said. "I have spoken to them all, all the staff families. Mostly they are so very sad at the death of their loved one but also the death of their *bwana* and his wife. Now that the farm and everything has gone they have no money only their *bomas* and *kibandas* are still liveable-in as they were some distance from the house. I hope that Jessica Langley is not going to throw them out just because there is no work for them anymore."

"I don't think so. She seems to me a kind person. So, did you learn anything?"

"Not much. They know very little of the life of the Langleys. As I said they lived quite a distance away, a fact which also saved their lives. I'll go through them one by one.

"First I spoke to Zarifa, the wife of Emmanuel the houseboy. They married five years ago but he has been working for Langleys since he was sixteen. Zarifa can make some money out of growing food on their *shamba*; beans, potatoes, tomatoes and *sukuma*. But she is alone now with two small children. She says her man spoke little about the Langleys, only to say that they were good people. He knew that *Bwana* Langley, as well as the farm, was working

42

on a project to save elephants but no more than that. She said that *Mama* Langley used to give her food and clothes for the children sometimes.

"Then I spoke to the family of Joseph the cook. His wife, Durah, does some work, she sews clothes and curtains for people but it is not a very regular income. Joseph knew even less about the Langley's affairs. He spent all his time in the kitchen and worked more with *Mama* Langley than with the B*wana.*

"Rachel had only grown-up children who are all working elsewhere. She was Jessica's *ayah* but stayed on to help even after the girl had grown up and gone away. Her family came to the funeral and are here now but they know nothing of life here and are soon going back up country.

"Samuel the gardener had no family living there with him.

"Now Jaba the cattle and odd job man has not been seen since that night. He came here only recently from way up country, near Somalia, and none of the others knows much about him. He seems to have vanished."

"Did they have bank accounts?"

"Oh, yes. It seems the Langleys were very fair and very modern about payment. None of that cash payment now. All paid straight into banks. Everyone has moved on since M*pesa* started. They all have mobile phones too so they can make payments that way."

"Did you get their account numbers?"

"No, boss. I didn't."

"It could be useful to check up on them."

"Why? You can't think that one of them could be involved."

"You have to check every angle. They might not have been directly involved but there could be a link – someone they knew or had contact with. You can get on to that in the morning."

"Right, boss."

"For now we will call it a day."

There is something special about early evening in Africa. There is a smell of dust, dry and spicy and an increasing quietness before the sounds of the night begin; the crickets and the croaking of frogs, the clack-clack of the palm leaves in the breeze. The shadows lengthen as the sun's power wanes. It feels as though the whole world is heaving a sigh of relief at the coolness of twilight. And the darkness descends so quickly as though the sun is rushing to get home after a hard day's work. It moves down across the sky at speed glowing a deep golden orange; a final glorious farewell to the day. The blackness grows behind it bringing a sliver of moon that shines a thin silver path across the land and the waters of the creek.

Jessica had known such sunsets all her life and never tired of watching them. It was at twilight that she finally met John's grandson. She had been in her room resting and having a refreshing shower before coming down to the terrace for the evening drink and meal that was almost a ritual in Georgina's household. She felt strong enough to face the evening and a new acquaintance.

John and his grandson stood up promptly to greet her. Lawrence Fletcher-Greene turned out to be a tall, handsome young man. What her mother would have called a fine figure of a man thought Jessica. She remembered her mother saying that her own mother had told her that a man should be handsome if he possibly could be but if not, he must be tall. Lawrence was both.

She watched him slip, slim and long-limbed, into the house to fetch her drink. It was obvious that he had a close relationship with his grandfather and was pleased to be helpful, to save him any trouble that he could. His deep blue eyes looked straight into hers from under a thick wave of black hair as he handed her a glass of wine, suddenly it seemed as if the air was filled with sweet music delighting her and troubling her in equal measure.

"Cheers, Jessica, I am so pleased to meet you. It will be nice to have someone young in the household, perhaps to go around with a bit. Normally, I am here on my own with Gramps and Georgina. They are great but they are not into all the latest news from the UK, and not too keen on sailing. Perhaps you don't sail either but before you tell me about yourself I must just say how sorry I am about your predicament. I didn't know your parents but it is a terrible thing to happen to anyone and I want to assure you that my sympathies are very much with you."

"Goodness, what a long speech. Thank you for your sympathy. I am afraid that's all anyone can offer at the moment. As for sailing, I have never done any in my life before but I suppose there's always a first time."

"I would be delighted to take you," said Lawrence with just the ghost of a bow.

It could be just what I need to take my mind off things, to take me out of myself as they say, thought Jessica. "How often do you come here?" she asked.

"About once a year. My parents had to move on. John, Gramps, was a lawyer and a magistrate in the colonial system. He decided to stay on after *Uhuru* in the 60s and my mother grew up here and married here but there was no land or farm that they could continue to work and of course there was no work for young white people by then so she and my father left to make their home in England where I grew up. But we came for frequent visits so I almost feel I belong here. Once you get to know Africa it grabs you, takes a hold of your heart and doesn't let go. How about you?"

"I came back this Christmas to see if I could make a life for myself here. I am a teacher so I thought there might be an opening somewhere in one of the schools. But I would like to try some new venture. Unlike you I actually grew up here and I feel a foreigner in the UK even after being at school and university there. But my parent's farm is not big enough for me to make a living out of. Not like the safari lodge that my friends Hugo and Cora are running. And I am no farmer so I don't know… it is all so different now. The land is still there but that's all. There is no house, no livestock, no farm buildings or machinery, all gone in the fire…" Jessica's dark, brown eyes began filling with tears, she could no longer speak.

"Oh, God, I'm sorry. I didn't mean to go back to things that would upset you." Lawrence was devastated by the effect that the turn of conversation was having on a girl he found heart-stoppingly beautiful.

"It's OK. I have to face up to everything somehow, sometime. There are so many decisions to make."

"Well, if I can help at all, apart from taking you sailing, let me know."

Take me sailing, thought Jessica pushing back her mane of dark hair. A fat lot of good that will do but I suppose it was kindly meant. I've lived here near the sea all these years and never been out in a boat. Perhaps I should try.

But before she could answer Georgina announced that supper was ready and they all went to sit down at the table where candles glowed in the warm darkness and plates of aromatic, dark red tomato and pepper soup steamed. By nine o'clock Jessica was ready for bed. She had had enough of polite conversation and needed some time alone to think. After coffee she made her excuses and left the three of them to enjoy the rest of the evening.

After saying goodnight to Jessica, the others gathered again on the terrace to chat for a while before bedtime. It had been a year since John had seen his grandson. He was keen to hear about his daughter in England and to catch up

45

on Lawrence's news too. But the conversation was all about Jessica. Lawrence naturally wanted to know what had happened and how Georgina had become involved.

"Do you think the police will be efficient?" he asked after he had been filled in on all the details.

"I don't know, they don't have a very good record of clearing up crimes," replied John.

"Yes," interrupted Georgina, "but now they have this new man, a new detective. Inspector Mona. It was he that brought Jessica here and what a sensible thing that was. He was sent to England to do some training with the police in London and I think he is keen to make his mark here. In the market they say he can be trusted which is more than you can usually say for the police here."

"I hope you're right, my dear. Meanwhile the girl has to try and come to terms with her new situation and decide what to do. I presume she inherits the farm and whatever savings and investments her parents had."

"She must do as she was the only child. Which makes things so much harder for her, no-one to support her or discuss things with."

"I thought she mentioned two friends. Wouldn't they help her?" asked Lawrence.

"You probably mean Cora and Hugo. They are brother and sister and went to school with Jessica. I think they will help her as far as they can but it's not the same as having family. She does have an aged aunt near her, so she isn't totally alone," replied Georgina. "And of course we are doing what we can."

"I am sure it was a lucky day when she was brought here. I know how kind and sensible you are. My favourite step-grandmother."

"Well, thank you, Lawrence, of course the day wasn't lucky, because of what happened but it was a good thing that Inspector Mona brought her here. The alternatives were a police cell or the hospital. Anyway I am off to bed, yawned Georgina. It's been a long day somehow. Goodnight."

"Goodnight," replied the two men. Left on their own they poured themselves another whiskey and carried on chatting.

"She is a wonderful woman, your Georgina," said Lawrence.

"Oh I know. I am very lucky to be with her. After your grandmother died I never thought I would find happiness again, but here we are, two old coffin dodgers together. And we still swim every morning and play tennis and snooker not to mention bridge. It all keeps us going. So far so good. But I had some bad news when I was in England. It seems I have Parkinson's Disease, very early stages yet. But I sometimes get terrible trembling, and pins and needles in my hands. Sadly it is also hereditary so you should keep a check on yourself."

"Oh, Gramps, I am sorry. There is no cure is there?"

"No, but there are drugs I can take to alleviate the symptoms and to keep me going as long as possible."

"Have you told Georgina?"

"Not yet. She has been too preoccupied with looking after Jessica. I will try to tell her tomorrow. I believe Jessica is going to be out all day visiting friends. Anyway, that's me done for now. I'm off to bed too."

"Well, me too. I have to try and get into the rhythm of life here."

The following morning Jessica's parent's friends, Martin and Sarah Davey rang again asking her once more to go back to their farm with them for a few days. "We are leaving today to go back up country.

"Just wanted to remind you, we meant what we said, come and stay, you will love the farm and it would do you good to get away from it all for a few days." Jessica thanked them and wished them a safe journey.

She had only just finished dressing when the phone rang again. This time it was David and Victoria Walker checking that she was still going to be with them for lunch, that she hadn't forgotten the invitation. As leading light of the social scene, Victoria being a born organiser was keen to be the first person in Jaribuni to have Jessica round for lunch. She would be able to gossip about it for ages after. David just did as he was told and would be glad to have a fresh audience to describe how he caught the biggest tuna ever on that part of the coast.

"You are coming to see us, aren't you? Bring your swimsuit. We can have a swim, nice and refreshing and lunch together. Come about 11.30. We need time to enjoy the pool before we have lunch," Jessica promised she would definitely be there at 11.30 that day. As instructed, she went and collected her swimsuit which had been in her overnight bag and so was one of the only bits of clothing she still had. She said her goodbyes to Georgina and John letting them know she would not be there for lunch.

Outside she jumped into her car and sped along the driveway past the many trees that Georgina had planted over the years, there were tulip trees, flamboyants, the pre-historic cycads, terminalias, teak trees, sausage trees and bamba koffis. The grass was dry and sparse, only greening up when the rains came as Georgina did not believe in watering her garden in an area where water was scarce. She passed through the gates onto the road and suddenly there was a car behind her. Strange, she thought, since Georgina's house was the last one at the very end of the road. After that there was only a sandy track leading down to the beach. The car followed her through town and onto the road where David and Victoria lived. As she turned into their drive it shot on past. A brown Toyota, very scruffy, whose number plate was illegible due to a thick incrustation of dirt.

Jessica shrugged. I am becoming paranoid, she thought. But even when I stopped to buy some flowers for Victoria it must have waited and then followed again. It's worrying but I won't mention it to David and Victoria they will make such a fuss.

And so, as ordered by Victoria, they enjoyed a refreshing swim and afterwards had lunch in the shade.

Victoria was very kind, talking about how her mother had been such a great supporter of the charities that Victoria espoused. The home for deaf children, the home for the elderly and the school for the blind were all recipients of money raised by Victoria through various social events, barbecues, jazz evenings, dinners and dances. She was anxious to make sure that Jessica knew she could always call on them for help.

David was keen to talk about her father. They had spent a lot of time together and both had belonged to the KAP. "I was just a foot soldier," said David. "Your father was the leader of our group, full of ideas. He liaised with the British Army because he could see that our rangers needed training to help them fight the poachers. He also worked with other groups exchanging information about known terrorist groups affiliated to the likes of Al Shebaab who often use money earned from poaching to fund their terrorist attacks. There are also people following up the supply chain finding out who the end purchasers are and getting them prosecuted in their own country."

"I had no idea that he had such international involvement," said Jessica.

"Oh, yes, and he kept meticulous records too but I expect all that has been lost in the fire."

"You need to speak to Inspector Mona. He must know about this. It is such an obvious line of enquiry."

"Don't worry. I already have. He interviewed me the day before yesterday. But I cannot remember any names that your father may have mentioned to me. I think all of us are in danger now because the poachers will be afraid that we know things that could identify them."

Then Jessica found herself telling David about being followed. "It's probably nothing but I found it quite alarming."

"I think it is alarming, definitely. You should absolutely go to the police about this."

"I'll think about it. Tomorrow, as I told Victoria I am going to Hugo and Cora's place for the night. It is well out of town so I should be safe there."

Going home, there, once again was the brown Toyota. But she soon forgot about it as her arrival coincided with Lawrence coming home from sailing. His face browned by the sun intensifying the colour of his blue eyes, his black hair salted, windswept, he was exhilarated, thrilled by the harmony of boat, wave and wind. The very air around him seemed to smell of the ocean. The sight of him took Jessica's breath away. She immediately felt her heart pulsing but at the same time guilt kicked in. How could she be thinking like this, feeling these emotions, so soon after her parent's tragedy.

Lawrence, for his part was also feeling his emotions stir. Jessica looked so fragile, her slender frame and long curtain of dark hair hiding her face from the world and her way of tossing it back when she looked at you, running her hand through her chestnut mane before speaking. Her brown eyes that filled so easily with tears at the moment. He wanted to scoop her up and look after her, if she would only let him.

Chapter 4

The day that Jessica was due to go to Zinj Safari camp to see Cora dawned bright and full of hope. Jessica's mood was lifted by the clear light of early morning, fresh before the heat of the sun makes the world glare and shimmer. Looking out of her window she could see the monkeys swinging in the trees and the dogs barking after them, all so unselfconscious and living only in the moment. She forgot about the car following her yesterday and how worried she had been.

That is what I must try to do, she thought, live in the moment, not dwell on what has happened but – that doesn't mean forgetting. Putting all her sorrows out of her mind she set about getting ready to go out. She was to be gone for two days, staying overnight at Hugo and Cora's place just as she had the fateful night of her parents' death. She began packing trying hard not to think about the last time that she had been out at the Zinj Safari Camp. This is different, she told herself as she threw sandals, safari boots, shorts and shirts together with a dress for the evening into an overnight bag. All of them "bend-down" boutique specials.

Over a quick breakfast she said her goodbyes to Georgina, John and Lawrence and then got in her car. "Ring us to let us know that you have arrived safely," they said. Nodding agreement Jessica switched on her engine, put the car in gear and set off. As she pulled out of the drive she was concentrating on her feelings about travelling back along this road and so did not notice the car which was waiting alongside the road and nosed out to follow her.

It was a journey of about an hour so she put on some upbeat music for encouragement. She crossed the bridge over the creek and soon came to the road barrier where she had been picked up by the police. She slowed down ready to stop but the duty policemen that day were more interested in stopping lorries and she was simply waved through. She breathed a sigh of relief, glad that she had not been stopped and had to spend any time in front of those terrible caltrops. Passing the turn-off to her family farm was another difficult milestone on her way to recovery. For recovery is what she needed, grief is an illness that never lets go but can only diminish with time. She looked briefly in her rear-view mirror as she drove on but thought nothing of it when she saw the brown Toyota saloon behind her. She continued her journey swerving round potholes and jamming on the brakes as the speed bumps loomed up at her and then turned off onto the dirt track that led across country to the Patterson-Smythes' farmstead, Zinj House and the safari camp offices. It was only here that the car behind did not follow her but carried on going. She vaguely wondered where but it was not particularly interesting, after all every other car in Africa was a Toyota. Then she remembered the car from yesterday. It looked the same. Same amount of dirt, both cars had illegible number plates and both were saloon cars.

Fifteen minutes later she was parking in front of the familiar old colonial house.

The dogs were standing, barking and wagging their tails in the pillared portico while jacaranda and bougainvillea tumbled over the white walls showing off their gaudy flowers of pinks, blues and whites. Cora came out to meet her. They threw their arms around each other in a great bear hug of an embrace that Jessica found immensely comforting. She knew Cora so well that there was never any need for pretence between them. Where Jessica was tall and willowy, Cora was short and though slim, curvy. They were exact opposites in physique. Jessica looked down at her friend's round, gentle looking face framed by short, fair hair, a practical style when looking after animals. She was pleased to be with her again. She always felt that Cora was the nearest thing she had to a sister.

"How was the drive?"

"It was fine. I didn't get stopped by the police at that barrier near the bridge, they just waved me through, thank goodness. I don't think I could have coped with any questioning and someone nosing about in my car. Too close in time, I shall have to get used to it all again, no doubt."

"Well, I am so glad to see you," declared Cora. "I have cleared my desk for the next two days, so no work, I am going to concentrate on us being together."

"That is so very kind of you. Before I do anything else I must ring Georgina, I promised her and I don't want her to worry. She immediately dialled the number on her mobile."

"Hi Georgina," Cora heard her say. "I'm here and everything went well. It took me exactly an hour. Not much traffic on the road and I wasn't stopped at the police checkpoint. What's that?" Then after a brief silence, "OK, I'll be careful."

"What was that about?"

"Georgina said that Lawrence, her grandson, left immediately after me and saw a car, a brown Toyota pull out from by the hedge at the side of the road and follow me. Perhaps not very significant but I noticed a brown Toyota behind me at the bridge and only when I turned down here did it take a different road. The thing is that Georgina's house is right at the end of the road going along the creek and there is no other building down there. Also I think I was followed yesterday when I went to the Walker's house."

"As you say it might mean nothing. There are thousands of brown Toyotas around. Still it might be as well to mention it to the Inspector next time you see him."

"Yes, I'm sure you're right. So, how are things at Zinj Safari Camp?"

"Let's go on inside and we can talk there. The staff will put your bags in your room. I have put you in a different room this time – the grand guest room normally reserved for my parent's guests. I didn't want you to feel that this was some kind of groundhog day to put it crudely."

"Thank you, very thoughtful of you."

"Come on then," and Cora led Jessica into the house and out onto the veranda. For the time being they were alone as Hugo and his father, Robert, were out on the farm somewhere mending fences, speaking to their workers and looking out for injured animals. Meanwhile Jenny, Cora and Hugo's mother, was in the office busy with paperwork. Coffee was brought, together with some delicious homemade biscuits which both girls declared they shouldn't eat but couldn't resist for, as Cora pointed out, this visit was for relaxing and enjoying.

"Don't forget," she said, "that we have one of the best cooks around and Mother is no slouch in that department either, so just tuck in and enjoy."

Jessica sat back and let the beauty of the scene sink in. The gardens were rich with flowering plants and trees, there were sculptural candelabra euphorbia, cycads and cacti planted beside desert roses while oleanders and hibiscus flowered pink, white and apricot nearby. There were trees giving shade, the fragrant camel's foot tree with its pink and white blossoms, flamboyants with their intense scarlet flowers, banyan trees and the mosquito-repelling neem trees. Near the veranda was a swimming pool, surrounded by fish-tail, butterfly and fan palms, its rippling waters sparkling silver and blue in the sun's rays. Beyond the trees running along the perimeter of the garden was the track that led to the safari camp. At the other side of the garden was a paddock where horses grazed peacefully and another track leading to the farm. Straight ahead the lush green lawns and careful cultivation of the garden gave way to the savannah where the tall dry grasses waved supreme and the sweep of land was interrupted only by the occasional flat topped acacia tree. This was where the safari camp was, but it was far enough away and over the other side of the distant low hills to be out of sight.

"Remind me what those trees over there are, they are quite magnificent. I used to know all the trees, we had to learn the names at school when I was little before I was sent to boarding school. But I have forgotten most of them."

"Those over there, beside the track? They are very old, as you can see by their huge size and spread. The monkeys love them. We call them *bamba koffi* but I think they are a kind of mahogany."

"So tell me how things are going here at Goshi." Jessica was anxious to keep the conversation light and easy, normal even.

"Well, it's quite difficult at the moment as a matter of fact. Like everyone else, we have been hit by the downturn in tourism. Every time there is an incident of unrest, or a murder the governments around the world, especially the British announce that their citizens shouldn't come here claiming that it is unsafe. Consequently, many of the hotels down on the coast road near where you are at the moment are closing so people are losing their jobs. And really it is no more unsafe than say America with all their mass killings or even some parts of the UK – London, Manchester, Glasgow."

"Normally I would have agreed with you. But horror has come into my life in a way that I would not wish on my worst enemy. Why would anyone take the risk of something so utterly horrific happening to them? Do you feel safe here?"

"This is my home and we take reasonable precautions like everyone else, you know we have BSafe security guards and an *askari,* but just lately things are becoming worrying. One of the problems we have is that the herdsmen keep driving their cattle onto our land. My father has given over a section of our farm that they can use but they are constantly demanding more. In Laikipia, up in the north, farmers have been shot for protecting their land – land that produces food for the country. Your father came here a lot to discuss farming problems but also to talk about the conservation projects."

"He was particularly keen to save the elephants and I know you have elephants here at the safari camp."

"We do, and my father is just as keen but he was concerned for all species. Rhinos and leopards, zebras and gazelles even snakes and pangolins all need protecting from poachers. He belongs to the same organisation as your father did."

"Then he will probably be questioned by Inspector Mona soon. Goodness, we have got very serious. Let's lighten up and talk gossip."

"Yes, you're right. Too serious. You are here to relax and recover. So, tell me about this grandson of Georgina's. What's he like?"

"I hardly know really. I only met him the day before yesterday and last night. He is tall and dark haired but he has the most amazing blue eyes. I think he is nice; he is very close to his grandfather which shows a good side to his character but he seemed a bit over-confident to me. Gave me a long speech about how sorry he was and wants to take me sailing." Jessica avoided mentioning the rush of feelings she had felt on seeing Lawrence the previous evening.

"Well you seem to have noticed quite a lot about him. I think you should take him up on the sailing thing."

"I've never been sailing in my life."

"Well, now could be a good time to start. You never know, you might like it. Come on let's go for a walk and see the horses." Calling to the dogs who were lazing under the shade of the oleanders, they set off, Taka-Taka and Shenzy running ahead. Arriving at the paddock they leant over the fence as the horses came towards them whinnying and swishing their tails. Jessica was particularly taken by one who was grey with black spots.

"His name is Domino." Said Cora.

"Of course, what else could it be," laughed Jessica, realising suddenly that it was the first time she had felt mirth of any kind for several weeks now. She held out her hand to stroke Domino's nose marvelling at his soft velvety muzzle. Cora had come prepared with some carrots which the horses crunched with gusto.

"Maybe you would like to go for a ride later or would you prefer to do a safari run in the land rover? Either way I think we should go back now. Mother will be expecting us."

As they strolled back to the house with the loll-tongued dogs panting behind, Jessica could see Jenny, Cora's mother on the veranda. When she saw the two young women approaching she stood up and came to meet them.

"Hello, my dear. How lovely to see you," she greeted Jessica giving her a long heartfelt hug.

"It is good to be here. I have always thought of this as my second home. And it is as always, just beautiful – my ideal house."

The three women settled down to drinks and a light lunch chattering together about this and that; the new supermarket which now, wonder of wonders took card payments, so much easier they all agreed, people getting divorced, people going away to visit family in Europe, people having their house renovated and other such gripping news. Eventually Jenny asked Jessica how she was and what her plans were but Jessica being unable to answer deflected the question with one of her own and asked about Hugo.

"Oh, he and Robert are out at the camp with clients. We have some American tourists, a group of six, so they are busy doing game drives and ensuring that the staff are keeping everything up to standard," explained Jenny. "They will both be back this evening. I'm planning a fine meal for us all."

Over lunch Jessica and Cora decided to opt for a mini safari rather than riding. They set off straight after lunch for their game drive through the safari camp. Zinj Camp was not one of the biggest parks but the Patterson-Smythes focused on quality. The tents that their clients stayed in were spacious and beautifully built in a style that most would recognise as 'old colonial'. They had wooden floors making them feel like a solid barrier against snakes but the walls were tough cream-coloured canvas that fastened with giant zips. Around the beds was a lot of trailing white netting some of which was for keeping out mosquitoes and some which was simply decorative. This was coupled with tribal patterned rugs and *kikoi* style bed covers. Only one of the tents was unoccupied and after a brief look at it, they moved on in search of game.

They saw plenty of Thomson gazelles leaping and pronking in front of the car, there were eland and water buffalos too and eventually they spotted some elephants, a small group of about five including one baby. Their grey backs were dry as dust as they plodded slowly by, seeming oblivious to the presence of the car. Not far on there were two giraffes stretching their long necks to graze gently at the top of an acacia tree where the softest shoots could be found. Then as they rounded a large bluff, on an outcrop of rock there was a lion lying lazily in the shade who also took no notice of the car. They hastily wound up their windows as lions have been known to rush at a car and take a swipe through the window at whoever is sitting there. Jessica and Cora felt lucky to have seen so much in one afternoon but decided to go back to the house, have a swim and freshen up for the evening.

Jessica's room, the guest room, was enormous and very elegantly furnished in the English country house style. No wonder Cora called it grand, she thought. It did feel a long way from her friend's room which was in another wing of the house. She threw herself down on the bed and closed her eyes feeling tired and suddenly very alone without Cora to chatter with. She had enjoyed the afternoon and especially seeing the animals, it was a long time since she had last been on safari. When a landmark or attraction is on your doorstep and becomes over familiar you tend not to make the effort to see it however interesting it might be. The elephants had made her think of her father and all the work he had done to protect them and as she thought about him her mind turned to what she must do to re-start her life. That was what it felt like, a new beginning. As plans and projects began to whirl round and round in her head she remembered her phone call with Georgina. She began to worry and fret about who could have been in that brown Toyota, possibilities were so hard to think about making her fretful and making a quick nap seem impossible yet somehow she did nod off to sleep to be woken sometime later by a knocking at her door. It was Cora wanting to know if she was OK and telling her that it was time to join the family on the veranda for drinks. Oh my goodness thought Jessica, it's later than I thought, the sun is setting. She showered and changed as quickly as she could and went downstairs to the veranda.

Hugo was sitting with a beer in his hand and leapt up as soon as he saw Jessica. His heart had leaped up too. She looked lovely he thought with her long hair brushed and shining under the lamplight, barefoot and wearing a simple white shift dress that made him think of Greek goddesses. He gave her a gentle hug and a kiss on both cheeks, trying to seem more casual than he felt.

"Here you are, your favourite tipple, I believe," he said handing her a glass of dry white wine chilled so that beads of moisture formed on the outside of the glass as she sipped.

"Where is everyone?"

"Mother and Cora are in the kitchen supervising the meal and Dad is just on his way. He is taking a phone call at the moment. So there's just me for the moment."

"Well, I expect you'll do," replied Jessica smiling. "How was your day?"

"Pretty busy. Our American clients are quite demanding and we took them on game drives this morning and this afternoon – that's a lot of driving in one day. Then they started asking about hunting. They seem keen to go out and bag themselves a lion or an elephant like in the bad old days. They were quite insistent so it took all my tact and courtesy to point out, in a way that persuaded them, that we only shoot with cameras on this reserve, and that we are all about conservation."

"They do love their guns, the Americans. I was reading a book just recently by Lady Genesta Hamilton, not that she was American, you know she was married for a while to Boy Long who was Lord Delamere's right-hand man, both of them were very 'in' with the Happy Valley set all those years ago. Anyway, in her autobiography which is a diary really she writes about her first experiences in Kenya and all the game she shot when on safari in those early days. Her book finishes in the 1980s and she has put a footnote in, something to the effect that it was sad to have killed all those animals and how shocked she was at the amount of killing her former self did."

"Yes, but 'former self' is the critical bit. We can't judge people of the past by the standards of our day. Things have changed and people's outlooks change. Look at those two old boys who run holiday huts on the beach not far from here. Do you know them, the Smithson brothers? They built their house years and years ago using the wreck of a boat that grounded on the beach and their doorframes are all made of elephant tusks. Their parents would have been here mid nineteenth century and it was they who killed the elephants, they and their friends. But it is old, old ivory so you can't be sentimental about it. The problem is that the trade in old ivory encourages the poaching of living animals. There are greedy people in this world that just want to acquire valuable assets, I'm not even sure that aesthetics comes into it. In any case you can't blame Sandy and Finn for keeping the frames or for the elephants that died a century ago. Even when they were young in the early part of the twentieth century no-one thought anything of big game hunting as it was called."

"I do know those two men. I went to visit them once with my parents to see the new snooker room they had built, with the latest air-conditioning even though their house didn't have any mod-cons. The kitchen was out at the back with an old *kuni (*firewood) stove for cooking and there was no electric lighting. The house was very ramshackle with all kinds of treasures piled all over the place. I remember the tusks and I remember the photos they had framed and put round the walls in the snooker room. Pictures of old time Kenya dating back to when it was known as British East Africa, so, pre-1920. A wonderful record of a past way of life. One of the pictures dating from soon after the First World War showed their sister as a little girl sitting with her arm round her pet cheetah. Apparently she had entered a copy of it in a competition for photos of children with their pets being run by an English magazine she subscribed to. They sent it back with a haughty dismissal saying that pictures of stuffed or toy animals were not acceptable."

Both began laughing at the thought of this just as Cora and Jenny came into the room followed by Robert.

"What are you two laughing at?" asked Cora. They quickly told her the essence of the story, then Hugo asked, "what about supper, I'm famished, will it be long?"

"No not very, we have time for another drink and I think Sami is bringing some nibbles that he has made and some nuts. That should stave off the worst of the hunger pangs for you."

At that moment Sami came in with bowls of macadamia and cashew nuts and some plates of bruschetta.

"There you are, Hugo," said Jenny and turning to Jessica explained, "He is always hungry. He once told me that the only day in the year when he doesn't feel hunger pangs is Christmas Day." Jessica laughed and said that she wished she had a brother.

"You can borrow mine any time you want," said Cora. "He can be a real pain."

"Thanks," said Hugo "But I don't think I want to be a brother to Jessica, I want more than that." Jessica pretended she hadn't heard the remark.

"Now, now," Robert cut in, "no need for bickering. Hugo, top up everyone's glass. I'm going to have a chat with Jessica."

So saying he went and sat down beside her. "Now tell me about this car that Georgina spoke to you about."

"There's nothing much to tell, really. She said that as soon as I left, her grandson Lawrence went out too in his car and just as he got to their gates he saw a car pull out from the side of the road and follow me. Apparently it was a brown Toyota, there was one following me yesterday too, but, you know, there must be hundreds in Kenya. What makes it worrying is that there are no other buildings down there. Georgina's house is at the end of the road, next stop, the water in the creek. So what was it doing down there? I didn't notice anything behind me, I was putting on some music and worrying about the journey, you know, the first time since the horror all happened. Also, further along that road you have to go past all kinds of local huts with women and children sitting outside them, chickens running free all over the place so I was concentrating on not running over anything or anyone. It was only after the bridge that I noticed the car behind me. It didn't follow me down your roadway so it is probably nothing. But I just don't know. There have been other moments when I thought I was being watched."

"When were they? Tell me about them."

Jessica took another sip of wine and then told Robert about the glimpse of something moving in the mangroves when she had walked on the beach with Hugo and Cora during the funeral and the time she had seen someone watching her when she came out of the police station after her interview with Inspector Mona.

"Robert listened very carefully with furrowed brow."

"Hugo did tell me that you had seen something down on the beach."

"At the time he said it was a monitor lizard rustling around in the mangroves but I didn't really believe him then and I am even more confident now that he was just trying to reassure me."

"Well, don't forget we're all here ready to help. Just call if you are worried any time, night or day. Now come on let's go and enjoy the meal that Jenny and Cora have prepared, it smells absolutely delicious and Hugo is not the only one who is famished."

Over the meal they talked desultorily of this and that, keeping the conversation light. But Robert had a worried distracted air about him. Afterwards, coffee was served on the veranda and Jessica was soon ready to go to bed. Cora followed her upstairs and the two of them went to Cora's room, "Come on," she had said, "let's talk just us girls. I've got some plonk to keep us going."

They threw themselves down, one on the bed, one on the armchair, and Cora poured out some wine.

"One thing I don't understand is where you were going when the police stopped you that day. Why didn't you come straight back here?"

"I don't know. I think I panicked; not my finest moment. And Jaribuni was closer too. I guess I thought I needed the police. A very English reaction."

"Mmm, I see what you mean. Now, tell me how things are going, I mean really going."

"Oh Cora, I don't know what to say. It's all locked inside me I keep thinking about what I must do next so as not to think about what has happened. I lie awake worrying. I suppose I must help the police first of all. But what can I do? Does finding and punishing the men who did this make me feel any better? I suppose it might, everyone talks about closure but I am not sure what that means. I know what happened, I have buried the bodies. In a way the criminals are peripheral to the emotions I feel. I can't hate them because I don't know them. Perhaps if they are found I will hate them meanwhile I must try to find out how and why this terrible crime was committed. The why bothers me more than the who. My parents were good people. They were kind to their neighbours of whatever colour, they cared for their staff, their animals and the wild animals of Kenya. Oh God I'm going to cry again. It's all your fault, I haven't cried for two days," sobbed Jessica.

"You just go right ahead and come here let me give you a big cuddle. Just remember I will always be here for you."

"You see it's bad enough when someone has a quiet clean in-the-sheets death with their loved ones all around. I know a friend of mine in London told me about being with her parents when they passed away and how she had flashback for some weeks afterwards, seeing their faces turn waxy and hearing the death rattle but when you know they have died in pain and terror it hurts so much deep inside." And she gave herself up to a fit of weeping against Cora's shoulder.

"Anything I can do to help; you must promise to let me know. And Hugo feels the same way."

"Thank you," sniffed Jessica. "It is good to be spending time together again," she said quietly pulling away from Cora's fierce hug.

"Here, have some more of that wine we brought up with us." The two women talked about other things for a while but every subject seemed to lead back to the same obsession until Jessica was exhausted with emotion and the wine bottle was empty.

"Oh God," she said, "that's it. I've had enough. It is time for bed. Goodnight, Cora, sleep well." And off she went along the corridor to find her room. But sleep did not come easily, she tossed and turned in the strange bed while her mind fretted and grieved until she got up and took one of the sleeping pills that Doctor Ngiri had given her.

Downstairs on the veranda Jenny, Richard and Hugo talked long into the night, mostly about Jessica. Hugo admitted that on the day of the funeral there had been evidence of more than just a monitor lizard moving in the mangroves, "but I didn't want to alarm either Cora or Jessica, especially as I wasn't sure. I didn't actually see anybody, just a footprint and an impression of someone moving swiftly through the undergrowth." Eventually, Richard said, "All we can do is keep an eye open for her. It seems she might become a target for some sort of attack too, why else would anyone be following her. If as I suspect this has something to do with Donald's work to stop poaching, any of us who were working on the project with him could be in danger too." He yawned and Jenny said, "Yes, we can't do anything now. It's time for bed."

Cora woke Jessica bright and early sounding cheerful and enthusiastic. She was a very straightforward practical person. She had no fears or dreams the way that Jessica did. They were very different in personality as well as looks which made for a good friendship.

"Come on, there's paw-paw for breakfast and tea and toast, then we can go off and do a game drive with Hugo. He knows so much more about the animals and where best to see them than I do. He's got the day off from our Americans because they are going to Mombasa for the day."

Jessica got up slowly, her mind still fogged by the sleeping pill she had taken. When she went downstairs, breakfast was all laid out on the veranda and Hugo was already sitting at the table with his sister.

"Morning," they all mumbled as Jessica joined them. "So, have you got your binoculars and camera ready?" asked Hugo.

"No I didn't even think to bring any, I would have had to borrow Georgina's or John's; I don't have any of my own anymore." And there it was again, yet another small thing that took her right back to the nightmare. Hugo was dismayed that his simple question had caused her any stress and hurried to reassure her.

"Well, don't worry. I was joking really. We have so many sets of binoculars here you wouldn't believe it. People are always leaving them behind in the lodges and the cost of sending them back is so prohibitive that it's cheaper for them to go out and buy new ones. I will give you a set as a gift. I'm sure your mobile phone can take some good photos. I sometimes find mine takes better photos than a camera although it's no good for birds. You really do need a telephoto lens and all the gubbins for that otherwise you end up with nothing but pictures of LBB's."

"What on earth are LBB's?" asked Jessica?

"Little brown buggers," replied Cora before her brother could answer. "It's his idea of a joke. OK, has everyone finished? Shall we go?"

Hugo's newly washed grey Toyota Land Cruiser was outside ready for them. It was a large comfortable car that was well equipped to deal with the rigours of any terrain. It gave Jessica a feeling of solidity and safety. Cora insisted that she should sit in the front next to Hugo as 'you can see better from there' she argued. Jessica did as she was told. The day was already warm but with the air conditioning on in the car they were shielded from the outside climate which was due to become very hot that day. Jessica felt that they were shielded from reality too and sank into the comfortable leather seat.

Hugo took a different route from Cora's of the day before. The way was much steeper and rougher. To begin with they saw nothing but as they drove further into the *msitu* (the bush) they began to see first of all dik-dik, little gazelles gently grazing, further on there were eland and frightening looking water buffalo who snorted and shook their horns. Then as they rounded a bend there was a herd of zebra with a cheetah stalking them. Hugo stopped the car to watch. Jessica couldn't bear to look. "I don't think I want to see this," she said. But fortunately on this occasion the cheetah was unsuccessful.

They drove down by the river where hippos were bathing and crocodiles lay basking in the hot sun, then down to an open plain. A herd of giraffe went by and at the tail end of the herd was an albino and her baby looking so beautiful and ethereal; ghosts moving slowly against the dark green trees. There were elephants too and eventually a pride of lions lazy and sleepy in the shade of an acacia tree with the remains of the morning's kill nearby. But here there was a problem. Hugo had forgotten that he had given a tour company, Sarai Tours, permission to bring clients in on a game drive. But there they were a whole mini bus full of Japanese tourists with the front wheel of their van stuck in a rock rabbit hole right beside the lions. The tourists all had their faces pressed to the windows and their eyes were made round as owl's by fear. How were they going to get out?

Hugo drove up next to the mini bus taking care not to get too close to the hole. He wound down his window to speak to the driver. "I think the lions have eaten," he shouted, "so they won't attack but we can't take any chances." Cora suggested that they could drive alongside and open the doors in each vehicle on the side away from the lions creating a corridor through which the people could get out but there were too many to fit in their car. In the end Hugo shouted to the driver that he would push the mini bus from the back and hope that it would then be able to clamber out of the hole. He backed his car to get behind the Sarai Tours bus and drove up behind it very slowly and gently. The driver of the bus switched his ignition back on and put the van in gear. Jessica was feeling very nervous by now. Suppose their car nose-dived into the hole after the van had got out? Who would get them out? Suppose the clutch burnt out with the struggle of pushing the van?

Hugo was very carefully nudging and pushing as the other driver gunned his engine and the van popped out of the hole like a cork from a bottle. Hugo rammed on his brakes so as not to end up in the hole after the van. Everyone breathed sighs of relief and the Japanese' eyes regained their normal almond shape. Thanks were exchanged and Sarai Tours drove on to more adventures. The lions yawned and stretched their warm, soft, tawny bodies in complete indifference.

After that Hugo felt it was time for a drink so he stopped the car on a high rock from where they could see any predators approaching. "As long as you stay very close to the car you will be fine," he told Jessica. Cora took out the picnic basket she had prepared and they all enjoyed much needed refreshment.

On the way back towards the house they saw plenty more game but by now Jessica was anxious to get back and drive home to Georgina's house before it started to get dark. As they swung into the drive a shot rang out and ricocheted off the wing mirror on the passenger side of the car. It was as if someone had known Jessica would be in the passenger seat. She and Cora screamed in fright; Hugo ducked but kept his cool. As he quickly sat up, looking in his rear-view mirror he spotted a brown Toyota speeding up the road in a cloud of dust going towards Jaribuni. So he thought, whoever this is, is based in the town where Jessica is staying and where the police are. To Jessica he said, "I think you are in danger. I wasn't sure before about you being followed but this is undeniable. You must take care and ask Georgina about her security arrangements."

"Oh, but I was thinking of moving on to a place of my own now that the lawyers are doing their bit and I know I have money to live on. It is the one thing that couldn't be burned being safely tucked away in the bank."

"I'm not sure it's a good idea for you to move and live alone, especially not in Jaribuni itself."

"I just don't know what to do. I must be on my own. I can't keep depending on Georgina especially now that Lawrence has arrived." And she began to cry again. Hugo reached out and held her hand in an attempt to reassure her but was thinking all the while who is this, Lawrence.

"Don't worry. We will all be looking out for you. Aren't you going to see James Denton tomorrow? He's a responsible sort of person, tell him all about it. I am sure he will give you good advice. He must have had plenty of experience with legal and criminal matters in his role as British Registrar."

"Small comfort," sniffed Jessica. "It's getting my life back together that I need help with."

Chapter 5

It was Thursday, the last day when Jessica could officially go to see James Denton, the British Registrar, to register her parents' deaths without incurring a fine. Or so she had understood from talking to everybody. She arrived at his house, which was also his office, early; anxious to have the whole officialdom ordeal done and dusted. The gates were closed so she hooted her horn and presently his gatekeeper opened up to let her into a wide paved courtyard surrounded on three sides by hedges, trees and shrubs. Opposite the entrance gates was the house, large and imposing, brick built with a tiled roof. It would not have looked out of place in Surrey.

The front door was opened by the house boy, "*Karibu, Mama,*" and he led her through the hall into a pleasant room with a big mahogany desk and large windows overlooking the garden at the back. It too was very clipped and manicured and Surrey-like with its sweeping lawns and tidy flower beds.

As she stood gazing out of the window a voice behind said "Hello my dear. How are you." James Denton took her hand and kissed her on both cheeks somewhat awkwardly. He was known to be shy in women's company. His own wife was rarely seen, being something of a recluse, and Denton was happier in snooker rooms and on his boat with male company than making small talk with ladies especially young ones whom he didn't understand at all. In fact, young people generally were like creatures from a different planet to him. He knew he had to show some kind of sympathy, even affectionate concern but he was of the generation that did not show emotions publicly or display their feelings so he followed the modern trend which did, but with reserve.

Jessica recognised him from her childhood. He had been at school with her father so they would have been the same age but where her father's hair had silvered elegantly framing his patrician features, James had a shock of unruly but still dark brown hair.

"I'm OK," began Jessica. Then she thought, actually I'm not. I have a whole bunch of problems. So she sighed and said, "Actually, I am still not sleeping properly except when I take Dr Mwara's pills. Apart from grieving, the pain, I can't stop worrying about the future and I think I am being followed. In fact, I know I am. what's worse is that yesterday when I was with Cora and Hugo outside their house we were shot at."

"But that's terrible. You must tell me all about it but first I should warn you that I no longer have any official position here. The British Government has decided that they no longer want to pay for there to be representatives looking out for the interests of their citizens in small far-flung places." As he finished speaking his glasses slid down his nose and he lifted his hand to push them back up.

"Oh, I thought I had to come and see you to register the deaths. Today is the last legal day according to what I have been told."

"Here in Kenya you have six months within which to register and the UK no longer requires registration there. You may want to have it registered there as it would simplify any legal procedures that may come about as a result of their death. I can give you the information as to where to find the registrar here in Jaribuni. Then you need to send a copy of the certificate with a translation to the UK authorities. I will give you the address. You see I still have all the information but I can't act for you in any legal capacity." And down went the glasses again just holding to the end of his nose.

"It's very kind of you to help. I am sorry to trouble you."

"No problem, my dear, he said pushing his glasses back up his nose. Now would you like a cup of coffee and you can tell me all about your troubles."

When she had finished telling him what had been happening to her, he was full of sympathy and after finishing their coffee began to tell her about her father's involvement on the KAP committee punctuating his sentences by pushing the glasses back up his nose, obviously it was a constant habit but he seemed to know a lot about her father's affairs especially his anti-poaching activities. She heard all about his initiative to bring British Army soldiers in to help and advise and how they were intending to trace the people behind the illegal trade in ivory, rhino horn and other exotic animal commodities.

"Now one thing is bothering me," said James. "The man Jaba. No-one seems to know where he is. Have you heard any more?"

"No, I haven't but why are you interested in him. I mean obviously we all want to know where he is, whether he is alright and whether he has any information. But how do you know him?"

"It's a long story. For some time I have helped in a charity which tries to set troubled youngsters on the path to a useful life free from crime. Some of them have been involved with drug dealing, others it is burglary and petty felony. Jaba was one of these lads. His parents died of malaria when he was six. His maternal grandfather brought him up. He blamed the white man's medicine for not curing his daughter and son-in-law, but more than that. He was in the *Mau-Mau* as a young man and was imprisoned by the British after being captured by a division of the King's African Rifles. He was very bitter against the white man, especially the British, a bitterness which he passed on to his grandson, Jaba. After his grandfather died, Jaba drifted into a life of petty crime and recently was recommended to our charity by the magistrate who found him guilty of theft for the umpteenth time. I thought that if I got him a job with a decent family it would help him to get on to the straight and narrow. So I sent him to your father who employed him as an odd job man and cattle man."

"Yes, he was new to the farm and he was good at fixing things around the house but, being away in the UK, I barely knew him."

"Well, my dear, no doubt he will turn up. He probably ran away in sheer terror and is now afraid of coming back either in case he is blamed or is himself attacked by the gang who attacked your farm."

Sometime later Jessica left James' house after listening to his advice. He told her to stay put at Georgina's, not to go and live on her own just yet and to tell the police about the shooting. For now she had to go to the registrar's office in town. She went in to a small waiting room with a clerk sitting fatly behind a large desk. In front of him was a ledger in which he wrote down the names of people as they came in. The room was squalid, with peeling paint and lacking any distraction apart from observing the other grieving relatives. The orange plastic chairs were all taken except for the broken ones that no-one had thought to replace. She leant against the wall and was soon feeling very uncomfortable. The room was a sweat box in which the only fan seemed not to work. The smell of body odour was overpowering and she was becoming tired of standing. Across the room from her was a woman with a baby at her breast. The infant suckled quietly but as the woman chattered to her neighbours turning to look at them her breast seemed to stretch in and out while the child continued to hang on. Near her was a man so vast in bulk that he engulfed the chair he was sitting on which seemed too flimsy to take such a great weight. No wonder so many chairs were broken. After two hours of watching and waiting she was called in to a large room which mercifully had a working fan. The actual process of registration only took a short time and she was soon back in her car with the air conditioning turned up high, a blissful coolness which dried the sweat that had been pouring down her body and beading her forehead.

She couldn't wait to get back to the cool comfort of Georgina's house. There was no-one in when she returned and she was glad to have this time to herself to think about what she should do next. She went to the kitchen to help herself to a much needed glass of cool water which she gulped back quickly. Then she thought first things first, I must have a shower and freshen up. I can't think while I feel so smelly and dirty. Then I shall have a drink and sit on the veranda. But when she came back to the kitchen to fetch herself a drink Lawrence was there. This took her by surprise she had forgotten all about him while she had been busy.

"Sorry, I didn't mean to make you jump," he said.

"It's OK. I'm just on edge with all that has happened. And my thoughts often detach me from reality, from my physical surroundings so I didn't see you as I came through the door. I am just so worried about everything."

"Have you had a problem today, been followed again or something?"

"Well, the day before yesterday coming back from our afternoon safari with Hugo we were shot at and there was a brown Toyota again. Today I didn't notice anything on my way home, I was a bit pre-occupied. I went to see James Denton who was the British Registrar here. I thought I had to register the deaths with him to make them official here and in Britain. It seems we are all behind the times. Britain no longer keeps any representatives in small out of the way places like this and the death only has to be registered with the Kenya authorities. UK registration is optional."

Lawrence was alarmed by her news and once again felt an overwhelming need to protect her, to prevent anything bad happening to her. He sympathised quietly and asked her if she had told the police but didn't tell her that he had seen a new blue Toyota lurking by the gate as he had driven in. She has enough to upset her already, he thought and instead he said,

"So any help James is still giving people here is entirely voluntary? I know he does help and advise still. That's probably why everyone thought he was still our representative."

"Yes. Well, he certainly was kind and helpful to me. I followed his advice and went straight to the registrar's office. What a nightmare that was. So hot and I had to wait ages standing up. The few unbroken chairs were all taken."

"Poor you. You must be exhausted. What can I get you to drink?"

"Just a fruit juice, it's a bit early for anything stronger but I am thirsty. I feel better having had a shower; I'm not hot and sticky any more. The thing that is so annoying is that when you go to these government departments you wait for hours in squalid stinky little rooms, real sweat boxes, but the business itself only takes a few minutes."

Lawrence went over to the fridge to fetch the drinks thinking about what he had just said, 'poor you', what a feeble thing to say. It doesn't express half of the concern I am feeling for her.

"Orange juice. OK?" "Here you are then. Let's go and sit on the veranda."

Jessica followed Lawrence out to the veranda where as usual the view across the garden and the flowing waters of the creek had a soothing effect. The two of them sat in companionable silence for a while. Lawrence noticed her long, bronze sun-kissed legs and fine-boned face that was almost heart shaped. She is heart-stoppingly lovely, he thought to himself yet again.

She began telling him how she had lost everything. "You know on the day that the police brought my car and bags back I sat and went through my overnight holdall to see what my remaining possessions were. I have my gold bracelet, some earrings and a necklace that I wore to the party. Some sandals, one pair for the party, one on my feet. I had my party dress and the one I was wearing when the police stopped me, but that was ruined by blood stains, I had a *kikoy* that I slept in and my toiletries, Oh and a bikini but that's not very useful for every day. That is the sum total of my worldly goods." It brought home to Lawrence what a terrible situation she was in. He felt again an urgent need to protect her, she seemed so fragile. Meanwhile, Jessica was wondering what this man who, despite all her troubles was making her feel alive again, was about. It occurred to Jessica that she hadn't asked Lawrence anything about himself. She felt a sudden pang of guilt that she was so wrapped up in herself she had failed to take any notice of others. So now she asked "What have you been doing today?"

"Compared to you I have had a very easy pleasant time. I am on holiday remember. I went over to the boatyard to plan some sailing with Jonathan – he runs the marina and fishing business. He has lovely boat called *Mkwaze*."

"That means fish-eagle, doesn't it?"

"Yes, I believe it does. I'm a real lotus eater when I'm here, I just enjoy the warmth and being out on the water without it being a survival exercise, not like sailing in Britain. You should come with me sometime."

"Yes, you mentioned it before. Perhaps I will. You must know James Denton then from sailing. I know he belongs to the club."

"I do. He has a fine forty-foot boat called *Blue Moon*. I have sailed on it with him, most notably in the racing at Lamu. We came second even though we made a poor start…" – and here Lawrence went into all the technicalities of a racing start with boats criss-crossing and shouting 'water' at each other and near misses with bowsprits behaving like javelins. Jessica didn't really understand most of it but she enjoyed his boyish enthusiasm and it was good to think about something other than her own affairs for a while. She found herself thinking that whereas Hugo was like a lion, tawny, solid and tough, Lawrence was more like a cheetah, agile, quick and lithe.

"As it happens I am going sailing with James tomorrow. I would ask you to come but he isn't keen on women on board. You probably noticed that he is quite old-fashioned in his attitudes. He knows the ropes when it comes to boats though."

"And when it comes to legal stuff. Tomorrow I am going to see my Great Aunt Miriam out at Abasheikh Farm. She is my closest relative now, and I did promise her. She will no doubt be full of advice and she does know Jaribuni well so she is worth listening to. As is James Denton. He may be old-fashioned but he keeps his ear to the ground. He knew all about my father's involvement with the anti-poaching campaign; how they are training game park wardens to fight off these poachers and how they are trying to follow the trail that leads to where the money is – the end purchasers as well as the suppliers."

"Are the police following that up? Because to my mind that is where the motive for this terrible murder is."

"I don't know. I haven't spoken to Inspector Mona for a few days. Perhaps I will ask him when I get back from seeing Aunt Miriam."

"You should go before you set off for Aunt Miriam's place. You need to tell the inspector about this car that has been following you and the attempt to shoot you."

"I dread going to the police station," said Jessica.

"Everyone is concerned for you. Georgina and John told me all about the shooting and they are very worried for you. I think they had a call from the Patterson-Smythes' as well. We are all very worried about you. In fact I will cancel my sailing trip and follow you to your Aunt's house to make sure that you arrive safely. On the way through town in the morning I will come with you to see Inspector Mona."

"That's very kind but I don't want to put you to all that trouble and I certainly don't want to ruin your sailing plans."

"You aren't putting me to anything. It is my choice." The need to spend time with her and to protect her were uppermost in his mind. Aloud he said "I would never forgive myself if anything happened to you. How long will you be staying there?"

"Just a couple of days; three at the most."

"Will you need a car there? Why don't I just drive you and pick you up when you're ready to come home?"

"If you are absolutely sure, it would put my mind at rest. It is quite a long way to Miriam's farm, sixty miles or so. It takes about an hour and a half with all the speed bumps and potholes. And I won't need my car there. She has a car and I know she will be happy for me to drive it if need be, I've done it before."

"That's settled then."

"What's settled?" asked John and Georgina coming in on the last bit of the conversation. Lawrence and Jessica explained their plan to them and all agreed it was the best way.

Meanwhile, on the other side of town Inspector Mona was following a tip-off that he had from the shoe seller in the market. He went to the "Glorious Off Road Café" where, according to his informant, Charo, a certain drug dealer was known to hang out and do business. It was a sweltering hot afternoon and Mona took out his big handkerchief to wipe the sweat from the back of his neck and his forehead as he walked towards the tin shack that was the café. Its veranda was held up at the front by bent and crooked poles and there were the usual scruffy plastic chairs and tables coated with dust and crumbs. Once inside, he was momentarily blinded by the sudden contrast between the bright sunshine outside and the shade inside. He stumbled slightly on the uneven dirt floor as he went to the bar. He ordered himself a Tusker and turned to look around the room at the other customers. He soon identified the man he had come to see from the description the shoe seller had given him. He saw for himself the many gold chains at the man's neck without doubting for a moment that they were real gold. Gold flashed also on his hands and when he laughed Mona saw that he had some gold teeth and that all his teeth were sharpened into points. He leant against the bar watching the customers come and go most of them ignored the bar; they were customers of the man with gold teeth. Money changed hands and the man's sidekick then handed out little paper packages. The men strode in, cool dudes swaggering their shoulders. The women shuffled in looking shyly down at the earth floor. The man with gold teeth appraised each one as she approached and the pretty ones were told to sit on his lap where he fondled them for several minutes before allowing them to take possession of the little packet they had paid for.

Mona waited for a lull in this commerce and then approached the table where the man was sitting, legs outstretched, crossed casually over, his crocodile shod feet resting on the table top which being made of flimsy plastic was bending under the weight. The man spoke first, removing his half-finished bottle of Tusker from his mouth, "Jambo Bwana, what you doing in this bar. I never see you before."

"No," said Mona, "I haven't been here before. I see you are a busy man, many customers so I will get straight to the point. I am investigating the deaths at the Shamba ya Tembo farm. I was told you might have some information."

"What, you some kind of policeman?"

"Yes and many people were killed at this farm."

"White people," said gold teeth contemptuously spitting out of one side of his mouth.

"Yes, white people, good people who cared for their farm and their workers but also many of their workers died too."

"Eh heh. What is it to me?"

"I was hoping you might know of someone who could be involved. I can see from your business here you are no respecter of the law. What else might you be up to? Let me start by taking your name."

"Tell him my name, Ali man," he said laughing to his sidekick.

72

"His name is Kahinde," said Ali. And Mona could see by the way he said it that it was a name to be feared.

Suddenly Kahinde dropped his legs to the floor and leant across the table towards Mona, eyes blazing he said. "I know nothing man. And if I did I wouldn't tell you." Kahinde and Mona were now nose to nose, blood rising. "I am doing this for the good people of this country. They need to know that murder cannot be got away with." Kahinde leant even closer so that his hot breath was burning Mona's face. "Take care he," he jerked out between clenched teeth.

Mona could see he was getting nowhere so he backed away from the defiance in Kahinde's eyes saying "I will find out who did this terrible crime."

As he walked away Kahinde, relaxed again and laughing said, "Not likely. I'll skin you alive first."

Inspector Mona went back to his office and wrote a report about Kahinde and his drug-dealing, highlighting also his suspected involvement with the murders at the Shamba ya Tembo Farm. Then he packed up his papers and headed for home, a simple one-storey building identical to its neighbours. The air was cooler now and he stopped off to buy himself a few beers on the way. Once in the house he switched his lights on, bare bulbs hanging from a flex in the centre of the ceiling. He settled down with the television and another Tusker beer to wash away the taste and thoughts of the man he had just met. He was glad he had bought himself the big bright orange moquette sofa from one of the sales on the side of the road. It dominated the room but was big enough to stretch out on. That and a plastic table with two chairs and a bed were the only furniture he had. He was proud of his *nyumba* although when he compared it to the houses of the white people that he had been in recently he could see that it lacked a great many things. Soon he realised that he was hungry so he went into the tiny kitchen and began to prepare his meal. He enjoyed cooking but often, like tonight, felt too tired to make much effort. He made some *posho*, a thick porridge of maize flour and water, then took out of his fridge a *maharagwe*, a stew of onions, tomatoes beans and spices that he had made the night before. After enjoying his meal he turned off most of the lights in his house to save electricity and sat in the glare of the television but quickly became tired of the strident voices and meaningless antics that he saw there. It was bedtime. As he prepared for sleep and was just getting into bed he was overtaken by the sudden rush of a man bursting through the door and bringing

73

a *panga* down on his head. His last thoughts were with Jessica and his sorrow at her plight.

The following morning Lawrence and Jessica set off to town early to see Inspector Mona before heading on to Miriam's farm near Kinango. Lawrence made Jessica keep her head down, hiding under the dash board in case the brown Toyota was lurking again. "If they think it's only me in the car they won't bother to follow." After a while Jessica began to feel very uncomfortable in her scrunched up position, "Can I sit up yet, I think I might be sick if I stay like this much longer." When Lawrence was sure that the danger was past he told Jessica, "No brown Toyota, a blue one, brand new, instead. But it didn't follow us."

They speculated idly as to whether the owner of the tatty old brown Toyota had been paid loads of money for spying on her and shooting at her and now had a new car. Or had he been sacked because he missed his target and this was now a different stalker.

They arrived at the police station in Jaribuni at eight-thirty. There seemed to be quite a buzz around the police station; numerous cars parked all over the place while policemen were going up and down the lopsided steps in a constant stream like ants round spilt sugar. Jessica and Lawrence threaded their way through the crowd to find Wanjiku in Mona's chair. "*Pole,* I am very sorry," he said, "but Inspector Mona was found dead, murdered, this morning."

"Oh, my God," Jessica's hand flew up to her mouth covering it as though not to let evil in.

"Where, how, why?" asked Lawrence.

Wanjiku looked at him as he spoke very quietly, "It was in his village and very brutal. They used a *panga.* As to why, I think it can only be connected with your case, or rather Jessica's."

Lawrence looked at Jessica to see how she was taking the news and could see that under her tan she was turning white. He put his arm around her to reassure her only to find that he was having to hold her up as she slumped over him in a dead faint. Wanjiku helped him get her into a chair and to get a glass of water. She came round slowly but as memory of what she had just heard came flooding back, she was overwhelmed with despair and terror. "He was such a nice man. So understanding," she kept repeating. "Why would they do that. He was only doing his job."

Lawrence tried his best to soothe her, holding her hand and attempting to be the voice of reason in the dark chaos that was making her head spin. "He must have got too close to someone who is utterly ruthless and doesn't care whom he kills or hurts. I am even more convinced that you need to be very careful indeed. Now tell Sergeant Wanjiku about being followed and shot at."

"I am Inspector Wanjiku now. They have asked me to take Inspector Mona's place. But, yes, you must tell me what has been happening to you," he said suddenly holding himself much straighter.

When Jessica had finished her tale including giving descriptions of the two cars that had followed her, Wanjiku shook his head. "You should have told us before. Did you get the registration numbers of the cars?" But neither she nor Lawrence had managed to notice them. "Well you had better get on your way. I have much to do. Two murder cases now. Inspector Mona did write a report and he was always punctilious about keeping it strictly up to date so I must go and study it. there is bound to be some clue there."

Lawrence took Jessica by the hand and helped her out of her chair and down the skewed steps to his car. She followed blindly so stunned by this new tragedy that she couldn't think. Lawrence thought that they were lucky there had been so much police activity at the Police Station; it probably deterred any would-be followers. When they arrived at Miriam's house the hug and affection that Miriam welcomed her with unleashed a flood of emotions. Jessica burst into tears as she leant on her great aunt's wrinkled shoulder. Miriam led Jessica into the house beckoning Lawrence to follow. Her house was a safe haven, so lost was it in the bush, far away from any roads. The only sounds were the loud rustling of the many palm trees in the garden and of the large terminalias, bamba koffis and neem trees. Birds were calling from their branches too. Miriam insisted that Lawrence should stay for lunch and they all sat down to refreshing drinks first.

"So, what is the news, my dear? Have the police found anything out yet?" asked Miriam.

"No. They haven't but something terrible has happened," replied Jessica fighting back more tears.

Lawrence took up the story. "When we arrived at the police station to tell them about Jessica being followed and shot at there was a great deal of hustle and bustle. Then we saw Inspector Wanjiku …"

"I thought he was a sergeant," interrupted Miriam.

"Yes, he was. But all this activity was because Inspector Mona has been murdered. So Wanjiku has been promoted to take his place."

"My God! What a terrible, terrible thing to happen. When was he killed?"

"Just last night. They, or he, broke into his house and cut him up with a *panga*. So no-one has had a chance to find out who or why yet. We left Wanjiku looking up Mona's reports on Jessica's case. He is convinced there is a connection."

"I think he may be right. Come on let's have our lunch and try to talk about something more pleasant. Jessica looks as though she needs to take her mind off it all for a while."

After lunch Lawrence took all Jessica's bags up to her room and then set off back to his grandfather's house. As he drove he found himself worrying about Jessica and wishing he could have stayed with her. He thought about how close he was beginning to feel to her and wondered if she felt the same way. But as soon as the thought crossed his mind, he realised that he was being foolish and perhaps selfish. She had no thoughts at the moment except for her deep distress and her desire to find the people who killed her family and destroyed their farm. With all these thoughts churning, he decided he would go sailing tomorrow to clear his head.

The newly appointed Inspector Wanjiku was feeling very worried, even frightened. He had been out to see the crime scene and ensure that all measurements were taken, fingerprint checks made and all other police procedures as he had been taught at police training college. The sight of his former boss lying in a mangled heap, with deep cuts in many places on his body including the main one that killed him nearly separating his head from his body, was deeply disturbing. He had now read Inspector Mona's report and he did not like the look of it one bit. The initial murders carried out at the Langley's farm were terrible enough but after reading the report of Kahinde and his dealings Wanjiku was now absolutely sure that he had either carried out the murder of Mona himself or hired someone to do it. Either way, he was responsible. Unlike Mona he had not had the benefit of university or going to London for training but he had learned a lot from working with Mona. He had been his protégé and had been much encouraged by the inspector, much as Mwangi had become when he in his turn joined the force. Now he was determined to do his best for Jessica and Inspector Mona. He sat in Mona's chair, now his chair, trying to think what he should do. He did not want to finish up like Mona. He had a wife and child to think about. Still, it was no use sitting in the office staring at papers; he had to get out there and start asking questions. Following people to find out who their contacts were and investigating this KAP. He looked it up in Mona's report – Kenya Against Poaching, Donald Langley was trying to save the elephants and the rhinos then. He checked the list of people that were connected to Donald in any way.

Wanjiku decided that he had to go and interview all these people again. He would draft in Mwangi to help him, he was a good man, reliable. Perhaps now after the death of Mona they would be more prepared to talk. It seemed certain people were beyond reproach, not suspects but none the less they might know something that would lead him to those responsible, especially anyone involved in the KAP. He checked through the reports that he himself and Mona had written up about the different contacts that Donald and Lydia Langley had. Even Jessica herself might have some bit of information that she didn't think was relevant but could lead him in the right direction. He shuffled his papers together, stood up, hitching up his trousers and adjusting his belt. He might not have had the same level of training as Mona but he had learned a great deal from his former chief. He put his sunglasses on with an air of determination and set out to talk to the people on his list.

First of all he drove out along Bahari Drive which ran along the length of the creek and out on to the sea. Several of the people he wanted to interview lived in the large luxurious houses on this road. The first house he came to belonged to Giles Harrison a member of the KAP committee who also had played snooker regularly with Donald Langley. The house was bright white, dazzling in the sunshine with its windows picked out in a turquoise blue colour. It looked more Mediterranean than African. The garden at the front was neat but had few flowers being mainly cacti and palms planted around a large sweeping drive currently occupied by two large cars. The front door was wide open as were all the windows; as was the case in most houses when anyone was at home, to let the breeze blow through the house. Wanjiku did not feel comfortable just walking straight in although he knew that this was what most people did. He stood on the threshold and called "Hello, anyone here?" Giles Harrison came to the door and invited him in. They went in to a spacious light room whose large windows looked out on to the sea. Fresh salt air breezed in making the room cool. It was furnished in a very different way from the

Hamilton's. No dark patina of much beloved furniture and rugs here. All was modern, light coloured and a bit intimidating in its perfection.

"You managed to park OK between my new Range Rover and my Mercedes then?" Wanjiku was quick to realise that the first thing Giles let anyone know when he met them for the first time was that he drove large expensive luxury cars. He simply asked if he could ask Giles Harrison some questions.

"I am happy to do anything I can to help. This is a terrible business. Terrible," replied Giles.

Giles was ten years younger than Donald had been. And Wanjiku could see straight away that he was a different type of person from the Langleys and the Hamiltons. He suspected that he had not been born in Kenya to an old colonial family. Questioning him Wanjiku found that he had been right; Giles arrived as a young salesman to work for Jaribuni Motors who had the concession to sell Land Rover cars. His manner of speaking was more casual and Wanjiku, though his English was good, did not follow all the colloquialisms that he used. He was one of those who had decided to shave his head as bald as a billiard ball rather than going grey which made it difficult to tell his age. The give-away was the large paunch that had been fed copious amounts of beer over a good forty years or more.

"I have known Donald and Lydia ever since I first came to Kenya – about twenty years ago. Great couple. I hear their daughter is still here trying to muddle through. Poor kid."

"Yes, that's right. She is very sad of course but she has some good friends helping her and looking after her. Now, I need to ask you some questions about your work with Donald Langley on the Kenya Against Poaching committee. I feel that could be the reason behind all this."

"Fire away."

"What?"

"I mean go ahead. I will answer what I can."

"Thank you Mr Harrison. Can you tell me what the committee had been doing just before the murders?"

"Yes, we had already organised some people from the British Army to help train our anti-poaching operatives."

"Sorry, what are they these operatives?"

"They are the game park rangers who are employed to protect wildlife."

"Ah, yes, of course."

"The soldiers were specially trained and are passing their knowledge on to the rangers. These poachers are all heavily armed with AK-47s as well as native spears, knives and *pangas*. The trade is worth enormous sums of money – as much as £17 billion a year and it is even worse in Kenya shillings. An endless stream of noughts. Some of this work was even sponsored by Prince Charles. Last year nearly a hundred park rangers were killed protecting the elephants and rhinos but now they have been shown military techniques we hope that won't happen so much. But when you have seen these wonderful animals with their faces cut away you just have to do something."

It crossed Wanjiku's mind that Giles' part was easy – sitting at a desk planning. He wasn't like the rangers going out, often at night, after murderous killers, jumping from helicopters and spending hours hiding and watching in the bush or crossing rivers swarming with crocodiles. But he made no comment. He also reminded himself that it was probable that Donald and Lydia Langley had been killed for their planning activities.

"So the rangers are now faster, as fast as the poachers perhaps and have better weapons? That is good."

"And we are using helicopters now. Yes, well you know, the tusks of a large bull elephant in his prime are magnificent and they are worth more than £75,000 on the black market. That is about 9,750,000 Kenya shillings. It is the ivory you see. It is highly prized for making carvings and jewellery. It can be very beautiful but when you know where it has come from it is the ugliest thing in the world. Rhino horn is valued as a medicine in China and South East Asia. There are now only 5,000 black rhinos left in the whole of Africa."

"So that is what you have already done but it sounded as if you had started working on a different area of concern."

"Well, yes. We discussed the fact that all the weapons the poachers use, their ammunition and their vehicles cost a great deal of money. I certainly know about the vehicles, being a car man myself."

"So what was decided?"

"Well, we think there is European or Asian money behind this. and we were planning to investigate."

"Did you find anything out?"

"Well that's the thing. Donald was the one with the report. It must have gone up in flames in his house. We haven't had a meeting since the murders, I think we have all been in shock. You might ask some of the others who were closer to him on the committee. You have the list of names I expect."

"Yes, I have. That is fine. Thank you for your help. I will certainly ask the others. There is just one other question, as a business man involved in car sales, do you have any knowledge of sales of Toyota cars in this area?"

Giles gave a short laugh. "You must be joking. There are hundreds if not thousands of Toyota cars on the road, it is the most popular brand in Africa and they are not part of my dealership. The Chinese are supplying the roads and the Japanese supply most of the vehicles. You need to go and ask the guys at the Toyota garage – I believe it's called Gari Jaribuni."

Wanjiku walked out past Giles' magnificent cars and climbed into his own dusty, rusty motor. He looked at his list of people to interview and added the Toyota dealership to it but as he was already out of the town centre and near to where James Denton lived he decided to go there next.

Walking up to Denton's front door Wanjiku had the feeling he had been transported to an English village. No longer a residency, an official part of British administration, it was Surrey-by-the-Indian-Ocean. He knew just what those villages looked like from the films and TV programmes he liked to watch. Only the flowers in the garden reminded him that he was still in Africa, bougainvillea, frangipani, flame trees and palms drew a sigh of pleasure from him. He looked up at the huge Beaumontia that was climbing up the wall of the house covered in large frilly trumpets of white flowers. As he did so he saw a face at a nearby window which pulled away as soon as he smiled. He realised that it must be James Denton's famously reclusive wife. He didn't give her another thought being sure that she could not possibly know anything helpful to his enquiry.

Denton quickly stood up and shook Wanjiku's hand. "How can I help?" he asked. Wanjiku, intimidated by such courtesy was taken aback but managed to stammer out his story. The death of Mona, his own sudden promotion to inspector and his mission to find the killers of the Langleys and their staff.

"I am convinced that it has something to do with KAP. Donald was the founder member and also the top man in the committee. We are all afraid for our lives now."

"I am sorry for that," said Wanjiku. "I spoke just now to Mr Harrison – he didn't seem frightened."

"No. Well he wasn't as involved as some of us."

80

"Tell me something of your work."

"To start with, we recognise that there are different kinds of poachers. There are the local *watu* (men) who just want some game for the cooking pot. The occasional rabbit, pangolin or gazelle. Small fry if you'll forgive the pun. They work alone and take little. Then there are the others who want skins for artefacts that they sell in the local tourist markets; in Malindi, Mombasa, Nairobi and other places. Again they take little though it is still damaging and when they go after larger animals like zebra or giraffe they act in a group. Zebra and giraffe are very popular for sandals and handbags. No, what we are after are the big gangs. Big time gangs financed by Europeans or Asians. They expect to export tons of elephant tusks, rhino horn, zebra meat and giraffe, as well as their skins of course which are seen as highly decorative. They go after pangolin too, for meat and also the scales are used in Chinese medicines. The hides may be good camouflage in the savannah but not in the eyes of poachers. They are poaching on an industrial scale and that is what is decimating our wildlife."

"What are you doing about it?"

"We are in partnership with Kenya Wildlife Service and some of the international wildlife protection agencies such as Big Life and Save the Elephants, we have had a lot of advice from Iain Douglas-Hamilton. And we now have Royal Marines and other soldiers helping to train our wardens and combat the poachers. We are identifying the routes they use to smuggle the illicit goods to the markets in Asia and Europe. We are trying to identify the financiers of this activity after all the equipment the poachers use costs a great deal of money. They are now using Kalashnikovs, AK45s, land rovers and other big 4x4s not to mention tracking systems, binoculars and so on. I am sure the poachers that we catch who are local boys are paid peanuts. We want them too but more important and as important as the finance guys are the end consumers. Without wealthy people wanting to buy these product there would be no poaching. And some of this illegal income is used to fund terrorist organisations such as Al Shebaab. Up to three tons of ivory is sold per month. Imagine what that is doing to elephant numbers and how much income is being generated."

There was silence while Wanjiku thought about all this and wrote down some notes. Then he asked,

"Do you have any names or suspects yet?"

81

"There have been some arrests but they have all been the local people, not the planners or the money men or those marketing the products. But you must have a record of the arrests made. We must start working on it again. We have all been in shock since Donald and Lydia were murdered. It has been brought home to us just how dangerous these people are."

"Yes. And now the death of Inspector Mona underlines that."

"When will his funeral be held?"

"I believe it will be the day after tomorrow. About 3pm."

"I would like to go and pay my respects. He didn't deserve to die like that."

"No," agreed Wanjiku. "No-one does. I had better go, it is getting late and I have to write up my report."

"Goodbye," said Denton shaking his hand, "and be very careful."

Chapter 6

While Wanjiku was busy interviewing friends and associates of the Langleys, staying at Miriam's house, Jessica was feeling less alone. Miriam was her only relative now and it was good to be with family. She had always been sad that she had no brothers or sisters and regretted it particularly now that she had no-one to share her grief with. But here was Miriam ready to listen and to talk about her parents in a way that no-one else could. Most people were all too busy tiptoeing round her afraid of saying the wrong thing. In the end, she thought, family is what matters.

She felt more relaxed here, she didn't have to be on her best behaviour. She and Miriam spent hours just talking, in the garden, at the dinner table, in the sitting room. And there was only one topic of conversation. *That is the other thing*, thought Jessica, after a while everyone else loses interest in talking about my family and the problems I am having. Here, we are both focused on the same feelings and worries. She looked at her great-aunt's face, the skin covered in freckles, sun-damage some might call it but thanks to her love of gardening and the constancy of African sunshine she did not have the pallor of old age. Her kind eyes were watery and faded and her white hair made her skin look darker than it was. I love this old lady, she decided, I love her rhinoceros hide skin, I love her courage in coming to the funeral with a broken arm and I admire the inventiveness of getting her houseboy to change gear for her, and now I love her for listening and telling me stories of my father's childhood and the early days of his marriage to my mother.

After a couple of days Miriam said to Jessica,

"Now we must talk about some hard facts. You know about your father's involvement with KAP I assume." Jessica nodded.

"Well, I happen to know, because he told me himself when they came to dinner before you arrived from England, that they had found out about a group of poachers active in this area. He seemed to think that they were funded by

Europeans, probably English. He didn't name names but he was sure that they were getting close to being able to make arrests of the 'foot soldiers' and then find out who was putting up the money for all their weapons and the shipping costs. Who was doing the marketing of these highly priced objects. Now I don't expect you to begin investigating for yourself, that would be far too dangerous but you could pass the information on to the police so that they go and question the others in the KAP. It seems to me that someone is afraid that you know something, otherwise, why would they follow you and shoot at you. And why would they murder poor Inspector Mona? If you start poking around they will be more convinced and become more persistent."

"I wouldn't know where to start investigating. But I can certainly talk to the KAP committee and the police. I just feel I need to do something. I feel so helpless. While I had the funeral to organise I was busy and it helped get me through those early days, now I need something else to be active about."

"Now, my dear, just stay away from the investigation. Your stay here at my farm is nearly at an end. I think Lawrence will be coming to collect you tomorrow but you are very safe here and would be welcome to stay on. I never had any children so your father was the nearest thing I had to a son and I see you as a grand-daughter…"

"Why was that? I've seen pictures of you and your husband and you look such a handsome couple."

"I did fall pregnant soon after we were married but it went all wrong. It was what's called an ectopic pregnancy. Afterwards, I couldn't have children but Quentin and I were very happy with our farm. I am only sorry that he is no longer with us to help us at this difficult time."

"I am so sorry. I'm sure you and Uncle Quentin would have made wonderful parents. But I can't stay here. It's too far from town. I need to be able to get to the police station easily among other things."

"I am sure Georgina looks after you very well; she is such a kind, strong person. Do you know what she did last year? You know the road that runs along the cliff top on the outside of the town overlooking the creek. Do you remember there was a big neem tree in the middle of a grassy patch, set quite well back from the road. The ladies from the town with their babies and m*totos* used to sit under its shade chattering. Somebody bought the land from the town council who gave them permission to build on it. People were incensed, it seemed quite outrageous to deprive the town of a lovely tree and spoil the look of the area as well as depriving people of an amenity that they enjoyed. Well, Georgina was one of those who was absolutely furious and the council took no notice of all the letters of protest and the petition that was handed in so she spoke to all the people whom she knew were unhappy about the loss of the tree and organised a march. She led them all right up to the governor's door waving banners and placards, shouting about their tree. Such a brave thing to do, the governor is known for his quick temper and quickness in taking offence. She could easily have finished up in prison. In the end he simply said yes to everything they demanded to get rid of them and then allowed the building to go ahead anyway."

"Yes, I do remember that tree and I had noticed something was different along that road but as it had been a long time between my visits I couldn't quite figure out what the difference was. I must say that Georgina is wonderful the way she took me in with no questions asked. And I feel that I can rely on her at all times. I was thinking of moving into a house on my own but now that I have been followed and shot at that doesn't seem like a very good plan. So I will stay where I am for the time being, besides," Jessica added, with a slight smile on her face, there is Lawrence there now."

Miriam's eyes twinkled with pleasure at this. "Aha, so that is the way the land lies. What about poor Hugo? He's had the hots for you ever since you were both m*totos*."

Jessica shrugged and looked a bit shamefaced. "I do love Hugo; he is clumsy and gauche always making stupid jokes but very warm and good hearted and I think brave too. It takes courage to look after all those wild animals and to face up to poachers. Yes, I do love him – very much – but as a brother. This Lawrence is new and exciting. He wants to take me sailing and is being very helpful, he is almost as good a listener as you."

"He's also very handsome. So tall too. Yes, I think you would make a lovely couple."

"Hang on a moment there, Aunt Miriam. We have only just met and he might not like me at all."

"Oh, I think he does. He has a way of looking at you that I noticed when he was here for lunch, a gleam in his eye. Well, he will be here again tomorrow to take you back to Georgina's. It will be nice to see him. Also remind me that I have put together some of my homemade jams and pickles for you to take to Georgina tomorrow."

Lawrence duly arrived the following day. His tall, supple body and handsome face gave Jessica a rush of pleasure which lent her tanned cheeks an extra flush of colour. For his part he had his emotions well in check and after greeting Aunt Miriam with a kiss on both cheeks he also gave Jessica a light kiss in the same way. But his eyes betrayed his feelings as he looked at her standing by the front door wearing her "bend-down" boutique shorts and large baggy, white over-shirt that was almost a uniform for her. Even in these "bend-down" boutique clothes she looked lovely to him.

Over lunch Lawrence told Jessica that he had a plan to get her back to the house without being seen by her followers who were still lurking out in the road even though the police had now set up a watch in the grounds of the house.

"So what is the plan?" asked Jessica as they set off waving goodbye to Miriam.

"We are going via the boat bar. From the bar I will take you across to the house in one of the water taxis that they run and then go back in the same boat to fetch your bags and my car which I can then drive back. I also thought we could go to the bar for a drink. It's time you started to try and enjoy life again."

Arriving at the boat yard, Lawrence parked the car in the shade of one of the boats that was in for repairs. He and Jessica kicked off their shoes to walk to the bar across the hot sand. Jessica enjoyed the feel of it trickling between her toes, much better than having it rub inside shoes or sandals. They made their way to a table in the shade of one of the palm trees at the water's edge. From there Jessica could see Georgina's house across the creek but it was too far away to see if anyone was in the garden. Lawrence fetched the drinks and they settled down to enjoy the view of the water and the boats and to feel the coolness of the breeze that was setting the palm leaves dancing and making a strepitous rustling sound. He watched as Jessica leaned back in her chair and held her chin up to the wind letting her hair ruffle and flutter on the breeze. It was the first time he had seen her look relaxed.

"So which is your boat?" she asked.

"It's not mine, I don't have a boat here. I just sail on other people's. The one I sail most on is Jonathan's. He is over there; I was talking to him while I got our drinks. I'll introduce you later. His boat is called *Mkwaze*."

"Oh yes, I remember now. It means fish eagle."

"He is happy for me to take it out on my own if I want. Mostly we sail together because it's more fun with two. Then I crew for James Denton. His boat is the large dark blue one on the mooring just over there. It's called *Blue Moon*."

"A lovely name," commented Jessica.

"Yes, she's a lovely boat. Last year we took part in the race to Lamu and won. It was all very exciting."

"But Lamu is a long way. It must have taken several days."

"Three each way to be exact. Oh look, here comes Jonathan now. He runs this place you know so he is everyone's friend but he doesn't do favours, strictly business. He might look like a hippy or sea gypsy but he has his mind fixed on the balance sheet."

Jessica watched Jonathan approach in his easy loping unhurried stride, she was looking to see if Lawrence's description was accurate. She saw a man in his early thirties, slim and tanned with longish brown hair held back by the sunglasses he had pushed onto the top his head. His t-shirt and shorts had seen better days, once blue they were now faded to a soft grey. Definitely a sea gypsy she thought.

"Hello Jessica," he greeted her.

She was a little taken aback at being addressed immediately by name. He was obviously someone very confident of his place in the grand scheme of things. Jessica envied him that.

Lawrence saw her flinch slightly, and stepped in to make the introductions and explain that he had already told Jonathan who she was.

"Yes," said Jonathan, "and of course we all here in Jaribuni know of your troubles. I am so sorry for it all. I hear Lawrence is planning to take you sailing soon to give you some distraction. I'm sure you will enjoy it. There's nothing like going out in a boat with the sea and the wind to blow away all the cobwebs cluttering up your mind."

"I've never been before. On the farm we were more interested in riding. We hardly ever came near the sea even though it isn't all that far to go. I remember walking on the beach occasionally and watching the dhows sailing by. They always looked so romantic."

"Well," explained Jonathan, "we mostly have modern boats here at the yard. There are one or two dhows and you can take a trip up-creek on one. A lot of tourists do that."

He turned to Lawrence and asked him when he wanted to take *Mkwazi* out with Jessica and between them they fixed a day.

"Just a minute," Jessica intervened, "you haven't asked me when it would suit me to go. I'm going to Inspector Mona's funeral that day."

The two men were a little crestfallen and apologised. Lawrence promised to go with her to the funeral.

"Thank you, that would be very helpful and we could go sailing the following day."

Just as they were finishing their drinks Jonathan's girlfriend, Annabelle, came slinking over.

"Do introduce me to your friends," she drawled. The introductions were made and Jessica had an immediate sense that Annabelle did not like her. It was something in the way she had said "So you're the sad person everyone is talking about," raising one elegant dark eyebrow in enquiry.

"I suppose I am," replied Jessica feeling more than a little irritated by the haughty and dismissive manner of this admittedly beautiful person. The two women eyed each other, Jessica feeling very much at a disadvantage in her "bend-down" boutique clothes. Annabelle was taller than her, and had the narrow hipped slenderness of a fashion model coupled with a mane of tawny blonde hair and large brown eyes. For her part, Annabelle could see that Jessica was attractive in spite of her apparent lack of dress sense. She compared her simple cotton shirt and shorts with her own designer clothes and it never occurred to her that these were the only clothes that Jessica had for the time being but she was always nervous when she saw Jonathan with attractive women. She sat down and busied herself with her phone, ignoring the people she was with and her environment.

Sensing the growing antipathy between the two women, Lawrence prepared to leave as quickly as possible. "Come on Jessica, it's time to get the boat. Don't forget I have to come back for the car and your bags, then drive around and through town. I don't want to be late back, Georgina's expecting us for supper." Lawrence led the way down the pontoon to where the water taxi was tied up. Taxi was rather a grand name for such a small dilapidated looking boat thought Jessica but she was too polite to say anything, not wanting to hurt anyone's feelings. The boat was just about large enough for four people including the helmsman and to someone like Jessica who had not had much to do with boats it seemed very unstable, listing from side to side at the least movement of its passengers. But it roared across the creek covering the distance in under ten minutes and she and Lawrence were soon clambering out of it into the shallow water and climbing the cliff back up to the house setting several monkeys skittering and chattering out of their way.

Georgina and John were sitting on the veranda with their sundowners when Jessica arrived with Lawrence. They both got up to greet them and seemed genuinely pleased to see Jessica again.

"So glad to have you back. We have missed your company." Jessica found this quite hard to believe as she knew that most of the time she had been pretty miserable but it was kind of them to say so. Lawrence added his own comments somewhat shyly to say that he too was very glad she was back.

"Well, I had better get back down to the boat. Amin is waiting to take me back across the river. I will be home soon with your overnight bag."

Jessica watched his tall, lithe figure disappear down the cliff with a small flickering of hope in her heart. She watched the little open boat make its way across the creek and when Lawrence was completely out of sight turned to go into the house and prepare for dinner.

Georgina and John had decided to go to the funeral too, feeling that it was the least that they owed to Inspector Mona. Hugo and Cora had also promised to be there to support Jessica. The funeral was held at the crematorium where Jessica was horrified to see that the body was placed on the open funeral pyre covered only with a white sheet. Mona's family were all there; he had no wife or children but his brothers and sisters and parents as well as his uncles and aunts stood sorrowfully by.

On the other side of the pyre stood a phalanx of policemen. Standing to attention in their dark blue uniforms and immaculate white shirts their faces were as solemn as could be. Young Mwangi was there keeping close to Wanjiku who was now his mentor; he was sniffing loudly. The men were contemplating the death of one of their own, a popular man but also it cannot have been far from their thoughts that it could have been one of them, and could still be one of them one day. They were wrapped up in the emotion and solemnity of the moment and did not notice the man standing under a shady tree to one side of the crematorium grounds.

Jessica was pleased to see that Hugo and Cora had come too, also James Denton, the ex-registrar. She assumed that the other people there were relatives and friends of Mona's. She nodded in greeting to Wanjiku who was with them but he seemed a little distracted and was staring over at some trees nearby. Under their shade Jessica could just make out that a man was leaning against the trunk of a baobab, chewing on a stick. She saw a flash of gold at his mouth as he chewed and more gold around his neck. He was obviously wearing a heavy chain necklace and seemed to be observing the ceremony but was quite apart from it. The sight of him made her feel suddenly afraid. She tugged at Lawrence's sleeve and told him to look too but she could see that Hugo had already seen the man and was now frowning and looking worried.

As the ceremony went ahead she became more and more upset as it brought back such raw and recent memories. When the policemen began to sing with their deep dark voices she remembered the moment when the Africans had all sung at her parents' funeral and the solemn beauty of that moment. Lawrence sensed her sadness and put his arm round her waist to comfort her. Her emotional state was such that she drew comfort and nothing else from his gesture. Lawrence however, was trying hard not to show the emotions he was feeling towards Jessica, especially his need to protect and take her into his arms and hold her close. On the other side of Jessica, Hugo shuffled uncomfortably on the spot making Cora nudge him into keeping still.

When the ceremony was over, Jessica went to speak to Mona's people to say how sorry she was at the loss of such a good man. They were tearful but polite and thanked her for her condolences except for Mona's younger brother. He was angry, "He would still be alive if it weren't for you *mzungus*. You Europeans are always interfering in African business," he raged.

His family rushed to stop him and apologise. "He is upset," they explained, "he and Daniel, Inspector Mona, were very close. He adored Daniel and looked up to him. The rest of us, we understand it is not your fault and we were sorry for your parents. Your father was a good man."

After saying their goodbyes to the family, Jessica and her friends went to the nearby Sarova Hotel for a drink. Jessica introduced Lawrence to Cora and Hugo hoping that they would all get along well. All was pleasant politeness and the asking of the usual life questions; jobs, origins and interests. Cora and Jessica talked about Mona and the tragedy of his death but soon moved on to Aunt Miriam and how things had been during Jessica's stay at the farm. Then Cora suddenly leaned over and whispered to Jessica, "You have been a dark horse lately, we haven't heard from you much. Now I know why." The two girls looked at Lawrence who was watching Hugo closely.

Hugo and Lawrence seemed to be involved in some sort of verbal sparring match, the two girls just caught the tail end of something Hugo was saying, "Known Jessica all our lives. We pretty much grew up together apart from going to school of course. It's up to us to protect her."

As for Lawrence, he looked disconcerted, realising the corollary to this speech was that protecting Jessica was nothing to do with him. It made him question what Jessica's feelings towards him might be just as he was becoming confident that she cared for him or at least felt attracted to him.

Partly to change the subject and keep the peace Cora suddenly asked "Did anyone notice a strange man standing over by the trees? He seemed to have a mouthful of gold and a great thick chain of gold round his neck."

"Yes, I did. And I didn't like the look of him," replied Jessica. "He seemed to be lurking. What's that phrase they use? Loitering with intent, that describes him."

"He didn't seem to know the family or friends at all. And he didn't speak to anyone. He was just being nosey," speculated Hugo.

"Or he was on the lookout," said Lawrence. "I didn't like the look of him at all and I don't think Wanjiku did either. I saw him watching that guy very carefully. I think we should speak to Wanjiku about him."

"Who is this 'we'?" asked Hugo.

"Well, myself and Jessica since it is about her parent's murders and if you want to help you could come too."

"We don't know that he has anything to do with the murders besides what use would you be, at least I can handle a gun," objected Hugo.

"As can I, retorted Lawrence, I'm in the Royal Naval Reserve so I do regular training." Hugo looked crestfallen.

Lawrence continued, "Don't you find it strange that he should turn up to watch the funeral of a man who has just been murdered whose main job was investigating what happened to Jessica's family?"

"Well, yes, when you put it like that. Count me in. I will come with you tomorrow to see Wanjiku."

"Not tomorrow. We have a date with a sailing boat tomorrow, don't we, Jessica? said Lawrence smiling at her."

"You're obviously not that anxious then," said Hugo not smiling.

Jessica woke the following morning feeling nervous. She couldn't think why at first then as the fog of sleep cleared she remembered it was the day that she and Lawrence were going sailing with Jonathan. She had taken a liking to Jonathan and was looking forward to meeting him again, the prospect of a day spent with Lawrence bent on fun rather than worrying about the serious issues that had been thrust on her so violently also filled her with pleasure but she hoped the superior Annabelle would not be on the boat with them. However, she was nervous about the sailing. She had never been on a sailing boat before and wasn't at all sure what would be expected of her. She lay awake for a while watching the sunlight peeping through the curtains dappling and playing on the wall opposite her bed. She could hear the birds calling and the monkeys chattering as they did every morning. The sounds of Georgina's garden were now so familiar and she felt more and more at home there but was also aware that she was eventually going to have to leave and set up her own life again. She couldn't stay in this limbo forever. For now she decided it was time to get up, shower, dress and go downstairs for breakfast.

As she came down the stairs into the open-air courtyard in the centre of the house she could hear the others were already at table. She was feeling so much less stressed and was happy to see them all smiling at her and welcoming her to breakfast. She sometimes thought that breakfast was her favourite time of day. It was such a simple meal and the day seemed full of possibilities. She realised that she hadn't thought that way for a long time and hoped that the day would fulfil its promise.

Lawrence was full of advice about the boat trip. Sun cream, hat, sunglasses and a long sleeved shirt were essential he told her. Also some light soft soled shoes that would not be ruined by a soaking in salt water. He finished by saying, "But you know, 'there is nothing so worth doing as messing around in boats'." She nodded happily while she ate her breakfast thinking that she had already thought of most of those things for herself. She didn't want to add painful sunburn to her problems, nor did she want to risk injury to her feet from sea urchins or other water creatures.

"The tide is in at the moment so we should get going quickly. We'll take the water taxi across the creek. Last time we managed to avoid being followed that way."

Soon they were climbing down the cliff to meet the boat on the beach. When it arrived they waded through the shallows to meet it, stowed their bags under the seat and climbed in. Ten minutes later they were walking up the jetty to the marina to meet Jonathan. Jessica was relieved to see that Annabelle was not there.

"Oh, she hates sailing," explained Jonathan, "it ruins her hair and she doesn't like getting her clothes all messed up. She loves the idea of sailing and being around a marina. She thinks that's cool but the reality of it doesn't appeal to her at all."

He certainly seems to know her well, pretentious warts and all, thought Jessica.

"Come on," said Lawrence, "this way to the boat." And the three of them trooped down to where the dinghy was waiting to take them out to the boat. *Mkwaze* was a sleek-hulled yacht of about 12 metres. She was low to the water but Jessica was relieved to find that being larger she was not as tippy as the water taxi or the little dinghy they had come out to her on. Nevertheless, she was bobbing and dipping on the water as though saying, come on hurry aboard, the sun is high, the wind steady, let's go. Jessica felt an excitement underlined by the sound of the waves slapping against the shore. She knew the names of some of the boats that sailed the world's oceans, the brigantine, the clipper, the yawl, the schooner and the ketch. Brave names that reflect the soul and the history of man but she had no knowledge of sailing or the sea. Moon and tide and their dark effects were a mystery to her. She had read of the Old Man of the Sea and the great leviathans of the deep, the sea serpents and giant squid. She stepped onto the boat and was immediately alarmed by its swaying and listing motion. She sat in the cockpit and watched as Lawrence and Jonathan busied themselves on board with ropes and rigging up sails. Jonathan started the engine and they putt-putted up the creek for a while until they were into clear water, away from all the moorings and boats that clustered near the marina. As they passed the tiny island that she had seen from the house, Jessica saw the fish eagle perched on its one tree ready to dive for his breakfast, or was it lunch by now. She waved in the direction of Georgina's house but wasn't sure whether she could be seen as they were quite a distance away. Meanwhile Lawrence was busy hauling up the sails and once they were up Jonathan switched off the engine. They seemed to move around the boat with such confidence as though they and the boat were one body. By contrast Jessica felt herself to be like a landed whale, unsteady on her feet and with no idea where anything was or what the various ropes did. They sorted out the cat's cradle of ropes and bare feet slapping along the deck they moved around checking the halyards and stays, opening hatches, stowing away mooring ropes. The quiet of the boat's progress through the water was pleasant after the noise of the engine. The only sounds were the wind in the sails and the lapping of water against the hull. Jessica turned back from waving at the shore to look at where they were going. The creek was wide and thick vegetation, especially mangroves, came down to the water's edge on both sides. Ripples of fish went by and overhead there were lilac-breasted rollers, egrets and cardinal birds flying. The carmine bee-eaters flashed red in the sunlight competing with kingfishers for speed and colour while herons, oyster-catchers, sanderlings and sacred ibis fished along the sandy selvages. The wind was light and warm as they sailed on. Lawrence explained that this was easy, sailing down wind, that's to say he explained, with the wind behind them, it would be more difficult on the way back as a sailing boat cannot go against the wind. "You have to tack," he said.

Tack, thought Jessica wonderingly, that used to be something we called the bridles and saddles for horses, it obviously has a different meaning here. "I've chosen a day when the wind is not too strong and we are sailing up river not out in the big ocean swell, we don't want to frighten you on your first time out," Lawrence told Jessica. "Are you OK? Are you enjoying it?"

"It's so peaceful now that the engine is switched off and it is lovely to see the creek from the actual water – to really feel it all around you. And the birds are spectacular. But I don't feel I am very useful on board."

"Here, have a go at steering," said Jonathan. They exchanged places and Jessica had to get used to the feel of the wheel and having to keep adjusting it, correcting from left to right and back again to keep a straight line to where they wanted the boat to go. "See that point of land over there, head for that," the two men said to her. She found she enjoyed the feeling of the boat's movement and being in control of it. "Keep the sails full, watch them all the time," she was told. Then laughingly, "You're such an expert now, we'll leave you to it while we have a beer."

"Hang on, I'm thirsty too," objected Jessica. "It only takes one hand to steer; I can handle a Tusker with the other." The two men laughed and Lawrence handed out the beers.

Soon they passed more islands much bigger than the one opposite Georgina's house. And from there the creek became much narrower. Jessica could now hear the grass and leaves rustling along the edge of the water. She wondered what creatures were hidden in those long grasses. Jonathan took the helm again now that the water was becoming shallower and Lawrence got the anchor out and brought down the sails so that they could stop for a picnic.

Jessica sat with her face turned up to the sun, another beer in her hand and said, "This is just marvellous. I feel I have been able to leave everything behind, here no-one can annoy us or hassle us. We have no worries, just peace."

"That is so true. Even here with land still nearby there is a feeling of total freedom. I am glad you are enjoying it," said Lawrence.

"It must be doing you good," commented Jonathan. "And who knows, we will make a sailor of you yet."

The way back was as Lawrence had promised more complicated. Tacking, Jessica discovered meant turning the boat to go across the creek one way and then the other way always at an angle to the wind and moving a little further forward with each tack. She became very nervous while the boat was turning as the sails rattled loudly, flapping angrily when they were pulled from one side to the other and the boat heeled over violently, or so it seemed to her. It was a relief when the wind re-filled the sails and they were off on a new tack. By the time they saw the marina she was tired and relieved and ready to get off. Lawrence hauled down the sails and Jonathan switched on the engine to motor back to the mooring.

When they arrived back on dry land she was amazed at how tired she felt considering that she had been sitting down most of the day. Also the world seemed to be listing from side to side like the boat had. As they walked towards the bar she stumbled slightly against Lawrence and he caught her to prevent her falling. He held onto her with such a gentle look on his face that Jonathan became suddenly very brisk, "Come on you two love-birds," he said. "I need a drink." Lawrence and Jessica looked at each other, "Love-birds?" they both said. And then, "Well, why not?" declared Lawrence thinking it was an opportunity to let his feelings be known, leaving Jessica feeling flattered but embarrassed. She wasn't ready for this and it was the wrong moment. She rubbed her arm thoughtfully where Lawrence had held onto her. I hardly know him, she thought.

In the bar they joined James Denton for a drink. "Well my dear, how was your first sailing experience?"

"Good. Very enjoyable," replied Jessica.

"Well done, well done. Perhaps you'll come out on *Blue Moon*, one day," said James with more courtesy than conviction, then pushing his glasses up his nose turning to the barman, "Ah, Jaali, can we have some of those fine oysters?"

"Not today, Bwana, *pole*, only on weekend. We have some *samosas*?"

Jessica and Lawrence went to sit down.

"So, did you enjoy it?" asked Lawrence.

"Oh, yes, Such a feeling of space and freedom. It takes you away from everything, lifts your mind onto a different plane altogether. I feel tired but exhilarated. And there were no scary people to frighten me."

"I don't know about that," laughed Lawrence, "you haven't met the crowd that hangs out around here yet."

James bought a large plate of *samosas,* hot, spicy and very crisp, for all to share which they enjoyed with their drinks. Jessica now discovered another thing about sailing, it makes you very hungry. The air was cooler now in the late afternoon, the world was breathing a sigh of relief that the intense heat was fading and all would be well for a night of clear skies and stars. James and the other two men talked boats for a while so Jessica sat back, relaxed and let it wash over her head. It was a chance to do some thinking of her own especially about Lawrence. So she jumped somewhat when Jonathan asked her a question, it was unexpected, she had been miles away. "Sorry," he said. "I didn't mean to upset you. I just wanted to know if the police had made any progress."

"I am not sure. They don't speak to me all the time. But there was a very nasty looking person lurking round the edges at Inspector Mona's funeral. You saw him didn't you?" Jessica said turning a worried look on James Denton and Lawrence who both admitted that they had seen him.

"We talked about him to Hugo. We are all going to suggest to Wanjiku, now that he is in charge of the investigation, that he should follow it up," said Lawrence.

"We were going to go today but the sailing seemed more important. It is time Jessica had some R&R."

"Thanks for that Lawrence. It is true, I think today has done me some good but I do want the case to come to a conclusion sooner rather than later. Hugo was annoyed that we put off going to see Wanjiku and maybe he was right. We should have gone today."

"I really don't think one day will make a great deal of difference," replied Lawrence feeling somewhat rebuffed. "I promise we will go with Hugo tomorrow."

"I could go on my own you know."

"Of course but both Hugo and I want to give you moral support."

"Is that what it's called nowadays," said Jonathan grinning. Lawrence gave him a withering look. And James Denton could see the conversation was becoming awkward. "Oh look," he said with relief to find a way of changing the subject, "there is Derek Foster."

Oh no, thought Jessica. Not that slimy bastard. But there was no escape Denton was beckoning him over and Derek was slithering along the sand towards them liver spots and all.

"Greetings all round," said Derek stretching his lips in a thin smile that revealed yellowing teeth as well as several gold ones. Jessica felt her insides withering but managed a polite smile in return.

"You do know each other, don't you?" asked Denton.

"Oh yes," said Jessica but Lawrence and Derek evidently had not met. So Derek, after offering his condolences to Jessica, began asking all the usual questions about what his new acquaintance did for a living, where he lived, in fact the usual third degree interrogation as he tried to decide where he was going to place him in his memory banks.

Suddenly Derek said, "Ah, there's my man now." Squinting against the low sunlight everyone followed the direction that he was looking and with sharp intakes of breath Lawrence and Jessica recognised the man who had been lurking under the baobab tree at the funeral. "Well, I must be off, I have business to attend to," said Derek. So saying he left the group and they all watched as he shook hands with Golden Boy as they had started calling him and the two of them went off together.

"Now what can he possibly have to do with that man?" asked Lawrence, speaking as much to himself as to anyone else.

"I don't know, he's a bit of a dark horse, Derek. Deals in gold, he says, on the net. He certainly can't be living on a pension, he came here too long ago for that, back in the sixties, he would have been about thirty," said Denton.

"Well, we will have to find out. Come on, Jessica, it's time to go home. I'll shout for the water taxi."

The following day Hugo and Cora came round just as Lawrence and Jessica were finishing breakfast with Georgina and John.

"Hello, all. Looks like you're having a very relaxing time. Come on, you guys, I thought we were all going to talk to Inspector Wanjiku about Golden Boy," urged Hugo who was irritated by the cosy domesticity being enjoyed by Lawrence and Jessica.

Jessica jumped up immediately and went to hug Cora and Hugo but Lawrence looked up at Hugo through narrowed eyes, "I'm just finishing my coffee. I'm no good to anyone until I have had my caffeine hit in the morning," he said. Then turning to Cora, "Hello, nice to see you again," he smiled.

Georgina intervened at this point to say that she thought they were more likely to find Wanjiku in his office first thing in the morning. "Later he might be out making enquiries," she said. John backed her up telling his grandson to hurry up with his coffee. By now Lawrence had finished so he got up, "Come on then, let's get going. Are you ready Jessica?"

"Yes, yes, let's go," she said as she noticed how Lawrence was once more making everyone dance to his tune.

"We'll have to hide Jessica as we leave the drive. Otherwise her followers will be after us again. If we take John's Range Rover you ladies can get in the back and Jessica can keep down on the floor so she can't be seen."

"Or we could take mine," said Hugo pointing to his large Toyota.

Eventually they all went in Hugo's car and were able to sneak Jessica past the blue Toyota which was still lurking, though further up the road now, away from the police watch. Hugo checked his rear view mirror as they went up the road to make sure that they weren't followed.

Twenty minutes later they were in Wanjiku's office telling him about the suspicious character that had been hanging around under the trees at Inspector Mona's funeral.

"You must have seen him, I saw you looking in his direction even though it must have been a difficult moment for you, he was there for the whole time," insisted Jessica. "We could see flashes of gold round his neck and in his mouth when he yawned. Also, we saw him again the other day at the boat bar."

"What was he doing there?"

"He seemed to have some meeting with Derek Foster."

"I don't know anything about him but I think the man at the funeral, from your description is the one that Inspector Mona spoke to just before he was

98

murdered. He wrote it up in his report," explained Wanjiku. "I'm afraid that he might be involved in the murder, he is known to be a drug dealer and a gang boss. A dangerous man. Kahinde is your Golden Boy. But I will follow it up, thank you for the information."

"One other thing," intervened Lawrence. "Jessica is still being watched. We have managed to smuggle her past the stalkers, as they are called but they are still there, waiting to pounce."

"Yes," added Hugo, "And we think it is the same ones that shot at us when she came to our place, only now they have a new blue Toyota instead of a tatty old brown Toyota, registration KCR578W."

"I will send some more men down your road to warn them off. But please leave it to the police. These men are dangerous."

"Well, we'll leave you to it then. I hope the information we have given you is helpful, goodbye," said Lawrence getting up to go.

"Just a moment there, Lawrence. You're not in charge. We only came to support Jessica." And turning to Jessica, Hugo asked, "is there anything else you want to add?"

"Only to say that this Derek Foster is someone I have known a long time. My parents both knew him too and he has always given me the creeps. He tells everyone he is a gold dealer, well if that is true maybe he supplied the gold for the necklaces and teeth to Golden Boy, as we have been calling the man at the funeral. On the other hand maybe the gold dealing is just a cover story and he is involved in other more sinister business. And I just want to mention that there is still no news of Jaba."

"Well said," encouraged Hugo.

"Right, that's it then. Come on, Jessica," said Lawrence taking her arm and taking charge of the situation again.

Seeing the tension building between the two men, it occurred to Cora that she should get them to be reconciled to each other. She could see her brother was seething with anger and frustration at the way Lawrence seemed to be taking over and seemed to be getting so close to Jessica. She knew he had always had very strong feelings for her that he hoped in time would be reciprocated but she thought that was unlikely especially now, with Lawrence around. It seemed to her that the best thing was for them all to be friends. With this in mind, as they left Wanjiku's office she said in a bright optimistic tone,

"Well, that went well. He has all the information now. Why don't we go out to our place and relax away from it all for a while?"

"That sounds lovely," replied Jessica, "but we don't have a car with us. We can hardly ask you to drive us all the way home afterwards. It's a long way."

"If you take us back now, we can come out to your place in my car, I mean John's or Jessica's," suggested Lawrence.

"No," insisted Hugo, alarmed at the thought of the two of them being alone together on the long drive out and home. "I don't mind driving. We'll all go together in my car."

If Cora thought she was going to bring the two men together in friendship, she was sorely mistaken. On arriving at the house they all decided to have a swim to shake off the heat of the town and the tension of their interview with Inspector Wanjiku.

Her swimsuit was the one of the few pieces of her own clothing that Jessica had but it was back in her bedroom at Georgina's house. So for now she had to borrow one of Cora's swimsuits. She and Cora went into the house to change. As they both appeared back on the terrace by the pool Lawrence felt his blood pumping faster, his fingers were tingling with the longing to caress Jessica's soft skin, the parts where it was untouched by the sun. Be still my beating heart, he thought. He asked himself what it was that made a person love someone. After all Cora was just as good-looking as Jessica but she didn't inspire in him the kind of emotions that he felt towards Jessica. For now he dived straight into the cool water closely followed by Hugo whose thoughts were quite different. He was full of anger against the interloper and wished that Lawrence had fallen for his sister Cora and left Jessica to him.

After doing a couple of quick lengths Lawrence stopped in the shallow end to watch Jessica. As she swam up and down he saw her slender arms coming out above the surface showering beads of water that were diamonds in the sunshine. She got out of the pool to dive, her body like an arrow slicing into the water.

While Lawrence was watching Jessica he was being watched by Hugo. "Come on let's have a race," said Hugo, keen to show off his superiority in the pool. However, it didn't work out that way, to his annoyance Lawrence beat him easily. The women joined in and there was much splashing and racing up and down the pool. Lawrence realised that he had not seen Jessica laughing and so evidently having fun before, not even when they went sailing. When Jessica emerged from the pool with the water running off her slender golden body Lawrence seeing her standing near the water beginning to towel herself dry imagined being close to her and gently licking the water from her skin. To escape his thoughts he dived in again and swam up and down till he felt calmer.

Afterwards they sat over drinks and talked. Lawrence asked all kinds of questions about running the safari park. Cora was happy to chat to him and tell him how much she enjoyed helping to run it. "I do a lot of the admin and paperwork with Mum while Hugo and Dad go out into the park and check on all the lodges and see that there are no problems. Mum and I oversee the cleaning and laundry for the lodges as well as the catering. We don't have to do any of it ourselves, we have staff to do the hard grind. My favourite bit is caring for baby animals that are orphaned or abandoned by their mothers. It is very hard work, getting up through the night, they feed every couple of hours, preparing bottles of milk and spending time with them, being a mother to them. I have hand fed baby hippos, elephants and rhinos, even lion cubs as well. Sadly some of them are orphaned as a result of poaching. The last baby elephant I helped to care for was found standing by his dead mother. She had been slaughtered and her face ripped off to get at the tusks. Have you ever seen a rhino or an elephant with its face ripped off? No, well, it's pretty horrible I can tell you. The poachers only want the horn or the tusk. So after they have slaughtered the poor creature they hack off the bits they need and leave the body where it has fallen. They have even been known to hack the face off while the animal is still alive. By the time we get there it is a mess of raw meat with hundreds of flies and hyenas licking at it. Sometimes the baby is standing there by its mother grieving."

"I have read about these things in the papers back home. Like most people I find it horrific but never do anything about it."

"You would if you could though, wouldn't you?"

Hugo was more interested in chatting to Jessica, reminiscing about their shared childhood; the ponies they had ridden, the journeys to and from school in England on the 'lollipop' flight, the barbecues, the friends they had shared, anything to keep Lawrence out of the conversation, to make him feel an outsider or more importantly to make Jessica see him as an outsider.

But Lawrence managed to butt in asking, "So all of you grew up here, you're not ex-pats as such."

"Good lord, no," snorted Hugo. "Not only did Cora and I grow up here but like Jessica, also our parents and grandparents. I suppose our great-grandparents could be said to be ex-pats but I think after three generations in a place you could be said to belong."

"So are you a Kenya citizen?"

"We all have dual nationality, so yes. How about you? Where do you fit in, if anywhere? Where did you get a name like Fletcher-Greene. It sounds more like the name of a village."

Lawrence laughed, "You know, it's a funny thing in England, if a place has a really lovely name like Rose Garden it will turn out to be a complete dump. If it has a name like Much-midden-in-the-Bog it will be gorgeous full of quaint thatched cottages and old Cotswold stone. Fletcher-Greene would probably be one of those dreadful places just behind a motorway service station, full of tin sheds masquerading as industrial units and those terrible flop house hotels, you know, Formula 1 and Premier Inn."

Cora, aware of the implied rudeness in Hugo's question rushed to say, "I think what my brother means is where do you come from and how is it you can spend so much time in Kenya every year?"

"OK," said Lawrence. "I'm a dealer on the stock exchange and I have my own tiny company. So I have a team of two people, if you can call that a team and I get away for long periods of time because I can do most of my business over the phone and on the internet. That's how come I can be in the RNR too."

"Oh, I see," said Jessica. "That's why you spend so much time on your computer and phone." Then she added with a smile, "When you're not talking to me that is."

Cora smiled at this but Hugo did not. He asked, "So where do you live, somewhere swanky, I suppose?"

"You can call it that if you like, I have a flat in Highgate," replied Lawrence. Feeling impatient with the questioning he tried to change the subject. "So what are we going to do about this man we saw and how can we find out what Derek Foster is up to?"

"I was just wondering," said Jessica, "if you have contacts on the stock exchange would you or your team be able to find out if he is dealing in gold?"

"If he is not registered on the London Exchange that doesn't mean that he isn't dealing through some other exchange, but I can certainly look into it. Perhaps we should go home and I can get on to it."

"Hang on," Hugo interposed, "we still haven't decided what to do about Golden Boy."

The discussion went back and forth but in the end it was decided that Jessica and Cora would try to find out about Derek Foster from their contacts while Hugo and Lawrence would follow Derek discreetly to see where he went and what he was up to. They would also follow Wanjiku in the hope that he might lead them to Golden Boy. Jessica was not altogether pleased with this plan. She felt it was not likely to lead to any information about her parents' murderers. Just because Derek was involved in some shady dealing didn't make him a poacher and murderer. Still, she thought, my friends are only trying their best and activity helps keep me sane.

Back at Georgina's house Lawrence and Jessica found that supper was already being prepared. A fragrant curry spiced the air making them realise how hungry they were. Lawrence disappeared to his room to chase up information on Derek Foster. Jessica went out onto the veranda to chat with Georgina. She was perhaps the most obvious person with whom to start her investigation. What she found out filled her with disgust for it turned out that Georgina knew Derek well as they had both lived in Jaribuni a long time and had frequently met at parties and especially at the boat yard.

"My dear, they say about him that he has very long pockets and short arms so when it is his turn to buy the drinks he suddenly develops diarrhoea and disappears to the loo. It's quite funny really but it also annoys people. He is a typical bar-room bore really. The other thing about him is that he came here under mysterious circumstances. He came here back in the 1960s. They say he had to leave America in fear of his life. That he was involved in the Ku Klux Klan. Something to do with bombings in Birmingham, Alabama and supplying arms or explosives. No, the less you have to do with him the better."

"But why would he come to Kenya, an African country full of black people whom he apparently despised and hated?"

"It was just before Uhuru, when the relationship between whites and blacks was very different from now. Yes, there are still some unreconstructed colonialists about, who show little respect but most people here see each other on an equal footing. We may have domestic staff but they are paid and free to come and go as they wish. He liked the way it was back before independence and he liked the way of life, the big game hunting especially. You really don't want to get involved with him; I think even the claim that he deals in gold may be false."

"Why does everyone tolerate him. They all seem happy to drink with him in the bar, even James Denton?"

"It's a very small community here, tolerance is essential for social survival. But also we have no proof, all is hearsay."

Then Jessica told her all about Golden Boy and his meeting with Derek which seemed to come as no surprise to Georgina. But then John joined them with some news which Jessica thought might be more useful. He had been playing snooker with James Denton who had mentioned that the colonel from the British Army who was in charge of the anti-poaching work was coming to Jaribuni again. "He worked with your father and the KAP so he might have some useful information for us and for Inspector Wanjiku."

Chapter 7

As soon as she could, Jessica phoned Denton to ask if she could meet his visitor.

"Ah, you mean Colonel Buckley. Yes, good idea, I was going to suggest it myself. It might also be a good idea if he talks to Inspector Wanjiku…"

"I am sure it would be. Can I come over to your house this morning? Say about eleven?"

"Perfect, my dear. We'll see you then."

As Jessica put her phone down, Lawrence came out onto the veranda where she was sitting. "I've been doing some research about Derek Foster and he certainly isn't registered on the London Gold Exchange but he could be affiliated elsewhere or be working through another company. So I am afraid we are no further on with that."

"He is such a creep, and after what Georgina told me about his connection to the Ku Klux Klan I find him even more horrible than before but it doesn't necessarily mean that he is a murderer involved in the poaching business. He just gives me the shivers."

"Well, we'll just have to start following him if we want to find out what he is up to."

"I can't do anything this morning. I am meeting a Colonel Buckley at James Denton's house. You know, the man that John told me about last night, who was in charge of the British Army training and support scheme for local anti-poaching rangers. He might know something about who is behind these activities in this area."

"Would you like me to come with you? Two brains better than one perhaps?" Lawrence was learning not to be too pushy where Jessica was concerned.

Jessica hesitated before saying, "OK, that might be helpful. After all Hugo and Cora can't be here all the time, they have to work today at the safari park."

"I guess I'm a poor substitute but hopefully I'll do," replied Lawrence. Jessica merely smiled.

As they got into the car Jessica said that she was glad to be able to sit upright now that the police seemed to have chased away the stalkers. They both waved to the police who were now parked by the gate. But as they drove on it soon became apparent that the stalkers had found another spot further on to hide, one that they knew Jessica would have to pass wherever she was going. It was much further up at a place where the road divided, one way took you to town, the other took you out along the coast road. As they took the fork towards the coast road where Denton's house was, the blue Toyota nosed out from under the shade of a large spreading neem tree.

"So much for police protection. Look what is behind us now," declared Lawrence. "It's a good thing I came with you."

"I don't think the police have what it takes to give protection," replied Jessica.

"They probably don't have enough to pursue the investigation either," said Lawrence.

"Well. here we are, Sussex by the Indian Ocean."

They were greeted by James Denton who as usual was very affable offering them a drink before taking them in to see Colonel Buckley. The colonel limped towards them; hand extended. "Good to meet you, So sorry to hear about your parents. We must do what we can to catch the bastards."

Jessica was surprised at the limp and the black eyepatch that he sported. It gave him a piratical air and she wondered how fit he was and how useful in combat. The same thought had obviously occurred to Lawrence because he asked, "Are you now the brains behind any campaign? Do you let younger men do the actual physical stuff?"

Buckley took the question in good part. "You're right. With a prosthetic leg and only one eye, I'm not as fit as I was. Both earned in the course of duty, Afghanistan, Iraq. Not Syria because I was already laid up from a bastard explosive device in Iraq, hence the leg and the eye."

"Crazy stuff," said Lawrence shaking his head. "I know you guys were only doing your duty, doing the government's bidding, but it's all so wrong."

"We're not here to clash swords over all that," objected Jessica. "Can we get back to the main event, my parent's death, their staff's deaths and the total destruction of their property, not to mention the connection with poaching."

"Sorry, Jessica. I only wanted to know how the Colonel was likely to be able to help us."

"Yes, these bastards must be caught." Jessica was soon to learn that 'bastards' was the Colonel's favourite word.

"OK," he continued, "You're right I am a backroom boy now but I have the medals to prove what I did in actual combat. I can still shoot straight though. And I do know Kenya, came here often for R&R with the army. Now I co-ordinate the different groups involved in the fight against this bastard poaching. So I oversee the training programmes for the local rangers and make sure that they have the technology to catch the bastards. The bastards are very well equipped which is why we think there is European or Asian money behind them. To level the playing field, the rangers need 4x4 vehicles, telescopic rifles, high spec binoculars and GPS systems every bit as much as the poachers do. We also train them in guerrilla tactics, jungle warfare."

"So, what was my father's role?"

"He liaised between us and the rangers. Not all of us speak Swahili fluently, he did. He also ran the recruitment programme for rangers, he knew the local people; who was trustworthy, who wasn't, and raised money, although I think that side of things was done more by your mother. Running coffee mornings and dinner dances is more woman's work."

Seeing the light of a crusading feminist in Jessica's eye at this point, he hurried on, "Another aspect of our work is to track down the end users. These guys on the ground here in Kenya, they may be bastards but they are the morons who are cannon fodder. They make a quick buck or two but telling them what to do are the big guys who sell the product on and they don't care who dies in the process. They are the real bastard bastards. All those rhino horns go to China for traditional medicines, souvenir hunters want the elephant tusks to hang on their walls. The skins of leopards, lions and cheetahs go to hang on the backs or walls of people with less sense than money and even less sensitivity."

"Mmm, I remember my mother telling me about a shop in Nairobi that she went to when she was a child. On display there was a waste paper basket made out of an elephant's foot and she asked her mother, my grandmother, how the elephant was getting about on only three feet."

"Oh that would have been Rowland Ward. They started back in the 50s selling something called 'animal furniture'. It was objects for the home, made out of animal parts. He was a taxidermist like his father before him, all very up-market and now highly desirable as antiques. But those were different times. Thankfully the camera took over from the gun as the main weapon of safari parties. His book carries on though, it is like a Guinness Book of Records for hunters."

"My Aunt Miriam already told me some of this. She helped Mum with the fund raising. But how does the end user as you call it come in to all this?"

"Without the end user there wouldn't be much point in hunting. There wouldn't be any way to make money out of it. As I say the products are sold for all sorts of reasons and some of the animals are captured alive and taken to the Far East to be eaten as exotic dishes, even things like snakes and anteaters. There is a woman we know about in Hong Kong, Li Wei Wang and a man in Shanghai, Chang Zhou, who have an international network servicing the market. We are watching the port of Mombasa at the moment but a lot is taken up through Somalia where they are less squeamish about these things and there are fewer checks on goods going through Kismaayo, the nearest port to Kenya, or Merca a bit further north. Both are places where Al Shebaab still have many supporters. And there you have another problem. Some of the money from poaching is being used to fund terrorist activity, in particular Al Shebaab and it works in tandem with the drugs market."

"Wanjiku told us that the man we saw hanging around the edge of the funeral was a known drug dealer so he could be involved," interrupted Lawrence.

"He certainly could. I will have to liaise with this Wanjiku."

"Inspector Wanjiku," corrected Denton and explained the full story of Mona's death leading to Wanjiku's promotion.

"He told me that Mona's last report was about a meeting he had with this man. Kahinde is his name and by all accounts he is very dangerous. But we at the KAP are convinced that there is European or Asian money financing the poachers."

"Well, it looks as though our next step is to see this Inspector Wanjiku and talk to him about the bastard Kahinde. Share our information. Maybe he has spoken to some of the Europeans here who might be involved."

"Yes, like Derek Foster," said Lawrence.

"Well, I don't know about him. He has lived in Jaribuni for years. I know him quite well. I think he is a bit of an idiot and a bore; he apparently left the

USA under a cloud and all that but I don't think he would be involved in something like this," objected Denton.

"No stone unturned, no stone unturned," moralised Buckley. "Shall we go and see your Inspector Wanjiku now?"

Jessica picked up her phone to ring him and make an appointment but just then it rang. It was Cora suggesting another get-together with Hugo. They agreed that she and Lawrence would meet Cora and her brother down at the boatyard. Jessica then dialled Wanjiku's number and an appointment was arranged for the next morning.

As they pulled out of Denton's drive, Jessica wondered if the stalkers would be in the road waiting for them and sure enough as Lawrence drove on, the familiar blue Toyota pulled out from the kerb and followed them. She pointed it out to him but he had already seen it in the rear view mirror.

"They don't bother to follow me when I'm on my own," he told her. "It's definitely you they are after."

"Very reassuring I'm sure. What are we going to do about it now?"

Lawrence had already decided against a heroic car chase. The thought of possible entanglements with *tuk-tuks*, kamikaze *matatus*, cyclists, children and even chickens was too nightmarish to contemplate. Then there were all those speed bumps, take those at high speed and you would be airborne. Heaven knows where you might come down or how. No, he decided, we will carry on safely home and then take the boat across the water. Especially now that the police are watching the house, the stalkers won't be able to get close enough to see what we are up to.

Cora and Hugo were surprised to see Jessica and Lawrence arrive by boat, they were even a little jealous, it seemed much more adventurous than taking the car.

It was a quiet time at the boatyard. Lunchtime on a weekday was not the most popular time for social gatherings but the yard was busy with its business of repairing and servicing boats. Johnathan came and joined the foursome bringing his girlfriend Annabelle with him. She was certainly more graceful than anyone else and had a radiance about her which was belied by her sharp, egotistical personality. She sat sipping her drink, long slender legs stretched out in front of her with her phone snug between her thighs almost as though she were making love to it. For once it didn't interrupt the conversation every five minutes but normally she would have been chattering or texting non-stop. Just now she was feeling threatened by the proximity of two very attractive women to her man. She wanted to stay on top of the conversation, to be sure of him.

Cora on the other hand was busy umpiring the word fencing that was still going on between Hugo and Lawrence while Jessica was simply sunk in her own thoughts and worries. What was she doing sitting in this idyllic place, sipping a glass of wine? She should be out there doing something useful, she told herself. She wished the wrangling between Lawrence and Hugo would stop too. It was too much of a distraction. She knew how Hugo felt about her. After all he was as subtle as a flying brick. But he had other qualities of kindness and loyalty and familiarity. But that last was the trouble, she loved him as a brother just as she loved Cora as the sister she never had. Now here was Lawrence. She couldn't deny she felt attracted to him but there was too much on her mind to think about it.

Her attention was caught by the arrival of Johnathan's business partner who ran the bar side of the business. Paul was dark with the deepest tan Jessica had ever seen. Barefoot and dressed only in a pair of faded shorts, he didn't look much like a business man but the place was obviously well run and he knew how to create the right atmosphere, both laid back hippy and serving good food. Oysters for free to anyone having lunch at the weekends and spicy *samosas* a speciality. He came and joined them with his girlfriend Sylvie. She was French, tall and slim with long straight hair that kept blowing across her face in the breeze. Jessica remembered her parents having an old record of Françoise Hardy's greatest hits. Sylvie looked like the picture of the singer on the cover. Jessica was amused to notice how Hugo seemed to be struck by her appearance. He couldn't take his eyes off her. Introductions were made all round and Sylvie embraced Jessica saying how sorry she was for the loss of her parents. "You must feel so alone," she said.

Jessica was grateful for her understanding. As the conversation went on between the others Jessica found she didn't feel like chattering. She stood up and walked away from the group to stand by the water and think.

Seeing her standing alone Lawrence got up and joined her.

"Are you alright?" he asked putting his arm round her shoulder.

Jessica gently removed it. "Not really. I just keep thinking about what has happened and how little I am doing here. I'm sure it will pass but I keep seeing the scene at the farm over and over again as if it were tattooed on the inside of my eyelids. And the smell of burnt wood and animals is still in my nostrils. I ought to go out there to the farm to see it. After all, it is all mine now. And I should go and talk to the families of our staff but I keep putting it off. It will be so difficult."

By this time Hugo had joined them followed by Cora. He heard Lawrence offering to go with her to the farm and quickly interrupted saying that he should be the one to go since he knew the area better than Lawrence. But Cora told them both off, saying that they should leave her alone to make up her own mind. She pointed out that she could go, or Georgina. Jessica gave her a grateful look.

Annabelle was now irritated that the party was no longer focused on her and seemed to be splitting up. In a loud voice she declared, "What is all the fuss about. Someone is spoiling our afternoon. What do you think, Sylvie?" But Sylvie merely shrugged and took another puff on her Gauloise.

"Oh, for God's sake someone take me home. Cora, you can drive Hugo's car, can't you?" By now the two men were looking like naughty schoolboys who have been ticked off and they sloped off back to the table where the others were sitting. Cora and Jessica left, pausing only to pick up the car keys from Hugo.

"She should be going home in the water taxi again. That way she can't be followed," said Lawrence regretfully. "I suppose they'll be alright."

Hugo was also worried. "It's a shame you haven't got your car here. I don't know these friends of yours but would they lend you a car so that we can follow the girls?"

Overhearing this Jonathan immediately handed over his car keys and the two men ran to his car and roared away in a cloud of dust oblivious to the mongoose who was quietly stalking his ophidian prey through the dry grass at the roadside. They could see the dust cloud that was Hugo's car and were soon catching up with it but Lawrence hung back slightly, he didn't want Jessica to know they were following her. Of course she won't recognise the car he thought but still it might annoy her.

At the junction a lorry bearing the motto 'The Lord will Save' lumbered out in front of them and crawled along the road making Lawrence slam down on the brakes. As it lurched from side to side, top heavy with a load of galana stone they couldn't see ahead to where the girls' car was, not least because of the amount of choking dust it was kicking up.

Suddenly, listing violently to the left it turned off down a side road and they were able to get moving. On the outskirts of Jaribuni they spotted a great crowd gathered round a car, Hugo's car, which was stationary at the side of the road, many, many people all shouting and gesticulating, a colourful screaming mass. Parked just behind was a blue Toyota. In the centre of the mêlée were Cora and Jessica being held by two men who were explaining to the crowd that the two girls had crashed into their car. If the crowd had taken the trouble to look they would have seen that there was not a scratch on either car but they were now wound up to a frenzy, thinking the *mzungus* were 'getting away with it' again. In fact the two girls had sustained a puncture that had forced them to stop. Lawrence felt completely useless, being unable to speak more than a few words of Swahili but Hugo strode forward and shouted at the crowd pointing out the obvious lack of anything on the cars remotely suggesting a collision. He told them that the girls were being kidnapped at which the crowd now turned hostile towards the two men. A shot rang out and Hugo crumpled to the ground. The two men were forced to run back to their car and drive away before being lynched by the angry mob. Hugo lay in agony on the ground, writhing and yelling and bleeding profusely. "Fuck, the bastard's got me," he shouted. Cora, Jessica and Lawrence all ran to him in horror and shock. Lawrence told him to try to keep still as movement would make the bleeding worse. A *bibi* who had been standing by went into her nearby *nyumba* and fetched out some water and a clean *kikoy* to wrap Hugo in while Cora held her brother's head in her lap. Lawrence did his best to wash the wound and staunch the blood with the *kikoy*. Several of the men helped Lawrence to get Hugo into Johnathan's car and leaving Hugo's car where it was, they all drove to the hospital. Jessica and Cora were both ashen-faced with anxiety whispering "Oh, please God, no," over and over again while Hugo was whispering faintly "fuck, fuck," over and over again…

By the time they arrived at the hospital Hugo had lost consciousness and Cora was frantically phoning their parents. Lawrence busied himself with calling to hospital porters to come and help take Hugo into surgery.

Hugo's parents Jenny and Robert eventually arrived in a great flurry and fluster of anxiety. Cora and Jessica rushed to kiss and hug them to try to reassure them that all would be well. Then they all sat down for the long wait on the usual grimy, orange moulded plastic chairs. Why orange Jessica kept asking herself.

Lawrence paced up and down for a while then said, "Look I can't do anything here. When Hugo comes out of surgery it's his family he will want to see, not me. Especially not me. I'm going back to where it all happened to talk to some of the people who were nearby. Find out what they know, especially who those men are."

Jessica looked at him, her eyes wild with panic. "Don't go. You might get hurt too; I couldn't bear it."

Lawrence looked serious at this outburst but inside he felt a sudden shaft of pure joy and hope. She cares after all he thought. Out loud he simply said, "I think I must. We have to know who these people are and who their contacts are."

"But you don't speak the language."

"Not enough to calm a crowd but I think I will get by talking one to one. There is always someone around with a smattering of English."

"Be careful, Lawrence."

"Yes," the others chimed in, "be careful."

As he reached the outside Jessica came running after him. "You could buy a replacement *kikoy* for that little old lady who gave us one of hers to wrap Hugo in. She won't want it back all covered with blood. I am sure she would be pleased to get a new one. she didn't look as if she has much."

"Fine. I'll do that," said Lawrence and with a brief squeeze of her hand he was gone.

In a small town news travels fast and Wanjiku had already heard about the attack on Jessica and Cora followed by the shooting of Hugo. He left his office quickly and went straight to the hospital where he questioned the two women about what had happened. Then he went to the village where he found Lawrence talking to some of the people who had been in the crowd.

"So, what have you found out?" he asked.

"Not a great deal. It seems the two men don't live here. They are from the other side of town. Only, this lady knows the name of one of the men." He pointed to a tiny, very wrinkly old lady clutching a brand new *kikoy*. "She says his name is Obama, you know like the last American president."

"Any family name?"

"Oh yes, it's Obama Ngina. He lives just outside Jaribuni in a village called Kitenga."

"I know it. I and my men will follow this lead, but that might not be his real name. Many *watu* call themselves by that name now…"

Lawrence let him go and phoned Jonathan to arrange for him to get his car back.

Sometime later he went back to the hospital in his car. The sun was setting and he was feeling anxious about Jessica, as well as Hugo. He may be my rival for Jessica's affections but he is a good guy, he thought, I wouldn't want anything to happen to him.

As he walked into the room where everyone was waiting Jessica leapt up to greet him, "Oh, thank goodness you're back," and in the heat of the moment gave him a great bear hug.

Hugo was still in surgery but Cora now had her parents with her so Lawrence tried to persuade Jessica to go home with him. It was only when he pointed out that she would be putting Hugo's family to more trouble if they had to give her a lift home that she agreed. The two of them left amidst a flurry of ring me's, tell us how he is, let us know straight away. Jessica hugged and kissed Hugo's parents and Cora and eventually they were on their way home.

Jessica sat in the car crying quietly, letting flow freely the tears she had held back so as not to worsen the situation for Hugo's family. Lawrence put a comforting hand on hers, the only gesture he could allow himself while driving. Unlike earlier when she had deliberately removed his arm from around her shoulders she simply left it there. But Lawrence wondered whether she had even noticed it, she seemed so distressed.

Supper was very subdued. Georgina and John wanted to know the whole story; they had only seen Lawrence briefly when he had called in earlier on his way with Jonathan to fetch Hugo's car. Now Lawrence told them the full story. Jessica was quiet, leaving the talking to Lawrence but when they asked her how she was she told them she was still in shock. "I've known Hugo all my life. I feel terrible that this has happened to him because he was trying to help me. I feel it is all my fault."

"Nonsense," said the other three in unison. "He was looking out for his sister too, don't forget but in any case the only people to blame in all of this are the two men who were attempting to kidnap you." John turned to Lawrence, "Do you think he was aiming at Hugo or was he just trying to scare the crowd away."

"Does it matter?" replied Lawrence. "He fired a gun in a crowd of people, someone was bound to get hurt. It may have been just bad luck that Hugo took a bullet in the belly but it might as well have been deliberate."

The conversation was interrupted by the shrill ring of Jessica's phone. All of them sitting around the table became tense and watched intently as Jessica listened to Cora. She let out a huge sigh of relief. Hugo was going to be alright. The bullet had hit him in the stomach but to one side and missed any vital organs. He had been patched up, given some pain killers and was now on his way home with his parents.

"Now we can all go to bed and sleep soundly," said John. "What a relief!" The others could only agree.

Most days in Jaribuni district morning dawned bright and clear encouraging early rising. Answering the call of the sun, Jessica got out of bed early and going over to the window was delighted to see the weaver birds creating a fluttering cloud of gold round the acacia tree outside her window. She could hear the shutters being opened downstairs and the staff calling out to each other as they prepared breakfast and opened up the house for the day. Sounds that she had heard all her life at home on the farm. She began to think about the farm and what she should do with it. She had wanted to come back to Kenya to live but it was difficult. It seemed that the only people who could make a life for themselves here were those with extensive farms, land where they could grow cash crops or run safari parks. Either that or they were NGO's working for one of the many charities or research facilities based in Kenya. Shamba ya Tembo was small, perhaps not suited to profitable farming. Coffee, tea, sisal, fruit, the main crops of the country all needed lots more acreage to make money than her parent's farm had. At least I already have Kenya citizenship, after all I was born here and my father was a Kenya citizen so they can't throw me out because I don't have a visa or work permit. Then she remembered her parent's friends, Kim and Sarah Davey, from up-country who had been at the funeral. They ran a farm that grew flowers. and they had invited her to go and see them. I think I could cope with flowers she said to herself but I am no farmer really. I think I might drive up there to visit them. I need a break. She spotted Lawrence going for his morning swim across the creek. She had dreamt about him that night. In her dream he had been kissing her passionately before tumbling her onto a bed and she had felt such desire and joy as she had never known before. If only it were that easy. She had to focus on her loss, not betray her parents. I need a break from him too, she thought. He is so full on sometimes and I feel he has muscled in on my problems. That seems ungrateful but I need some space to think. I'm not ready for more than friendship especially now. Also I don't want to upset Hugo now that he has been hurt. I know how he feels about me, he doesn't hide his feelings, but I can't feel the same way about him, I see him as a brother only.

All these thoughts were going round in her mind while she showered and dressed for the day. She was still wearing her 'bend-down' boutique clothes but she was too preoccupied to worry about going to Mombasa to shop for new outfits. She heard Lawrence, back from his swim, calling and knocking on her door.

"Are you ready? We need to have breakfast promptly if we are to get to Wanjiku's office on time."

Jessica opened her door suppressing the slight feeling of irritation at Lawrence taking charge once again, "Here I am, ready as you see and starving," she smiled. He smiled back and Jessica's resolve not to get involved just yet began to waver but she inwardly shook herself down and told herself there would be time for love later. Then realised as she went downstairs that she was admitting that what she felt might well be love. The kind of love that she couldn't give to Hugo.

As they walked over to the breakfast table she said, "I see you were enjoying your daily swim this morning. Very early."

"I like to swim across the creek and back every day to keep fit. There is no training military or otherwise, here. It's about half a mile across so it's a good workout."

"I see, but you often go when the tide is low so you walk part of it, it's not so far to go as at high tide," Jessica teased. Lawrence took the teasing in good part and said,

"Come with me and try it, you seemed to be a pretty strong swimmer when I saw you in the pool at Cora and Hugo's place."

"I have only ever managed to make it as far as the island in the middle. Besides Georgina tells me there are snakes in there, sea snakes that kill you with an electric shock."

"I swam in races against other regiments in the RNR, so I did a lot of training. It's a question of building up the distance. As for the snakes I haven't

116

seen any. If they are as shy as land snakes they will be frightened away by your splashing."

Over breakfast with Georgina and John on the veranda they discussed the meeting they were about to have with Wanjiku and Georgina agreed that she would go with Jessica to her farm afterwards. Cora was busy at the safari park and looking after Hugo, and Jessica had already told Lawrence off about it. He hadn't dared repeat his suggestion of the day before. He was still holding that early morning smile close to his heart.

The two of them drove out past the police car that was still keeping watch and past the fork in the road where the blue Toyota pulled out behind them again. When they turned off to park outside the police station, it sped on past.

"Good riddance," they both yelled at the windscreen and then laughed at their stereo exclamation.

Colonel Buckley and Denton were already waiting for them and knew about Hugo and what had happened the day before. "Sorry to hear about your friend, I told you the bastards will stop at nothing."

"How is he?" asked Denton and on the two of them being reassured that Hugo was recovering they all went inside to see Wanjiku.

Wanjiku was able to tell them that they had arrested Obama Ngina and were now looking for his accomplice.

"He has just followed us here. That blue Toyota again. Do you know who owns it?"

"I did a check on the number plate you gave me. It belongs to a Rod Wiley who lives at Kwale. I spoke to him and he claims his car was stolen but he hadn't bothered to complain because he doesn't think the police would do anything."

"That doesn't seem likely. It's brand new."

"I can't do anything, I have no proof," said Wanjiku. "Do any of you know this man?"

Denton admitted that he knew him and had done for years. Pushing his glasses up his nose he said,

"He is one of those loud bluff types, hangs around the boatyard a lot. Guffaws noisily at the slightest joke and slaps everyone on the back. I think he annoys the ladies most. I just always thought he was an idiot."

"How do you mean he annoys the ladies?" asked Jessica.

"I am told he has wandering hands but he also embarrasses them. For instance not long ago, a young woman came into the bar at the boatyard, a local, Kikuyu I think and very er well-endowed, er physically if you know what I mean. He was at the bar with a group of his cronies, including Derek by the way, and he said in a very loud voice 'My God look at the knockers on that.' Most of us thought he was completely out of order. So embarrassing."

"He sounds like a total dinosaur," said Jessica.

"Well, I have had an idea," said Lawrence. "We shouldn't get ourselves involved in following people, putting ourselves in danger, we've already seen what happened to Hugo but I can do some investigation on the internet. If this poaching is on such an international scale there must be an internet trail. I could try and follow that up, even if I have to go onto the dark web."

So it was agreed that Wanjiku would continue his enquiries among the people of the town and known criminals while Lawrence carried out an investigation on the internet. While Buckley promised to put two of his best men on the trail of Derek Foster and Rod Wiley.

"What should I be doing?" asked Jessica. "After all it is my affair before anyone else's."

The men all looked from one to the other. "We don't mean to leave you out of it," explained Lawrence in an apologetic tone, "and I will keep you up to date with whatever I find, and you can help me. But you have enough on your plate with lawyer's visits, seeing the families of your staff and deciding what to do with the farm. And there's Hugo. Maybe Cora and his parents need some support. I'm sure he will want to see you."

Jessica had to admit that he was right though she was somewhat disgruntled.

"Right, well, we had better go. I have to get back to the house and then Georgina and I are going over to the farm."

That afternoon Jessica and Georgina set off together for Shamba ya Tembo Farm. Georgina was anxious about Jessica and how she would react to being back at the farm where all the horror had happened. "What do you want me to do exactly?" she asked, more by way of distraction than real need to know.

"My Swahili is coming back but there are still times when I forget and don't understand a word so you can help me with that, otherwise just being with me is a help. That's strange, no follower today."

"Perhaps Wanjiku has managed to arrest him," suggested Georgina.

"Oh, no, there he is. He must have got stuck behind the *matatu* that I saw just now."

But Jessica didn't notice that there was another car following behind the blue Toyota. Both cars pulled off the road behind her to go down the track to where the farmhouse was. She heaved a great sigh as she stopped the car under a shady tree some distance from the ruins of the house. As they walked towards the blackened skeleton of the building the blue Toyota pulled up hard in a cloud of dust in front of them and a young man jumped out waving a gun at them.

"You come with me, now. Now," he yelled.

The two women looked at each other for reassurance and hesitated. The man fired a shot in the air. "You come, now," he repeated. This time they began to walk slowly towards him, hearts pounding. As they got close he pushed Georgina out of the way with one hand and she fell hitting her head as she crumpled to the ground in a fragile unconscious heap. Jessica tried to go to her but Ali waved his gun at her again saying, "You, take your clothes off." As she stood frozen in horror he said, "Take off your clothes or I shoot your friend."

Jessica slowly took off her clothes hoping blindly that something would happen to stop this terrifying man carrying out his so obvious intentions till she stood, naked, shivering in spite of the heat. She couldn't look at her attacker. Was this one of the men who had raped her mother? Her heart beat as though it would burst through her chest and her limbs felt weak. Stand upright, don't show your fear, she told herself. She was terrified for Georgina and had no idea how she was going to find a way out for both of them. Screaming would achieve nothing, there was no-one to hear. The man was now close to Jessica running his hand up and down her body. Jessica took a step back away from his rough hands but the man followed her grinning to himself. "Nice, very nice," he kept saying. With her next step back Jessica stumbled and fell back against the steps of the house. "Good, you lie down," he said as she squirmed in the dust to try and get away from him. He was already undoing his trouser belt. Georgina began to regain consciousness and was shouting loudly thinking to draw his attention. He turned towards her, lifting his gun to aim straight at her when suddenly the other car that they had not spotted on the road pulled up behind the Toyota and Inspector Wanjiku jumped out. "Put the gun down, now," he yelled. Kahinde's man, Ali, swivelled round to face this new arrival and Jessica took the opportunity of that momentary distraction to leap up and knock the gun out of his hand. She and Ali both ran to pick it up but Wanjiku already had his gun out and was shouting at Ali, "Stop or I'll shoot you." At this Ali stopped and put his hands in the air. Jessica picked up the gun and Wanjiku sent his sergeant, Mwangi over to handcuff Ali while he went to help Georgina up.

In the flick of a geckos tail, Jessica dived for her clothes but as she dressed herself she found her trembling fingers fumbled and struggled with her bra hooks and she stumbled standing on one wobbly leg after the other to put her pants and shorts back on. Georgina came over to help her rubbing her head where it was sore from her fall. She and Jessica hugged one another sobbing with relief and thanked Wanjiku for rescuing them.

"How come you were here?" asked Jessica wiping away her tears.

"You mentioned at my office where you were going this afternoon and I know these men have been following you, so I thought if I waited to see them following you I would be able to follow too and catch them. Of course there is only this one. His partner is already in custody thanks to your friend Lawrence and the information he found out."

"Well done Lawrence!" declared Georgina and Jessica could only agree. Wanjiku sent his sergeant off with Ali and stayed to make sure that Georgina and Jessica were well enough to get themselves home. "Are you sure you OK and can drive home?" he asked. Jessica said "I think we just need to sit quietly for a while and take time to calm our nerves. We'll be fine." Having been reassured that they could manage Wanjiku drove away in the blue Toyota.

Jessica and Georgina went on over to the house. Jessica sat at the top of the steps leading to where the front door had been, tears in her eyes and shoulders heaving with the effort of choking back her sobs. Georgina took her hand gently saying, come on I think we must go home. You can come and see the families tomorrow. I will come with you again. For now, I don't think you are fit to drive. I'm sure I am not either; we could ring Lawrence and John to come and get us.

"I'll be alright. I just need to sit quietly for a bit. I keep thinking how it could have turned out and how it must have been for my mother. All those men. What horror. But what about you, are you feeling alright?" Georgina put her arm round Jessica's shoulders and hugged her wordlessly. Silence and physical comfort are worth more than words at a time like this she thought. The two women sat quietly for a while watching the sun, a ball of orange fire, dropping through the sky towards the horizon.

Jessica stretched out her legs and then stood up offering a hand to Georgina. "Come on, time to go. I don't want to end up driving in the dark."

On the way home Georgina rang John to tell him what had happened so when she and Jessica arrived at the house he and Lawrence were standing on the front door step waiting for them. Georgina went straight to John who wrapped his arms around her as though he would never let her go. Lawrence held his hands out towards Jessica, "Oh, Jessica, my God," he blurted out.

"Lawrence, I was so frightened," she replied.

"Come here," She went towards him hands outstretched and he took her hand then drew her towards him and folded her into his arms where she sobbed with relief. He held her close stroking her hair and saying "I'm so sorry. I can't bear to think of what happened. I should have been there."

At that she pulled away from him. "No you shouldn't, you would have been shot for sure and where would that have got us? Nowhere."

Lawrence sighed, the moment of tenderness was over but it was a good sign that her sparkiness, not to say prickliness was back.

"So are you hurt?" he asked.

"Just grazed and bruised from where I fell and was squirming about on the ground. Georgina is the one we should be worried about, he knocked her out, you know."

Georgina was stoical and refused to let anyone make a fuss. "I'll just go to bed and rest," she said.

That night Jessica went to bed thinking about how she had felt in Lawrence's arms. Safe was the first word that came to her mind but that may have been just being back at the house and away from danger. She had to admit that she had liked being held by him. Like, she thought, such a weaselly word but I'm not going to think any more about it. As Scarlett O'Hara always said, "I'll think about it tomorrow." That night Lawrence visited her dreams once more.

Georgina and John were already at breakfast when Jessica came down stairs. There was no sign of Lawrence. Jessica was feeling a little frazzled after a night of tossing and turning, full of fear for what had so nearly happened and emotionally drained by her vivid dreams of love with Lawrence. She was half way through her first cup of coffee when he joined her at the table. Georgina and John had finished and left to take a stroll around the garden. "You look a bit frayed at the edges this morning," Jessica told Lawrence.

"I didn't sleep well last night. I was thinking so many different thoughts my mind was whirling."

"What about?"

"Well, you mostly. I had such dreams, like paradise was all mine."

"Oh," said Jessica, not admitting that she too had been dreaming. She finished her coffee and stood up with an air of determination. "I have to go; Georgina and I are going to the farm again today." And she walked out of the dining room. Lawrence followed trying to say that he thought it a really bad idea for them to go alone in case they were attacked again. Just as he went into the hall there was great volley of barking making any comment impossible and a man walked in surrounded by the dogs jumping up at him.

"What the hell are you doing here?" demanded Jessica.

"I've come to see you."

"It's a bit bloody late."

"Who is this?" asked Lawrence.

"That is my ex-boyfriend, emphasis on the ex," Jessica spat out. "His name is Daniel Parker."

"Sorry, Daniel, I don't think she wants to see you."

"That's my business not yours." Lawrence held up his hands, "OK, I'll leave you to it," and he walked out on to the veranda hoping that this wasn't one of those instances so beloved of romantic fiction where two people initially hate each other but soon fall in love.

"Come on Jessie, I've come all the way from London to see you."

"Well, you can fuck off back there and don't call me Jessie. You know I hate it."

"I can't go back. I'm booked for a two week stay. I'm in a hotel that I thought was near here but it seems to be miles away."

"You can go straight back there then. Go and turn yourself into a human lobster like all the other tourists on the beach. Leave me alone."

"I'm sorry, I know I should have called more often but then you blocked all my calls."

"You shouldn't have just called; you should have been on the first plane to come here and give me some love and support."

"But I had this big project, I was being paid shedloads of money. I couldn't walk away from that. My career was on the line and I would have been able to buy us a decent house."

"You know when something as horrific as the murder of your entire family happens your perspective is quite different. Get your priorities right. Now go away I have too much else to do and I know now that I don't need you."

"No well, you've got lover boy there now," said Daniel pointing in the direction of Lawrence.

"Why does everybody assume we are an item. He is a good friend and he has stood by me in a way that you didn't even begin to do. Now fuck off and get out of my life." She shrieked. So loud was the shouting that Lawrence came back to see if she needed help. The dogs were barking again announcing the arrival of Cora who was very confused by the situation.

"I can't go anywhere the taxi has already gone," said Daniel.,

"I'll give you a lift," offered Lawrence. "Oh, I'm Lawrence by the way and this is Cora another friend of Jessica's."

By now Jessica was in tears and calling to Cora to come and talk. "Georgina and I were going to come and see Hugo this afternoon, and you of course after we had been to see the families. How is Hugo?"

"He is still very sore and finds moving painful but he is making a good recovery. But how about you, what is all this commotion and why these tears?"

Jessica told her what had happened the day before first of all, at which Cora was deeply shocked and sympathetic. "Just think what might have happened if Inspector Wanjiku hadn't turned up when he did. It's all too awful and poor Georgina, I really felt terrible for the fright that she had. After all she's no spring chicken. She could easily have had a heart attack or something."

Cora hugged her friend and then asked what the problem was now. Jessica felt as though she were in a confessional. She told Cora all about Daniel Parker who had not come out to support her when she needed him but was here now. "I'm so angry, how dare he come now." Then she broached the question of Lawrence. "I think he is in love with me. I keep pushing him away, he might turn out to be just as flaky as bloody Daniel. Anyway, he seems to be always trying to take over, to be in charge even though all the troubles are mine."

"He is only trying to help you. I am sure he does love you; I've seen the way he looks at you, and naturally he feels he wants to look after you," soothed Cora. "He is a lovely guy. Be nice to him."

Jessica sniffed and wiped away her tears admitting to Cora that she couldn't stop dreaming about him.

"Look, I'll take your Daniel Parker back to his hotel and you can spend some time with Lawrence before you go to the farm."

"I am dreading going back there to tell you the truth. It feels cursed, such awful things have happened there. And I am still worried about Jaba, our cattle man. Maybe he was kidnapped. Maybe I will be kidnapped this time, I don't understand why they want to follow me otherwise."

"They probably want you out of the way because as long as you are here pushing, the police will continue to pursue their enquiries."

"We had better get going, you with Daniel to his hotel and me to the farm with Georgina."

"Just the two of you again. Is that wise?"

Jessica merely shrugged her shoulders in reply.

Chapter 8

Once Cora and Daniel had left, Jessica asked Lawrence how his internet searches were going. According to what he told her the Chinese and Hong Kong end of things was quite easy to pick up. The goods were advertised quite openly on the Chinese websites and he had found Li Wei Wang. She had her own site advertising both live animals and animal parts for sale. He also found Chang Zhou in Shanghai offering horn and tusks as well as skins, apparently with impunity. Where it became more difficult was tracking through to this end. The trail goes off into the dark web and names became difficult to find. He promised to keep trying and Jessica went to find Georgina and see if she was ready to drive out to the farm.

Finally, as planned Georgina and Jessica set off once again for the farm but in some trepidation. They knew the two stalkers had been imprisoned but were fearful that Kahinde might have a whole boxful of other foot soldiers to do his dirty work for him.

They weren't the only ones who were fearful. John and Lawrence set off after them to keep a watch over them without letting them know. They kept quite a long way behind, Lawrence did not want to annoy Jessica again especially now he had seen what her anger was like. He didn't fancy being shouted at like Daniel had been. He had been astonished at the rage and passion that Jessica had displayed. He had never heard her really swear before though it was understandable in the circumstances.

The two women arrived at the farm and walked slowly up to the house. Both of them kept looking around to make sure there was no-one else there.

"I have to say I am so sorry about what happened to you yesterday," said Jessica.

"Nonsense, my dear. It wasn't your fault and you had far worse than I."

"I don't think so. You were the one who was knocked unconscious. Thank you for being there for me. You have been so helpful in so many ways. Jessica paused on the doorstep. Oh shit, this is so difficult, at the moment I feel I never want to have anything to do with this place again."

"Come on you have to face this and think what you are going to do with all this property. I am sure your parents would have wanted you to have it and make a life for yourself out here. It's not only the rich who can make a go of things here."

"You mean like Sylvie the French girl who is with Paul at the boat yard?"

"I do. Her father is a multi-millionaire who owns all kinds of enterprises including oil companies and pharmaceuticals. She is on the pay roll in some obscure capacity that doesn't require much effort beyond drifting around looking gorgeous."

"So that's how she manages to live, I did wonder when I met her the other day. When I asked her what she did she shrugged her shoulders and said 'Sometimes this and sometimes that'. Thinking about the farm though, I can't see myself rearing and milking cattle. The farm is too small to yield much from most crops so I don't know what to do. I don't seem to have any ideas."

"Why not set up a workshop of some kind. You know making goods, like dresses or bags or leather goods? Shoes and handbags are always in demand. Or what about a honey farm, that doesn't take much land."

"Gracious that's more ideas than I have had in all the time I have been here. They are good ideas too. I will think about that. I am planning to go and see my parent's friends upcountry. They run a flower farm and might have some advice. I thought perhaps I could cope with flowers."

The two women walked on into the burnt out shell of the house crunching over the blackened floors. Jessica was thinking how she would have to rebuild the house from scratch but according to the letter she had received from the lawyer she was able to afford that. With her own money as well she could start some kind of enterprise.

"Oh my God, look at this. That was the sitting room, where we are standing was the dining room. Upstairs has all gone, crashed through the burnt rafters. We are walking on it I guess."

"Come on, let's go and see the families now. There is not much we can do here."

Together the two of them walked through the farmyard and over to where the families were still living a half mile distance from the house.

The nearest *kibanda* was where Emmanuel, the houseboy had lived. His widow was outside in the *shamba* picking tomatoes.

"*Jambo, habari?*" shouted Jessica from the edge of the vegetable patch. Zarifa straightened up saying "*Nsuri sana.* (I am fine.) Hello, Mama Jessica how are you?"

But when she had put down her *kikapu* full of tomatoes and came over to Jessica the two women wept and hugged each other. She has lost a lot of weight thought Jessica and asked Zarifa how she was managing. Zarifa soon ran out of English words to explain and continued in Swahili with Georgina prompting Jessica when needed. "It is very difficult. my three m*totos* are hungry. We have this bit of land and I grow food but only vegetables. We need some meat but it is too much money and even *posho* and flour are expensive. I don't know what we would do without our *kibanda* here." Then with a look of alarm, "you haven't come to tell us we have to go, have you?"

"No, no, for the time being you can stay, this is your home. I am trying to decide what to do. I don't want to sell. I don't want all of you to have to leave. Emmanuel was with my parents a long time. I remember him from when I was a m*toto* and before you and he were married. A loyal man and a good worker."

"Yes, not like that Jaba. Shifty and lazy he was."

"Was? You mean you still haven't seen him?" Zarifa shook her head. "No mama, I have not seen him."

"Where are your m*totos*?"

"At the school. they will be home soon."

"I am sorry not to see them."

Jessica left Zarifa with some money for food and went to look for Durah, the wife of Joseph the cook. She was sitting outside her *kibanda* cutting sukuma, for her evening meal. She was sitting on a stool with a *kikapu* full of the dark green spinach-like leaves that she had picked from her *shamba.* In one hand she held a bunch of leaves tightly scrunched together, in the other she held a sharp knife with which she was cutting the leaves so that they fell in narrow ribbons into the cooking pot held between her feet. She worked so fast and the knife went so close to her fingers that Jessica was afraid to speak in case she was distracted into cutting herself.

"*Jambo*, Durah, how are you?"

"*Jambo*, Mama. I am not so well. Very sad since my man died. Very sad for you too and this place. The smell of burning is in my nose and throat every time I pass the house. I have only my sewing work now, very small money and no-one to protect us here. Mingati, our *askari* was a good man, very strong, kept us all safe. He had only just been given that name after killing his first lion but lions are not the same as evil gangs. Even he was not strong enough for that."

"Have you seen Jaba? He wasn't killed with everyone else but no-one has seen him. I am worried about him."

"You should not worry about him. He was no good."

"Why do you say that?"

"We had a girl working here in the house with Mama Lydia. She wanted to be a cook. Jaba kept pestering her, then one day I heard her crying. When I went to her, her clothes were ripped and she told me that Jaba had forced himself on her. Bwana Donald was very angry when he heard about it and told Jaba he must go. He is a bad man; he probably just ran away."

"Well, if he does come back tell him to come and see me. Here take this money to help you out a bit. I am planning to do something with the property and will need workers for whatever project I can create. So don't go away. *Kwaheri,* Durah."

"*Kwaheri,* bye bye, Mama. Thank you."

As she strolled back to the car with Georgina, Jessica breathed a sigh of relief that she had finally made contact with Durah and Zarifa and made sure they were alright. She hoped that they were pleased to be asked to stay on and that she would be able to fulfil the promise she had made them.

Georgina was very relieved when they got back into the car again without incident and said as much to Jessica.

"Yes. Me too. Now how do you feel about going to see Hugo? It's only another twenty minutes down the road."

"That's fine but I don't want to be too late back. John isn't so well you know. He has been told he has Parkinson's, it's why he went to London, for tests."

"Oh my God, I am so sorry to hear that. You should have told me before. Here I am taking up so much of your time and energy, not to mention putting you in danger."

"He only told me the other day. And at the moment there is not much to be done. Just take the medicine and carry on as normal."

"Does Lawrence know?"

"He does. He is very close to his grandfather so he is very concerned. Anyway, let's go and see Hugo. I'm sure he will be pleased to see you."

They were so busy talking they didn't notice John's car hiding in the bush. The two men drove out behind them, "Where the hell are they going now?" said John, "Jaribuni is in the opposite direction."

"I think this is the road to Zinj Safari camp. I went there the other day with Jessica."

"You have really fallen for her haven't you?"

"Is it that obvious?"

"Afraid so."

"She makes me think of Bronzino's Lady in Red, especially in her swimsuit," he grinned. Then looking serious, "I think she could be my forever woman but she won't let me near her."

"I thought you millennials or whatever generation you are supposed to be were more into the likes of Beyoncé than classical beauties. She seemed very willing to be embraced by you yesterday when she and Georgina came home after their ghastly attack."

"I think she was just pleased to be hugged and sheltered by anyone after that, even me. And if you notice she pulled away as quickly as she could on the pretence that I had said something annoying."

"Remember, she has been going through hell. Romance is probably the last thing on her mind. Just be patient and persistent, keep on helping her. Things may change as time goes on. Now what are we going to do? Should we follow them into the safari camp or just go home? They could be there some time and I don't fancy sitting waiting in the car. It's too hot for that."

"We could just go in to the house saying we have come to see Hugo which is probably what they are doing."

And so much to the surprise of Jessica and Georgina, John and Lawrence turned up at Zinj just after them.

Hugo was happy to see them all, as were his parents and Cora. The women all kissed each other fondly while the men shook hands. Jessica interrupted all the greetings to say to Hugo "I wouldn't for all the world have wanted anything to happen to you. I am so sorry; this terrible murder is now bringing disaster to my dearest friends."

"It's fine," said Hugo. "I just want to help you to be safe and find who is behind all these dreadful, absolutely awful crimes."

"Good to see you looking so well," said Lawrence. "Are you still on the painkillers?"

"Yes and having to have the dressing changed every day. I must thank you for helping to look after me that day and Cora tells me you were great at the hospital getting the medical orderlies organised with a stretcher and so on. Thanks, man."

"Let's hope you will soon be out and about and able to help us."

"I'm sure I will be. Perhaps you can even take me out sailing one of these days."

Lawrence smiled and nodded, pleased to get the message that hostilities between them were over.

The conversation turned to what Georgina and Jessica had gone through on their previous visit to the farm. Jenny was horrified at the thought of what almost happened. They all agreed that the one good thing to come out of both violent incidents was that now the two men who had been following Jessica were in custody and could no longer do any of them any harm. Robert was serving drinks all round when Daniel Parker walked into the room.

"What the hell is he doing here?" exploded Jessica.

"I invited him to stay," explained Cora. "His hotel was miles away and he seemed so forlorn on the way there I felt sorry for him so he's spending the fortnight with us."

Jessica was dumbfounded, how could her friend, knowing that she didn't want this man around, do that. She didn't know what to say and Daniel took her silence to mean acceptance. "Hi Jessica," he said being careful not to shorten her name to the hated Jessie.

"I'll have to put up with you being here, I suppose but you can keep away from me and my affairs."

Jenny, ever the perfect hostess stepped forward to smooth things over saying, "Thank you all for coming to see Hugo. Let's raise our glasses and wish him a swift return to perfect health."

Conversation got back onto its normal, pleasant, even keel, during which Jessica announced her plans to go to stay up-country with Kim and Sarah Davey on their farm.

"By yourself?" everyone said in horror.

"Of course. They have asked me twice to go there and they are my parents best friends... or rather were," she added bitterly.

"But it's a six hour drive," said John. "I'm not sure that's wise for you in light of all that has happened."

Georgina added her voice to the chorus of protests suggesting that Jessica should take Lawrence with her to share the driving at least. Lawrence nodded in agreement. "Yup, I can do that," he said with alacrity.

"It's no good. I've made my mind up and I've already agreed with the Davey's that I will drive up tomorrow."

"Is her car up to it?" Lawrence quietly asked Hugo.

"I think so. It is a 4x4, one of those little Suzukis, well, you know it. Small but tough. Also the road is tarmac for most of the way but there are potholes."

"And lunatics and morons out on the road," added Lawrence. "I don't suppose there is anything we can do. Her mind is made up." "Not a thing," replied Hugo.

In the end they did manage to persuade her to follow the method that had worked so well so far, to leave Georgina's place without being followed. It was decided that she would drive her car to the boatyard and leave it there, going across the creek by boat to get home. Then in the morning she could take the water taxi to pick up her car and drive up country.

Once all that was settled Georgina and John set off in their car and Lawrence and Jessica in hers.

"You seemed to get on better with Hugo," Jessica said.

"He was really very nice. I never had anything against him as a man in the first place. Just his obsession with you and being jealous got in the way of friendship. He seemed genuinely grateful to me for helping out when he was injured. Slightly embarrassing because I don't think I did much at all."

"You stood by him and that's all that matters."

"Do you really have to go tomorrow. I'm very worried about you driving all that way alone. Not just me. All of us."

"I must start standing on my own two feet. I have been depending on everyone for too long. I hope to find some ideas for what do with the farm. The Davey's grow roses on their farm. I could see myself doing that rather than dairy farming."

"Both involve large amounts of manure," said Lawrence teasingly. "I will miss you. These last few weeks have been both wonderful and awful. I love being with you but I am tortured by sleepless nights thinking about you. When

I do fall asleep I dream of you and I'm in heaven. Then I wake up and I come back down to earth especially when you keep being so distant."

"Oh, God damn it, Lawrence, I'm concentrating on driving at the moment. You do pick your moments. I feel so mixed up just now. I don't feel I have a right to be happy or to indulge in romance after what has happened. I still see my parent's bodies every time I close my eyes. Every breath I take is tainted with the terrible smell of burning. I think I need some space and that is another reason for me to go. I will miss you. You have been a good friend to me and stood by me."

"That's all I am then. I do get it, but you know I am sure your parents would want you to find happiness. They couldn't want you to let your grief get in the way of living your life."

"How the hell do you know what my parents would think or feel? Just let me come to things in my own time."

"Sorry. I didn't mean to presume what your parents might think. I am trying to be the voice of reason and of love if that doesn't sound too cheesy."

"So you can ditch me at will like Daniel did. I can do without that kind of love."

"Not all men are like that."

"Hmm," was Jessica's reply and they drove on to the boatyard in silence.

It was nearly dark when they got the boat across the creek and the spray in the boats wake and at her bow was like thousands of fireflies as the phosphorescence danced its magic on the water. Jessica looked across to where Lawrence was perched on the gunwale looking down at the water; his face looked solemn, she thought. But looking at him silhouetted against the darkening sky her limbs felt as solid as the water that the boat was floating on.

Dinner that night was quite a sorry affair. Lawrence was not his usual cheerful and amusing self. The only positive moment was when Georgina and John reassured Jessica that they had not seen any cars lurking in the roads leading to the house. Both of them were tired from their long day and all the driving so they retired to bed early.

Jessica and Lawrence were also only too happy to go to their separate bedrooms.

That night Jessica slept only fitfully; she didn't admit it to her friends but she was nervous about doing such a long drive all by herself. She kept thinking of all the pitfalls, most of them had been enumerated by the others. She was most worried about breakdowns or flat tyres when she would have to stop and get help, that is when she would be most vulnerable. At least when they had got home last night there was no sign of any watchers and she would be able to drive off from the boatyard without any followers.

As daylight dawned Jessica got up and packed the few things she would need for her stay. After breakfast Lawrence insisted on going with her to the boatyard. "I can hook up with Johnathan and we will probably go for a sail," he told her.

"And what about your internet searches?" she reminded him.

"Don't worry that is well underway. Now listen," he said as they were standing by her car, "You must ring me when you arrive. I, we all, need to know that you have got to the farm safe and sound. Promise?"

"I promise."

"And I shall ring you every day whether you need it or not. I am going to miss you Jessica Langley."

"I'll probably miss you too, and all the others. But I am looking forward to seeing the farm and the Davey's are very good friends and fun to be with."

Lawrence leant down to kiss her goodbye but she made sure that it was only her cheek that she offered.

As she drove off Jonathan stood next to Lawrence. "Where's she going?" So Lawrence explained her plans to his friend. "That was a very restrained kiss, you gave her. I can tell she means more to you than that."

"Yes, but she is keeping me at a distance. Says she can't think about romance at the moment. It's as though she is protecting herself with this great, black cloud of grief and guilt."

"Come on, you need cheering up. Let's go out on *Mkwaze* for the day. I don't have anything urgent to attend to and the wind is perfect, not too strong. We could sail out to the reef."

Jessica's drive was long but uneventful. All the way she was constantly aware of how nervous she was, kept telling herself to relax her grip on the steering wheel whenever she noticed that her knuckles were turning white. When she arrived at the Davey's farm she was exhausted by her own tension as much as by the actual drive which had been hot, dusty and noisy with large antiquated trucks rattling all around her, grinding gears and generally getting in her way. Overtaking was always terrifying as you never knew whether they might not swerve into you as they lurched along from side to side.

Finally she arrived at the gate to the Davey's property. She drove up the drive admiring all the beautiful hibiscus that grew along one side. On the other side were teak trees and palm trees and nearer the house frangipani trees perfumed the air. The house was large and covered with bougainvillea of many colours, white, pink, purple and orange. It was obvious Sarah and Kim did not feel the same way about watering their garden as Georgina did. The grass was a lush green.

Kim and Sarah welcomed her with open arms and a long cool drink with plenty of ice. Sarah then showed her to her bedroom where she would able to take a refreshing shower.

She looked around the large, cool room. There were lovely big windows on one side that looked out over the garden. The ceiling had beams that looked dark and old but otherwise everything was white, walls and ceilings white. The tiled floor was a neutral stone colour and felt smooth and cool underfoot. The bed was enormous because, as Sarah explained later, when there are two of you and it's hot at night you need some space around you to breathe easy. The bed linen was all white except for the throw on top which was a vivid red and white pattern. There was a very handsome carved chest against one wall and a dressing table and chair in Queen Anne style, bandy-legged thought Jessica. Built-in wardrobes took up most of another wall and an archway led into the bathroom, privacy being afforded by a red curtain matching the throw.

Jessica put her one small bag down on the sofa at the end of the bed. It looked lost in all that space. She felt a bit lost herself. She hadn't seen Kim and Sarah for years until the funeral so although she had known them well as a child she now felt they were almost strangers. They were very kind. They had both given her such big hugs and treated her as if she were their own daughter coming home. A knock at the door broke into her reverie. It was Sarah telling her that dinner would be in an hour and they were having drinks on the veranda if she wanted to join them when she was ready. So Jessica undressed, had a shower and changed her clothes regretting that she hadn't been to Mombasa yet to buy herself something decent. Sarah was so smart with her linen shirt dress and carefully groomed hair. Jessica put on a pale blue cotton kaftan that she cinched in at the waist with a wide belt. With her long hair freshly brushed and silky and the new *ndara* (sandals) that she had bought at the market on her feet she felt refreshed and ready to face the evening despite her weariness. Then she remembered that she hadn't rung Lawrence. Just then her phone rang and there he was on his phone, his voice coming across the ether sounding muffled but still recognisable.

"You didn't ring," he accused.

"No, well I only arrived about an hour ago and I was speaking to Kim and Sarah, settling into my bedroom and taking a shower. After that long, hot drive I needed to freshen up. I was literally just going to pick up my phone to speak to you that's why I answered so quickly."

"Well, so long as you're safe and sound. That's all that matters. I'll tell Georgina, she and John have been as worried about you as I have. Enjoy your evening. Bye for now. I'll ring again tomorrow."

"Bye," whispered Jessica suddenly feeling lost without him. She told herself to get a grip, put her shoulders back and stand tall. Then she went downstairs to join her friends on the veranda.

"Now come and sit next to me," said Sarah patting a comfortable looking chair with lots of soft cushions. Kim went to get her drink and they enquired how the drive had been, how long it had taken her and whether she had stopped anywhere. Jessica was pleased that they were focussing on the small details of everyday life. Having a dull conversation about the mundane things that everyone discussed was just what she needed now. Sipping her drink she relaxed into their friendship and the comfort of their beautiful home.

During dinner she asked them how they had got to know her parents. It seems that it was Sarah and her mother who had known each other first. Kim and she had lived near Jaribuni when they were first married and the two women had met at the East Africa Women's League meetings. "Not my cup of tea, really, my dear, nor your mother's either but we didn't know anyone and it seemed like a good way to meet other women."

Jessica remembered that her mother had been a staunch supporter of the League which raised money for charity. "She didn't go to many of the meetings though. She was always either too busy or too tired. After all she worked hard in the house and helped out on the farm."

"She was always very practical," said Sarah. "She also welcomed everyone into the house with great generosity, all waifs and strays could count on her. She and I were very sad when Kim and I moved here. But by then we both had babies to look after and we just kept in touch by phone and the occasional visit."

"That explains why I never got to know Gemma very well. How are the twins these days?" asked Jessica.

"Matthew is working in London. He's a junior doctor and Gemma is married and has just had a little boy."

"Wow, so you're a grandmother. How exciting!"

"Yes, I am thrilled. I can't wait to see them. They are coming over when the baby is six months old so I have to wait a while to have a cuddle. I have seen him on FaceTime and they send photos, would you like to see?" She smoothed back her already tidy hair and got up to fetch her iPad. Jessica remembered Sarah as being tall but that was years ago before university and work when she herself was smaller. Both she and Kim were much stouter than she had expected too but still attractive people. Sarah had a lovely smile which lit up her face now as she showed Jessica the pictures of her new grandson. Jessica made all the appropriate comments but was interrupted by Kim telling them that the staff were calling them to dinner.

The mood changed as they sat down at table and Sarah asked Jessica how things had been going in Jaribuni. So Jessica told them everything that had happened since she had seen them at the funeral. She could see they were both shocked to the core to know how close she had come to horrific violence herself. And the violence done to Hugo and Inspector Mona.

"I am surprised you were prepared to drive here by yourself. Weren't you nervous that you might be attacked again?"

"Yes, I was. But I am determined that I should stand on my own two feet as soon as possible. I only stopped once on the way and that was in a petrol station with plenty of people about and I know that the men who had been following me, especially the one who attacked me, are in jail."

"Well here you are now and you made it without any problems. Who is this Lawrence you keep talking about?"

Jessica explained that he was the grandson of Georgina Hamilton's lover.

"Her lover, don't you mean her friend?"

"No. She insists that he is her lover not a mere friend."

Then she went on to tell Sarah and Kim how she was hoping to make use of what was now her farm and had come to them looking for ideas and inspiration.

Kim was very happy to talk about the farm, "...more of a market garden really. We grow beans and sweet corn that are exported to Europe, and roses. I am the bean-waller and Sarah looks after the roses. We can give you a guided tour tomorrow and tell you something of the practicalities."

"That would be perfect," said Jessica. "Right now I think I am ready for bed, if you don't mind."

That night she slept soundly and dreamlessly waking in the morning feeling more refreshed than she had for a long time.

She came downstairs to find Sarah already bustling about organising the household as she was going to be busy on the farm that day. As she told Jessica when you have live animals or plants to take care of there are certain jobs that cannot be put off.

"But I hope you will come with me to see what we do."

After a quick breakfast Jessica set off with Sarah. She was looking forward to seeing the flowers which cannot grow in the climate of the coast. She had always loved seeing the roses in England and France, summer beauty. She could see the greenhouses up ahead covering acres of land. Inside, the perfume exuded by the flowers was overpowering, she felt quite choked by it. Sarah was busy explaining how it all worked. The drip feeding of water and fertiliser in exact quantities, the prevention of disease and insect infestation again by carefully measured chemicals. "Oh yes, Lawrence said that growing roses is as much about manure as dairy farming is."

"He is right in a way but nowadays we don't shovel shit it is all distilled into very carefully produced and purified chemicals in liquid form. Of course the roses do well here because we have rich volcanic soil and plenty of sunshine. It doesn't get as hot and humid as you have it down at the coast. The climate is more like an English summer day."

"It seems very scientific," said Jessica as they walked up and down the rows of roses watching the workers pruning and tidying the plants to ensure healthy growth and cutting the long stemmed blooms to take to the packing shed. Moving on to the packing shed she saw more workers, mainly women cleaning the stems and putting together the bouquets. "We have about 400 workers here just for the roses. We make sure they all have mosquito nets for their families, that they are vaccinated and we even have a small school for the little ones. You are a teacher aren't you? Perhaps you would like to see it tomorrow."

"What are they doing over there?" Jessica asked. "Ah, they are taking off all the thorns so that the customers don't prick themselves. We have to avoid any Sleeping Beauty scenarios," explained Sarah. Jessica laughed, "I always wondered how come the roses you buy in supermarkets in England have no thorns."

"Over there you can see the flowers are being wrapped in cellophane, they will be flown out to arrive in the supermarkets of Europe tomorrow."

"How many acres do you have here?"

"We have about a thousand acres but only 60 dedicated to rose growing. The rest is down to Kim. He grows French beans and baby sweetcorn for export. Do you want to see his fields?"

"Why not."

After a morning in the fields Sarah and Jessica were ready for lunch and went back to the house where they were joined by Kim. As he went to fetch drinks for them both Jessica thought how pleasant it was to be with them. She was accepted, welcomed readily without having to explain herself since they already knew where she came from and most other facts about her. They were both so down-to-earth. She couldn't imagine them being phased by anything. Silver haired now, distinguished looking, their eyes were as friendly as ever and full of humour.

Jessica accepted her drink from Kim and told him how impressed she was by their farm. "Lot of hard work of course," he said, "but we enjoy it. I gather from what you said last night that you are thinking about what to do with your parent's farm, well, yours now and I gather you don't want to do dairy farming like Donald."

Kim went on to ask some very practical questions about Shamba ya Tembo farm, acreage, type of soil, climate and so on. He came up with some very practical suggestions for Jessica to mull over.

After lunch Jessica left Kim and Sarah to get on with their work and took a book to her room. She lay on the bed in the peace and quiet and tried to read but now she was unoccupied her mind kept drifting back to Lawrence and wondering when he would ring. She was determined not to ring him but her fingers were itching to pick up her phone. Instead she rang Cora.

"So how's it going up there?" asked Cora.

"Ya, fine."

But Cora knew her friend only too well. "You don't sound exactly ecstatic. what's up?"

"I am feeling lonely. Sarah and Kim have been very welcoming but they are my parent's friends not mine. I miss all of you."

"You mean you miss Lawrence. If it's any consolation I think he is missing you a lot."

"Yes, I suppose I do. He has been so good to me but so annoying too. I think about him all the time."

"I think you would be crazy to let him go."

"You think he might give up on me?"

"You haven't been very affectionate towards him to say the least."

"I guess not. I've only known him such a short time and with my mind full of all my problems... Also I feel guilty every time I think of being happy again."

"Don't be silly."

"OK, OK. What are you up to? Is that bloody Daniel still with you?"

"He really makes you angry doesn't he? You can't speak of him without swearing. Personally, I like him. we have had a good time together. He's going tomorrow so he'll be out of the way by the time you get back."

"You haven't fallen for him have you?"

"Maybe. Maybe not. We intend to keep in touch. He doesn't want to leave London and I couldn't possibly leave Kenya so there isn't much future in it. We might have some fun together every so often but that's about it. You just keep thinking of Lawrence, those beautiful eyes, those slim snake-like hips."

"Don't mention snakes. That is a real off-put. I'm terrified of them."

"Don't be so awkward. You know what I mean. I've got to go. I have to feed the baby hippo that's been orphaned and I promised Daniel he could come with me."

Somehow the room seemed even more silent than before once Cora had rung off. Jessica thought about ringing Georgina but she knew that she and John would be having their siesta. She lay on the bed and thought about Lawrence. She had intended to think about the ideas for her farm that both Georgina and now Kim had suggested but Lawrence got in the way. Damn him! she thought, I must try and find somewhere else to live. It's the only way to escape.

Time ticked on and Sarah and Kim were back. That evening was another night of reminiscing and family news but then Sarah asked, "Last night you kept talking about a man, Lawrence was it? You mentioned him again when we were looking at the roses. Is he someone special to you?"

Jessica sighed and told Sarah how he seemed to be in love with her but she wasn't ready yet. She talked about her feelings of guilt at the thought of being happy after what had happened to her parents. "I still see that horrific scene every time I close my eyes."

Just then her phone rang. She apologised to Sarah and Kim, "…so rude but I have to take it. It's Lawrence on a video call."

"Let's see him whispered Sarah," and she came over to look over Jessica's shoulder.

The conversation was brief since they could not speak in private but Jessica promised to ring back later.

As she switched her phone off, Sarah simply said, "Wow, You want to hang on to that one. Not only does he look great but he has kindness in his eyes. He looks like someone you can trust. I know it sounds a bit crazy but there are men I look at and think how could any woman put their life in his hands. Because that is what you are doing when you form a relationship, marriage or otherwise. Of course his life is in yours too but you are perhaps more vulnerable. Forgive me if I am speaking out of turn but I did know your parents really well, especially your mother. I was probably her oldest and closest friend. I am certain that they would want you to be happy. They wouldn't want you to let the nightmare you have endured ruin the rest of your life…"

"Lawrence said something very similar to me just before I came here. I got angry with him because he didn't know my parents so I didn't think he had any right to speak for them. It's different coming from you. Perhaps you are both right."

"I am sure we are. You are denying yourself a life and love. The way you keep talking about him, the way your eyes lit up when you were on the phone just now, I can see you are passionate about him and you are keeping him at arm's length because you are afraid of what life might yet do to you."

Jessica went to bed with her mind in turmoil. Perhaps Lawrence and every one else was right, and Lawrence was a very different person from the flaky Daniel. Perhaps she should trust him. For now, she dialled his number and felt a thrill of pleasure at hearing his voice and seeing his face on her screen. They spoke for half an hour, all the news from Jaribuni, the progress Lawrence was making on the internet, tracking down the poachers' connections. Jessica told him all about the roses and the suggestions that Kim had made for her farm and then it was time to say goodnight. "*Lala Salama (*sleep well*)* I love you, Jessica Langley."

"I love you too," she replied.

At his end of the phone Lawrence couldn't believe his ears. Did she really mean it or was it just a casual line such as one good friend might say to another? What had suddenly changed her mind if it was changed? He forced himself not to ring back, I'll speak to her again tomorrow and then she will be coming home the day after that, he thought. But he spent an uncomfortable night of fitful sleep worrying about what Jessica had said.

It was Jessica's last day at the Davey's farm. Sarah took her to see the little school that was housed in an immaculate white building at the edge of the farm. Jessica was impressed by all the smiling children sitting in neat rows looking cleaned and polished to within an inch of their lives. Their faces were shiny with hygiene and excitement at having a visitor, a *Mwingereza* – an Englishwoman. Jessica shook hands with their teacher who introduced her to the class. "Good Morning Miss Langley," they all chanted just as they had been practicing since early morning. She replied in time honoured fashion, good morning children, and spoke to the class encouraging them to try out some English phrases. They responded with enthusiasm, "Hello, How are you?"

"I am fine." in delightful singsong piping voices. Then Jessica asked the teacher, Mercy, if they knew any English songs. It seemed they had all learned *The Wheels on the Bus* and *Old MacDonald had a Farm*.

"They like the sound effects," explained Mercy "and they all know what a *matatu* is and a *shamba*." So Jessica led the children singing those songs and loved their excitement when they made the animal noises, especially the boys snorting like pigs.

That evening was her last and though she was sorry to leave Sarah and Kim she was anxious to go back to Jaribuni. After dinner and liqueurs out on the veranda under the stars Jessica went up to bed. Her phone rang just as she climbed into bed. It was Lawrence. "Hi there," then there was a long pause, he hardly dared speak, not wanting to say the wrong thing that might turn her off. He resorted to chitchat; he had been sailing with Hugo as he had promised.

Sylvie and Paul had broken up so Cora was busy consoling her. Finally, he asked if she had meant what she had said last night. Jessica played dumb. "What did I say last night?"

"When we said goodnight I said I love you and you answered I love you too."

"Well, I do. I have missed you these few days and I am glad I am coming home to you. There will that do?"

"That will do very well. I can't wait for you to get back so that we can be together again. Drive carefully tomorrow. I love you. Goodnight, *lala salama*." "*Lala salama* to you too."

After bidding Sarah and Kim a fond farewell during which they pressed a gorgeous bouquet of roses on her to take to Georgina, Jessica set off for Jaribuni and Lawrence.

She felt so much less anxious now that she had made up her mind to let her feelings flow naturally, to obey her heart and body. The return journey was uneventful and seemed to fly past as her thoughts were now entirely focused on seeing Lawrence again. Halfway along the road she noticed her surroundings and wondered how she had got there. She had been driving blind she realised, reacting to the road and its hazards on auto pilot. But the urgency of the journey and the sense of excitement rising from deep inside her spurred her on.

It was early evening when she arrived at Georgina's house. As she went in she saw Georgina moving between kitchen and dining room organising dinner for them all.

"Well, look at you," said Georgina. "You look like a particularly fragrant Birnam Wood. Who is to be vanquished I wonder?"

"Hi Georgina, these are for you courtesy of Sarah and Kim. Wow, it's good to be here and to see you again." And somehow despite the bouquet they embraced one another fondly. Jessica was now anxious to see Lawrence. She could hear voices coming from the veranda so she followed the sound. As she arrived on the veranda she saw Hugo grinning and then Sylvie kissing Lawrence. She froze on the spot momentarily and then with a look of pure pain she turned and ran upstairs to her room.

Lawrence pushed Sylvie to one side and ran after her. He managed to wedge his foot in the door as she was closing it. "It's not what you think."

"No? You men are all the same. You're as flaky as bloody Daniel." Lawrence wriggled his way into the room through the narrow gap between the door and the jamb.

"Goddammit, Jessica, I told you I love you and I meant it. Sylvie came…"

"I don't want to hear your excuses. Get out of my room," and to her own annoyance she began to cry. "This isn't what my homecoming was meant to be like, I thought we would be so happy to see each other," she sobbed. "Don't touch me," she yelled as he tried to put his arms round her. He took a step back holding his hands up, palms outwards as though she were pointing a gun at him.

"OK. Now just listen, will you?" he was sounding angry now. "Just listen. Sylvie and Hugo came round for a drink and a chat. They have only been here an hour or so." Jessica was crying too hard to interrupt him so he soldiered on. "We went sailing the other day and I think I told you that Paul and Sylvie have split up. It seems Hugo has quite taken to her and they came round for a friendly chat. She is French and is enthusiastic about kissing people to say thank you, to say goodbye, any old excuse. In this instance it was both thanks and goodbye, Hugo is taking her home."

As if to prove the truth of his words they heard Hugo and Sylvie calling goodbye to Georgina and John and the sound of a car engine firing up. "There now do you believe me? Come here," he went towards her and finally managed to put his arms around her waist and pull her to him. "Come on now, stop crying. It was bad timing, unfortunate that you came in at that very moment but you misunderstood big time." All the while he was stroking her hair. His hand moved down, lightly touching her face till with his fingers he lifted her chin towards him and kissed her on the mouth. She pulled back to begin with but soon began to respond despite herself. They kissed as though time itself had stopped. After a while Lawrence whispered, "Oh Jessica, I have longed for this moment. You are in every fibre of my being, every last corner of my soul. You have taken over my mind and my heart. My thoughts are with you in my waking and in my sleeping."

She murmured, hardly daring to speak, "All those nights when I wasn't sure, sleepless nights when I thought only of you. And when I did sleep, what dreams I had. Disturbing and pleasurable. All over now. I will be yours and you will be mine."

And they kissed again. Only their social conscience, aware that the others were waiting downstairs for them to join them for dinner, put an end to their embrace. Over the meal Georgina and John could both see the change in the mood of their two guests and anxious not to be in the way went to the sitting room to watch television instead of having drinks on the veranda.

Lawrence and Jessica went out onto the veranda and walked into the garden holding hands. The night was heavy with stars. The trees rustled in the breezy darkness and the sounds of crickets and frogs filled the air. There was the call of the owl and the cry of the secret tree creatures of the night and the shy bushbaby. The evening cool was sweet with scents of flowers and dust.

"All those stars are enough to make you believe in love," said Jessica. Lawrence took her in his arms again saying, "I love you more than I can say. I would steal your soul and take it into my heart. Let me come to you tonight and I will make you believe in love." And they kissed again. Georgina came to the door and saw them but crept silently away, not wanting to disturb the moment. They were wrapped up in their desire for each other and did not see her.

That night Lawrence went to Jessica's room where they lay together, bodies and souls entwined. There was no outside world for them, nothing else existed until morning.

Chapter 9

Morning was the sound of Lawrence breathing gently in her ear. It was the warmth of tangled sheets and limbs, the happiness of letting her heart have its way, allowing her body to love the beauty of the man beside her. A ribbon of sunlight slipped through the curtains lightly touching his hand and caressing her shoulder. Soon it would be time to get up but for now she was cradled in a moment of pure pleasure. From now on my every waking will be like this and the final pleasure of each day will be the moment when the bedside light is switched off and we are wrapped in the darkness of each other, she drowsily mused.

Several days of lotus eating followed, days of sunshine, swimming, sailing and relaxing, days of holding hands, and making love until one morning when Inspector Wanjiku called announced by the usual cacophony from the dogs. That morning Jessica had gently slipped out of Lawrence's arms to get up and start the day. She told herself she mustn't lose her focus, must get back to pursuing her parents' killers so she was already feeling purposeful. Lawrence had woken up to find himself alone in bed and seeing her emerge from the bathroom and bustle about understood that she was intent on getting back to business.

Wanjiku arrived just as they were finishing breakfast. "It seems you haven't been around for several days," he began. Jessica looked a little embarrassed and explained that she had been to stay with friends and then spent a few days taking a break from her troubles.

"Well, I came to tell you that we have interrogated Ali and Obama and tested them for DNA. I thought you ought to know…" and here he looked suddenly very solemn, "… you ought to be told so here I am. They are two of the men who raped your mother."

Jessica gasped and went quite white. She slumped over the table knocking over cups and plates. Lawrence went straight to her and held her close while her whole body was racked with sobs. Then she leapt up and ran out of the room to the loo where she was violently sick. Lawrence followed her to see if he could help. He held back her hair, fetched her water and mopped her forehead only going back into the dining room when she stood up and began to tidy herself up. Wanjiku was still there. "I am sorry. It is not an easy thing to tell. *Pole*," stammered Wanjiku. "She will be alright in a moment," said Lawrence. "By the way, I have had some success with my internet research perhaps we should come to your office to talk."

Wanjiku looked at Jessica who was still evidently distraught. "Yes," he agreed, "I think that is best. Shall I see you in an hour?" And he walked out leaving Lawrence to console Jessica until she was in a fit state to speak.

"The nightmare is starting again," sniffed Jessica. "These last few days I have been so happy, not thinking about all the horror but it's all closing in on me again."

Speaking soothing words, Lawrence assured her that he was there to help and in time they were able to go to Wanjiku's office.

Up the rickety stairs and along the corridor there was Wanjiku shouting down the telephone. He brought his conversation to an end and invited them to come in and sit down. He mopped his brow with a large colourful handkerchief. Jessica had noticed him doing that before. His first thought was to ask how she was. "I am alright now I suppose," she replied. She had her emotions under control by this time.

"Well, Lawrence, what have you found out?"

"So, I went on the internet pretending to be a buyer of animal parts and even of live animals. I thought that would bring traders to me and once I had their details in my system I would be able to follow up their contacts some of whom might be suppliers. They in turn could lead me to the money men, the investors who supply the cash to finance the poaching operations."

"And did it work?"

"Yes, up to a point." Lawrence explained how he had found Li Wei Wang in Beijing and Chang Zhou in Shanghai offering horn and tusks as well as skins, quite openly. They had sites advertising both live animals and animal parts for sale. Where it became more difficult was tracking through to this end. The trail goes off into the dark web and names became difficult to find. There was a link with Kahinde however.

"How about you Inspector, have you or your men found out anything?"

"We have been busy with our two prisoners. They didn't give us information easily."

Jessica shuddered at the thought of what this might mean but then remembered what these men had done. They got what they deserved she thought.

"It seems they work for this Kahinde but he takes his orders from a big boss. A m*zungu*, they said. Kahinde never speaks his name so they don't know it."

"And you believed that?" asked Lawrence.

"Oh, yes they were ready to tell us everything. My men can be very persuasive. They gave us other names including Jaba, your cattle man. It looks as if he might have been part of the gang with them and let them loose on the farm."

"Jaba, Jaba! How could he?" raged Jessica.

She leaned froward and spoke in a low voice "So, Mona told me that you found five separate footprints and five sets of DNA. You have identified two of them. Do you think that Jaba was one of them? If so there are only two more to find."

"We have not found Jaba yet. They said he was in Mombasa. He will not be easy to find."

"And what about Colonel Buckley? Have you spoken to him, he was going to get his men to follow Rod Wiley and Derek Foster. Do you know if he came up with any useful information?"

"No, we were busy with our prisoners."

"Perhaps we should go and see him," suggested Lawrence. Jessica agreed that was a good idea. She turned to Wanjiku, "Thank you, I feel we are getting closer to finding the bastards as Colonel Buckley would put it."

"We'll let you know if we get anything from Buckley," added Lawrence as they left.

"Come on, time for a drink, I think. We could go to the boatyard or the Sarova hotel."

"The hotel, it's nearer," said Jessica.

They chose a table overlooking the water and settled down to discuss their next move. Music from Mali, Ali Farka Touré and Youssou N'dour from Senegal were being piped on a loop across the almost empty room. Jessica sipped at her chilled white wine tracing with her finger the drops of condensation as they ran down the outside of her glass. Lawrence drank his Tusker beer down quickly and before he called the waiter over to order another suggested that they have something to eat. Over a dish of Swahili prawns piled high with spicy rice, they planned their next move.

"First of all we must go and see Colonel Buckley or meet him somewhere," asserted Lawrence.

"I'm worried about Jaba," countered Jessica. "We need to find him, or at least the police do. He hadn't been working for my parents for long. He joined them just before I came out for the Christmas holidays. He was introduced to Dad by James Denton as being a lost boy in need of help to find his way in the world. Inspector Wanjiku said they think he is in Mombasa; he will be well hidden there; we are talking needles and haystacks but I need to go and buy some decent clothes anyway."

"I think I prefer you in indecent ones," interrupted Lawrence grinning.

"Stop it, I'm being serious," said Jessica giving his knee a slap.

"OK, OK."

"We could use the shopping trip as cover and while we are there we can just ask around. We could ask Cora and Hugo to come too, four sets of eyes are better than two. I'll ring Colonel Buckley and then Cora."

It was quickly organised. Colonel Buckley would come over to the hotel and meet them there. "Time for another drink then," smiled Lawrence.

Cora was pleased to be asked on a shopping trip, the real purpose of it was an added thrill. She was sure that Hugo would be able to come, now that he was recovered and since the downturn in tourism the Safari camp was not so busy but... she said "He will probably want to bring Sylvie."

"That's fine. We can have lunch somewhere nice. But remember I really do need some clothes and we really do need to look for Jaba so we can't spend too much time eating and drinking."

"What about Lawrence? Is he coming?"

"Of course."

"So it's 'of course' now is it? Is that why I haven't heard from you for days since you got back from upcountry. I guessed as much. Well. I'm very happy for you both and I know Hugo will be fine now that he has Sylvie."

"That's all settled," Jessica told Lawrence. "Tomorrow we go to Mombasa."

"Just a minute, you haven't asked me if I'm free tomorrow," Her face fell and Lawrence laughed, "I'm just remembering how cross you were when Jonathan and I tried to arrange a sailing trip without consulting you."

"You're a rat."

"Who's a rat?" asked Buckley arriving just in time to hear the last of the conversation.

"Hi, there, it's OK we're just larking about," said Lawrence getting up to shake his hand. "What will you have to drink?"

The waiter was already by their side, "*Tusker mbili, mvinyo nyeupe moja tafadali.*"

"Wow, your Swahili is better than I thought," Jessica told him.

"I can only do the important things like ordering drinks," replied Lawrence, sitting down again. They all laughed when the waiter came back with the two beers but had brought a lemonade instead of wine. "It must be your pronunciation," teased Jessica.

"I guess, *maji ya limau moja* could be mistaken for *mvinyo nyeupe moja.*" The waiter was very apologetic and soon corrected his mistake after which they began to talk business. Lawrence told Buckley everything he had found out. The colonel then told them what he knew. His men had spent a week following both Rod Wiley and Derek Foster. They had come to the conclusion that Derek Foster was dabbling in drug dealing and Kahinde was his front man. The gold exchange was his cover story and on a small scale was genuine. "Now Rod Wiley... we can't make out what makes him tick. Seems to spend a lot of time on the internet. One of my men is going to break into his house and take a look at his computer tonight. We happen to know he's going out. Bastard's got some girl in one of the villages just outside town."

"It still sounds dangerous. He might have a burglar alarm and he's probably got staff keeping an eye on the place and guard dogs."

"Bound to have. Bastards like that always do. But then nothing venture nothing gain."

"Hang on a minute, you're talking as if you already know he's guilty. Shouldn't we wait and see," objected Jessica.

"I don't know how you can think that way after what's happened to you. Put it this way, the bastard's up to something, I can feel it."

"Yes, but I also want to be sure we get the right people. We could catch someone who has nothing to do with it while the real criminals go free."

"This isn't England you know. No neat well equipped police force, no incorruptible judiciary. If you think you're on the right track you have to go for it. Strike hard. Right I'll be off then. Lawrence, don't forget to email me those details you talked about."

Lawrence and Jessica also left and spent the rest of the afternoon swimming the creek.

They were up before the sun the next morning so as to get to Mombasa by ten o'clock. They met Hugo, Cora and Sylvie outside the Mombasa Club – easy parking and we can have lunch there later, we are members and can take in guests. "Yes, good idea," Jessica had replied, "Mum and Dad were members there. I know it well."

Dusty and fraught with *matatus,* ancient God-fearing lorries, *tuk-tuks, boda-bodas* (motorbikes) and death-trap cars the journey took them over the many speed bumps, through the higgledy-piggledy towns where the shops and restaurants were forever threatening to engulf the road. Towns redolent of dust and chaos such as Gazi, Mwabungu and Ngombeni sped past. As planned, they were at the club by ten. Sylvie showed her usual enthusiasm for kissing everybody, especially the men but this time Jessica did not mind. Somehow it made the expedition seem festive. Lawrence pointed out that none of them knew what Jaba looked like so would be hard pushed to find him. Jessica took out her mobile phone and scrolled through her pictures. "These are the only pictures of my life I have left; this phone is very precious to me. Here we are, it's not the clearest picture because he is in the background, behind my father but I can send this to you all now."

They spent several minutes studying the photo and deciding that the women would go off to shop while Lawrence and Hugo would explore around the old Arab quarter where the houses were all tumbled on top of one another and people were packed in so tightly that it would be easy to slip by unnoticed and to fade into the shadows of the ancient crumbling walls.

The women took a taxi from the club which was in the old town standing in the shadow of Fort Jesus. Built by the Portuguese in the 17th century, it was a solid construction squaring its shoulders to the world with a commanding view of the sea. The white and blue of the main town seemed to sparkle in the sunlight by comparison with the muted yellows of the old town where the narrowness of the streets kept out the sun. The taxi took them down Moi Avenue passing under the huge, more-than-life-size elephant tusks that arced

150

over the road. "Maybe once they were seen as the gateway to the city," mused Cora, "but now the city is so vast. There are so many parts to it. Look at all the traffic. We are such country bumpkins living where we do." The taxi drew up outside the City Mall where the driver assured them they would find the finest of everything. Having purchased a few items there, they moved on to the Nyali Centre, behind it were some small shops run by Indian or Arab traders. Several of them were jewellery and curio shops. Jessica found the things she needed at the centre, new underwear, some shorts, tops and dresses, and then the three of them went to explore the intriguing looking little shops. They were covered in centuries old layers of dust and had none of the shiny, brash, bright colours of the malls that they had been in. *Imani* seemed to specialise in *kikoys* and other fabrics, all neatly folded and piled high according to size. There were also some lovely sandals, both Sylvie and Jessica bought a pair. The shop that attracted them next was called *Lulu*. "It means pearl," Cora explained to Sylvie, "from the Arabic." Inside there was a range of curios, seashells, wooden salad bowls and servers, carved animals, Masai head combs, 'all *mvuli* wood' the young boy in the shop assured them. There was also a selection of Masai style jewellery, big beads and deep red colours combined with blacks, whites and vivid yellows. Next to that was a locked cabinet containing antique pieces according to the label on the front of it. The three women looked at it closely. These pieces were all very much European designs, rings, bracelets, chains, earrings and pendants in gold and silver, some embellished with precious stones, some plain. As they were all looking into the cabinet, the shop owner approached, dressed in a grubby looking, white *kanzu,* feet shuffling in a pair of ragged looking slippers, and wearing an embroidered *kufi* cap, "Old, old but very fine, very nice pieces for very nice ladies like you." He stroked his grey beard as he watched them, But then Jessica went quite white and drew in her breath sharply. "What is it?" asked Cora, "You look as if you've seen a ghost."

"It feels like it," replied Jessica through clenched teeth and emotions. "See that ring there, the large solitaire diamond? That was my mother's I'm sure of it. Her killers stole it." Cora looked at it carefully. She had been so close to Jessica and her family throughout the years she was sure that she too would be able recognise Lydia's ring, she had always worn it. "I think you are right," she said, "but we need to be careful here. What is the best way to deal with this. First of all we need to take a closer look to be absolutely sure."

"There was a dedication engraved inside the band. It said 'Lydia & Donald Forever'. That should make it easier to identify." Cora turned to the shop owner and asked if they could take a closer look at the ring and try it on. While he went to fetch his keys she suggested to Jessica that it might be a good idea to buy the ring but to insist on a proper written and signed receipt so that the police could question him later. "Without buying it and getting a receipt we will have to leave it here and hope that it is still here when the police can come and interrogate the old rogue."

"There is another way," said Sylvie, "it is probably expensive, *cher*, so we could say we want to buy it and put a deposit so that we can come back when we have more money. *Comme ça* we can make sure the ring is not sold to anyone else so the police will see it in the shop."

"What do you want to do Jessica?"

"I would like to take it with me now if we can, just to be sure."

The man came back and unlocked the cabinet. He handed the ring to Cora first but she waved towards Jessica who took the ring from him with trembling hands. To carry out the charade that they were just interested in buying it, she slipped it on her finger. It fitted perfectly and Cora and Sylvie both admired it in the way that ordinary shoppers would do. Jessica held her hand up at arm's length, fingers splayed letting the diamond catch the light, flashing fire. Finally she took it off and looked inside the band pretending to look for the hallmark. There, were written the words 'Lydia & Donald Forever'. "Oh my God. It is, it is." She handed the ring to Cora to look.

"It is beautiful," said Cora continuing the charade.

"I think you should have it. How much is it?" she asked looking at the owner of the shop.

His wrinkled face became deeply creased as he smiled at the prospect of a sale, "This ring? Very expensive, very special diamond 390,920ks," he drew out the sound of the word very as he spoke, for emphasis.

"That's about £3,000. I haven't got that kind of money available. All my finances are up in the air until the solicitor has done his stuff."

And so they began to negotiate with the shopkeeper about giving him a deposit. He agreed to give them a written, signed receipt for when they came back to collect it. But Jessica was worried that he might not hold to his word, that he might sell it to another customer even though she had paid a deposit. At that point Sylvie stepped in saying "I will buy it for you. I have my card, no limit thanks to Papa. You pay me back later when your money arrives." Jessica was too anxious to rescue the ring to argue and promised to pay Sylvie back as soon as she could. Sylvie merely shrugged.

"Ca va, *Ca va*. It's OK, I am happy to help." After getting the receipt they left the shop with Jessica still wearing the ring. She gave Sylvie a huge and heartfelt hug. "Thank you from the bottom of my heart, this means so very much to me." Sylvie kissed her enthusiastically.

"It is nothing." She shrugged.

Jessica sat in the taxi on the way back to the Mombasa Club holding on to the ring on her hand, silent tears were running down her face. Cora tucked her arm into Jessica's, "Come on now, don't cry. You must be happy that you found it against such formidable odds and we weren't even looking for it."

"It's silly I know, but I have so little left of my parents. This ring means so much to me now. It's as if it was meant to be. I can't believe Sylvie could be so kind and generous."

"She can easily afford it, so don't worry too much about that."

When they arrived at the club, they walked through its cool, white walled corridors hung with spears, shields and native blankets, its floors dark and worn with the patina of centuries. Going up the polished wooden stairs they found Hugo and Lawrence sitting at the bar on the top terrace looking out across the sea that sparkled vivid blue beneath.

Jessica ran straight to Lawrence tears streaming freely. Seeing she was distressed he took her into his arms and held her close. Cora was so excited about the ring that she rushed up to them and blurted out the whole story. "It's amazing. We weren't actually looking for it. Who could have imagined that we would be able to find it even if we were searching," she finished. Lawrence looked at Jessica who was unable to speak through her tears. Silently she held her hand out so that the two men could see the ring.

"You bought it? You didn't think it would be better to leave it where it was and let the police go and talk to this shop owner?" was their reaction. But Jessica explained that she didn't want to risk it being sold to someone else.

"I just never want to let it out of my sight. We do have a written, signed receipt that we can show the police and they can take a picture of the ring so that the shopkeeper can't pretend he doesn't know which ring they mean."

"Time for a drink and some lunch," said Hugo. "I'm starving."

"You always are," laughed his sister.

"Just remember, I'm still a wounded soldier, I need to build up my strength."

Drinks were soon brought and after studying the menu and making their choices they all sat back and relaxed watching the shape of the land where it met the sea and the movement of light on the water. The gateway to the Indian Ocean was shoaled with boats from the traditional *dhows* and *jahazis* to the smoky old ferry and the vast container ships running in and out of the port of Mombasa. Threading their way between these were the little *ngalawas* and *mtumbwis* bouncing on the wake being left behind by the big game fishing boats and the speed boats.

"Wow, this is lovely. With such a fabulous view and such a wonderful place to see it from, it is hard to think that anything bad can happen here."

"Hugo, you are just such a sunny side up kind of person. Sadly I see it differently. There is always a fly somewhere even in paradise," countered Lawrence. "So Jessica did you manage to find all the things you needed?"

"I absolutely did, I think we have all had enough of shopping now, it's too hot and dusty, not to mention noisy in town after the peace and quiet at Georgina's. How did you get on in the Arab quarter? Did you find any trace of Jaba?"

But Lawrence and Hugo had not found anything. Just then a group of people arrived at the bar talking loudly and ordering the bar staff around with the voices of entitlement. The man at the centre of the group was especially loud and brash. Among the group was Derek Foster.

A hush fell over Jessica and her friends as they moved closer together to be able to talk more quietly and avoid eye contact with Derek. He spotted her though and came over bringing the loud brash man from the group.

"Hello guys, I didn't expect to see any of you here. You're a long way from Jaribuni. what brings you here?"

"Shopping," Cora told him. "Jessica lost everything in the fire at her home and needs some decent clothes, not "bend-down" boutique specials."

"Ah, yes, a bad business that. Let me introduce Rod, Rod Wiley, he's another escapee from Jaribuni, often to be seen down at the boat bar. I'm surprised you haven't met before. Rod this is Jessica, Cora, Sylvie, Lawrence and last but not least Hugo."

"Good to meet you all. I have heard all about your troubles, Jessica. I offer my condolences."

Lawrence took hold of Jessica's hand to reassure her and spoke up for her. "Thank you for that."

"Well, I can see you are in good hands," said Rod. "Enjoy your lunch." And he and Derek went back to the bar where they continued laughing uproariously and slapping each other on the back.

Lawrence turned to Hugo and said, "Are you thinking what I am thinking? That we could follow Rod Wiley and see where he is hanging out and what he is up to, who his contacts are even."

Hugo agreed that that would be a good idea. "Meanwhile we will have to stay here until they leave so we'd better have another drink."

Over their drinks they decided that Jessica, Sylvie and Cora would go back to Zinj Safari Camp in Jessica's car while Hugo and Lawrence took Hugo's car to follow Wiley. They saw the party over at the bar begin to break up, soon only Rod Wiley and Derek Foster were left huddled together in a conspiratorial fashion.

After watching them closely for a while Lawrence stood up. "Time to go I think," he said, "you ladies can go on ahead."

They all went down to the car park where they hung about chatting. Soon, as Lawrence had anticipated Rod Wiley and Derek Foster came to fetch their cars. "Haven't you young things gone yet?" inquired Wiley.

"Just saying goodbye," responded Hugo and they all watched as he walked over to the brand new Range Rover opposite Hugo's Toyota. As he approached his car a man stood up and stepped out of the shade from behind the car where he had been sitting watching over it. He was not very tall, thin as a rake with close cut hair and eyes that never stopped darting about, like a rodent. Jessica drew in a sharp breath but said nothing. She could see that the others had also recognised the man. He got into the Range Rover with Wiley and the two of them drove away leaving a cloud of dust in the car park.

"I think that was your Jaba, Jessica, wasn't it? and Cora checked the photo on her phone."

"It was definitely him," asserted Jessica, "but he is not my Jaba."

Lawrence was already jumping into Hugo's car to follow them. Hugo climbed in too a little more slowly being mindful of his recent wound which still jabbed him with pain on occasions.

Cora took charge of the women, "Come on you two let's get going. I'd like to get home now."

Lawrence and Hugo continued to follow the dark blue Range Rover. It was heading back towards Jaribuni but then turned off to go to his farm near Kwale. Hugo, grunting with pain at every speed bump, was holding back, not getting too close in case they were spotted. Luckily, as they drove off the main road there was no tarmac and on the murram road the Range Rover kicked up so much dust it was like a smoke screen. When they could see the farmhouse ahead Lawrence suggested to Hugo that they stop the car behind some conveniently placed bushes and continue on foot but keeping behind the bushes and trees that lined the drive. As they got close to the house they could hear the dogs barking, large dogs by the sound of it but they were obviously locked inside for now. Closer still and they could hear Wiley talking to them, "Hello, my beauties, Daddy's got a snack for you," and the noise of slobbering jowls as the biscuits were devoured with eagerness. Just then Wiley's phone rang. The two men listened so intently they didn't notice that Jaba was calling to the dogs to let them out. Wiley seemed to be planning a meeting of some sort but a night time meeting. Then they heard him say, "Yes the boys will all be ready. We have all the guns we need. Should be easy as pie, Zinj is a synch," he said laughing at his own almost-pun. "See you on Saturday. Or at least we won't see each other, it'll be dark and we'll be well hidden."

After hearing this Lawrence and Hugo turned to creep away but could hear the dogs barking excitedly at the back of the house obviously now outside. "Leg it," breathed Hugo as loudly as he dared. And the two men ran as fast as they could towards their car. Adrenalin leant wings to their feet and in Hugo's case made him oblivious to pain. They had a head start on the dogs but the Rottweilers caught them up just near the car and pinned Lawrence against the side of it. Hugo, who was more used to dealing with animals, showed extraordinary aplomb, standing in front of them and using a firm voice to order them down. He also happened to have a snack bar in his pocket, something he always carried as he was always hungry. He shared this between the two dogs and he and Lawrence leapt into the car and drove away before the men in the house came to look for the dogs.

"Whew, that was a close shave. Those dogs nearly had me. You seem to have a way with animals."

"I do spend most of my working life dealing with animals in one way or another. But bloody hell, it sounds as though they are planning to raid our safari park. We have to protect it; we need to get in touch with that Colonel and with the police so we can stop them."

"You certainly put an impressive turn of speed on for a wounded soldier."

"The adrenalin of the moment. Fear turned my legs into pistons."

He put his foot down on the accelerator and the car surged forward as the two of them drove back to Zinj to catch up with the women.

Once they were all together Hugo and Lawrence told them what they had heard and what had happened to them. "So we now know for sure that Jaba is working for Wiley," said Jessica, mulling over the new information.

"Yes," said Hugo, "but more to the point we also know that the bastards are planning some kind of raid on our safari park. Presumably they are after elephant, rhinos, lions and zebras for export. They seem to be the favourites."

"More than that, we know when," added Lawrence. "I think we should contact Wanjiku and Colonel Buckley, we need to put together a group of armed anti-poaching rangers."

"Probably a bit late now. We'll have to see them first thing in the morning. You said it was Saturday that was being planned for. Today is only Tuesday which gives us time to get organised. I'll ring Buckley now and fix a meeting," said Jessica. "We can tell him the gist of it all over the phone."

While Jessica was talking to Colonel Buckley, Lawrence was talking to Jonathan who had rung him to tell him about a party that was to take place at the boat bar the following night.

"I hope you can come. Bring that gorgeous girl of yours. It's all in aid of charity so bring other friends too."

Lawrence grinned broadly and told him that he thought it was exactly what he and his friends needed to relax them and have some fun. "We've had rather a tense day today but I'll tell you about it later. And by the way you're right we are an item now Jessica and I, but I will have to ask her if she wants to go before I say yes. Remember how irritated she was when we tried to plan our sailing trip without consulting her first."

It was soon agreed that they would all go to the party. "That's great," said Jessica, "I will have somewhere nice to go to wear some of my new clothes. But, Sylvie, are you sure? Paul is bound to be there; you might not want to see him." Sylvie shrugged, "It's OK. I will come. I have Hugo now."

Wednesday morning Jessica and Lawrence were out early to meet Wanjiku and Colonel Buckley. When they arrived at Denton's house, Hugo and Cora were already there and Wanjiku followed soon after. James Denton welcomed them all in and organised coffee for everyone. Meanwhile Jessica told Wanjiku and Buckley all about finding her mother's ring. Wanjiku assured her that he would contact the police in Mombasa to check up on the shop where she had seen it. "I have paid for it, or at least Sylvie did on my behalf. Since it was stolen and is mine by inheritance should I not be able to get the money back?"

"I am not sure that you will get the money back but we can find out what the connection is between this shop and its owner and Kahinde and Wiley. Then Hugo and Lawrence told him how they had followed Wiley to his farm and Jaba was definitely there working, it wasn't just by chance that he was sitting by Wiley's car in the carpark. They told him how they had heard Wiley say that the raid was to be this Saturday.

"I will get some men together and we will come to Zinj even if it is only to scare them off."

"Scare them off," exploded Colonel Buckley, scare them off. "We need to do a bit more than that. I can put together a team of 10 men. How are you with a gun, Hugo?"

"Fine, though I am more used to shooting tranquilliser darts. I will certainly be with you on the night, apart from anything else I know the terrain and where the animals are likely to be. My father could help too, he has had even more experience with guns than I have. What about you Lawrence?"

"Yes, I'll definitely come to help. I have done training with the RNR so I know my way round a gun too."

Denton said that he would leave the physical stuff to the younger men, "don't think I'm quite up to adventures of this sort now."

"You all make it sound like some Boy's Own Adventure," said Jessica.

"Well, my dear, it is," declared Buckley. "We have to catch these bastards and unless you are handy with a gun you won't be much use out there. In fact you could make it more difficult. I will be there in the background; with my gammy leg and only having one eye, I won't be much use either. Though, as I've said before, I can still shoot straight."

"OK, OK, I'll stay out of it. I have never fired a gun in my life. I just can't believe that you all sound so light hearted about it."

"It's no good being gloomy and expecting the worst. We have to go in with full confidence," said Buckley.

"I am afraid he is right," Lawrence told her. "If you come and are in danger it would be a distraction for us." Turning to Buckley he pointed out an obvious problem, "We don't know what time these people are likely to attack."

"We'll just have to wait in different positions around the reserve. We know it will be after dark so that is a starting point. We must make sure we all have our phones fully charged, communication will be crucial. I suggest we have another meeting when we have all our manpower together."

"Good idea," said Hugo and with that the meeting was over.

On the way home Jessica voiced her alarm to Lawrence. "You're all putting yourself in so much danger. I am really frightened for you. What will Georgina and John say when they know what I have got you into."

"You haven't got me into anything. I love you and am determined to help you find the men who murdered your family and to stop the poachers. I am choosing to do it out of conviction that it is the right thing to do on so many fronts. Don't worry I will be careful. Just think we have the party tonight to look forward to. Concentrate on having some fun."

Back at the house Lawrence told Georgina and John all the news and what they were planning to do. They were very concerned for his safety. John spoke regretfully, "We've already seen what they are capable of. These are very dangerous men. With my condition I can't offer to help you, I'm sorry."

"Of course you can't," said Georgina with some asperity. "Even without your Parkinson's you're much too old. This is a young man's game and I for one think all the more of Lawrence for being prepared to help."

"We're off to a party tonight. I guess we had better enjoy ourselves while we can. Come on, Lawrence, let's go for a swim in the creek and then we can dress for our night out," urged Jessica.

That evening Lawrence was dressed and ready to go long before Jessica. Navy shorts and a light blue linen shirt with a pair of deck shoes were his easy-going outfit. Jessica was having trouble deciding which of her new outfits she should wear. In the end she decided on a simple linen shift dress the colour of burnt orange and a pair of leather and bead sandals. Lawrence whistled when he saw her. "You look fabulous. Let me give you a kiss before we go," and he reached out and pulled her to him.

"Wow," said John coming in just as Jessica was pushing him away saying "Don't mess up my dress,"

"What a couple you make. You look stunning Jessica."

Lawrence asked her if she would like to go across to the boatyard by water taxi or round by road in her car.

"Water taxi is more fun and it's quicker but I don't want to get my dress wet."

"No problem. You could get into a plastic bag to sit on the boat and I can carry you through the shallows to the boat."

They found a suitably robust plastic bag in the kitchen and set off down to the beach. They could already hear the sounds of the party drifting across the water. Jessica felt foolish climbing into her plastic bag but it did the trick. Ten minutes later they were climbing up the jetty to join the party and her dress was unharmed.

Jonathan and Paul had worked hard to make the place look festive. There were strings of coloured lights and lanterns around the perimeter. All the tables and chairs had been pushed to the edges to leave space for dancing in the middle. There was already quite a crowd gathered. People from all parts of local society, Kenyans, Italians, French, Germans and English, all of whom would normally keep to their own nationality groups, were all mingling together. The music was loud with an insistent beat making it necessary to shout directly into people's ears. Over to one side a young Indian woman was decorating hands with henna patterns. Soon most of the women were sporting *mehndi* decorations on their hands.

Jessica was surprised at the number of women who seemed to know Lawrence. "How come you know all these women? They seem to think they know you rather well too."

"I have been coming here to stay with John for years. You didn't think I had lived like a monk all that time, did you? Anyway they're all past history now."

Just then they spotted Hugo, Sylvie and Cora in the crowd so they went over to join them. "Drinks all round first, I think," said Hugo. He and Lawrence went off to fetch drinks while the women watched the dancing. "I don't know who I'm going to dance with," said Cora. "Since Daniel left I haven't had anybody to take me out and about."

"You might meet someone tonight, someone new," Sylvie reassured her. "Maybe Lawrence and Hugo will dance with you too."

"Absolutely," agreed Jessica. When Lawrence and Hugo came back with the drinks they grabbed a table near the water rather than too close to the dance floor. They wanted to be able to talk so the further they were from the speakers the better. Hugo and Lawrence were full of their plans for Saturday when they hoped to arrest the poachers while Sylvie, Cora and Jessica chatted about clothes and gossip and whether there were any likely men for Cora to hook up with. The speakers began piping out 'Into my Arms'. "Oh my god, that's my favourite song," declared Jessica.

"Come on Lawrence, you and I have never danced together before. Let's go." So the two of them went to join the heaving crowd on the dance floor. Hugo and Sylvie soon followed while Cora danced with one of the Italians. The music changed to 'Happy' and a hundred people were bouncing up and down in unison. After a couple more tracks all of them went to sit down and have another drink, out of breath and thirsty in the heat of the night. Hugo went to buy more drinks and Sylvie went to help him. After bringing the drinks to the table she said, "I must go to *les toilettes*. Back in a minute." As she left, Hugo saw Kahinde on the other side of the room and saw that he followed Sylvie signalling to two other men who were near the door. "I think Sylvie might be in trouble, quick, Lawrence, come with me." The two men ran across the dance floor and arrived outside the bar area just in time to see Sylvie screaming and kicking being pushed into a Toyota truck by Kahinde and two other men. "*Laisse-moi, dégage, putain. Au secours, au secours, aidez-moi,*" she was shouting. Hugo yelled back, calling her name 'Sylvie, Sylvie' and running after the car. Lawrence was just behind him and made a note of the car number plate. "Come on, man, you can't do anything. They've taken her. We must get onto the police."

Jessica and Cora arrived at that moment after threading their way through the dancers with some difficulty. The four of them left immediately, Cora driving, Jessica trying her best to comfort Hugo while Lawrence tried to reassure him saying, "At least we know who has taken her and he is already known to Wanjiku, that has to give us a head start."

"Yes, but suppose they treat her the way they tried to treat Jessica the other day. Oh my god, poor Sylvie. Why? That's the other thing, why?"

"I'll ring Wanjiku now to make sure he is at his office to meet us," said Lawrence. When they arrived at the police offices in town the four of them ran full tilt up the crooked steps stumbling and panting heavily. Wanjiku was there but had obviously only just arrived from home. "Trouble again?" he asked. And they explained that Sylvie had been kidnapped at which point his phone rang shrilly. It was Sylvie's father arriving from Nairobi in ten minutes. His helicopter was going to land on the town football pitch. "I can hear it now," said Wanjiku. "I'll go out to meet him. You wait here."

He was soon back followed by a tall heavy set man with a dark five o'clock shadow. Jacques Arouet shook everyone by the hand then "*Alors*?" he asked with eyebrow raised. He seemed remarkably calm for a man whose daughter had just been kidnapped. Lawrence explained what had happened at the party.

"Do you think they knew that Sylvie would be there or was it a, how do you say? ...opportunity crime?"

"We don't know. We only decided to go to the party yesterday but she may have mentioned it to someone," replied Lawrence.

"Yes," said Jessica, "but equally she has been Paul's girlfriend for some time and known to be so. They may have assumed she was bound to be there with him. How did you get here so quickly?"

"I had a phone call. The kind of call that everyone in my position dreads. You know, we have your daughter/son/wife *n'importe qui*. No police. Bring money. Come alone etc."

"OK, we must organise. We know the man who has taken her," Wanjiku told him. "He is a known drug dealer and we think is involved in poaching too."

"Yes," broke in Hugo, "and the other day one of his men tried to rape Jessica here. And is known to have raped Jessica's mother together with several others. They are very dangerous men. Pure evil. We must find her quickly."

"You must be the young lady that Sylvie has told me about, whose family was killed and home burnt in a terrible fire."

Jessica nodded silently. Lawrence held her hand to comfort her. All this was bringing back horrific memories.

"I am sorry for you," said Jacques. "For now we must think about Sylvie. Inspector Wanjiku, I can tell you that they have asked for five million dollars for the safe return of my daughter."

"Do you have that kind of money?" gulped Wanjiku.

"As the head of a multi-million corporation, yes, I do. You probably know of my companies Afrigaz and Afripharma. They are the Kenyan branches of my international oil and pharmaceutical businesses. I was in Nairobi at a conference about supplying drugs, vaccines etc. to Africa. I was in my hotel when the email came through."

"And do you plan to hand over the ransom?" asked Wanjiku.

"I don't want to but I may have no choice. She is all I have in the world. Sylvie's mother died of cancer five years ago. We had no other children. What would you do in my position, Inspector Wanjiku?"

"The official line is that we do not give in to ransom demands. But I can understand your feelings," said Wanjiku, wishing that Mona were still there with him to take charge. He felt things were escalating wildly.

"But," Hugo interrupted, "It could take some time to set up the meeting and hand over the money with no guarantee that any agreement you make with the kidnappers, Kahinde and his men, will be honoured. Sylvie will be in danger of harm every moment of that time." He spoke with urgency and emotion so that Jacques asked him, "Are you her new boyfriend?" Hugo admitted that he was. "*Eh bien*," said Jacques, "What do you all suggest?"

Wanjiku spoke up saying that he and some of his officers should immediately go to where Kahinde was known to live. He picked up his phone and dialled a number, a short time later three of his men turned up. "I will go now. And I will let you know what happens in the morning." They swapped phone numbers and then Jessica and Lawrence turned to Jacques and invited him to come back to stay at Georgina's, confident that she would be happy to make him welcome. So he sent his helicopter back to Nairobi until he might need it again. Cora drove them all to Georgina's house and then took her very distressed brother home.

By the time they arrived at Georgina's house it was late. She and John were about to go to bed. But she made the unexpected visitor very welcome and offered her sympathies. "So, we will know more in the morning, goodnight, Madame, and thank you," said Jacques.

No one in the house slept well that night. All were fearful of what the morning might bring.

Chapter 10

Wanjiku rang early the next morning, Thursday, to speak to Jacques. The conversation was not a happy one, the others could see by the way the Frenchman was running his fingers through his hair, walking up and down, up and down, like a caged lion and saying *"d'accord, d'accord,* and I don't understand," over and over again. He came off the phone and sat down with a huge sigh and ran his fingers through his hair yet again till it was sticking up in tufts. His five o'clock shadow had deepened and darkened and his eyes were sunken into sockets, dark from lack of sleep, giving him a wild look.

"What's the score?" asked Lawrence.

"It seems the police were out all night searching the area where Kahinde is known to live and operate. They found nothing. Nothing. They questioned people in the village who might have seen or heard something but that was a negative too. All I can do is wait until this Kahinde contacts me with instructions for handing over the money."

"I wonder if the police have thought of looking out at Wiley's farm. If Kahinde is working with Wiley he could have taken Sylvie there to hide her. I could ring Wanjiku and suggest that the police look round the farm if you like."

"Thank you, Lawrence. I think that would be helpful."

"Also, have they thought to question people who were at the party?" asked Jessica. "Jonathan and Paul must have a list of who was at the boat bar last night."

"I think there was too much noise from the music for people to notice anything, but we should explore every possibility," replied Lawrence.

He picked up his phone and spoke to Inspector Wanjiku first. The policeman had only just gone to bed after being up all night searching but he agreed that someone should go out to Wiley's farm. Lawrence suggested that he himself should go on some excuse or other rather than the police which might alert Wiley that he was being watched and make him call off the poaching raid he was planning. "Just make sure I have back-up. Perhaps a few of your men could be out there on the main road so that I can call them in an emergency." He then asked Wanjiku if he had thought of questioning the party goers. The inspector admitted that he hadn't but promised to see Jonathan and get a guest list so that he could follow up any possible leads.

"Right, I had better get going. Can I take your car, Jessica?"

"You can't go alone. Take someone with you, me for instance."

"Absolutely not, if you end up in danger we would be worse off than we are now. I can't take Hugo or Jacques; they are too emotionally involved. And though he is a lot better, Hugo is still injured. No, I am better going alone, I shall simply pretend I am a tourist who got lost and wandered into the farm by accident."

Just as he was about to leave Jacques's phone pinged to announce a message coming through. It was Sylvie, a recorded video message. "Papa, papa, I am OK. They want money only. Nothing but money. If you don't do what they say I will die, they will kill me. *Au revoir*, Papa." She sobbed.

The phone pinged again and this time it was a text message with instructions about handing over the money. Jacques was told to put the cash in a blue hold-all and bring it to Ndong village, the road that ends at the rock of the same name at 9pm the next day. We will hand over your daughter when we have the money. Come alone and no police or else, the text said.

"All you can do is agree at the moment, to make sure they keep her alive and unharmed," said Lawrence. He put his hand on Jacques's shoulder, "Come on man, it'll be fine. I'm sure with all of us working at it we will get her back. Let's have another look at that video message, maybe there is something in the background that could give us a clue as to where it is."

They all examined the video desperately looking for some defining feature but to no avail. The background was a dark brown, probably a mud hut which could have been anywhere. "I must go now. Wanjiku is texting me a number to call for help and you need to contact your bank I expect, to arrange to get the money."

"Oh, yes. Thank you, Lawrence. Thank you for your help and be careful."

"Hang on a minute Lawrence," called John. "How are you going to make sure you look like a lost tourist?"

"Oh, Gramps, I was going to ask you, can I borrow your big camera with the zoom lens, also your binoculars?"

"Of course, but are you sure that Wiley won't recognise you? Didn't you meet him the other day?"

"I did but only briefly and I intend to wrap a scarf round my face like a Bedouin, as though to keep out the dust, together with my sunglasses it will obscure my features."

John handed over the camera and binoculars and wished Lawrence well. "Just be careful. We want to see you back here in one piece."

"Amen to that," added Georgina.

Jessica handed over her car keys and followed Lawrence out to where her car was parked under the shade of a *bauhinia* tree, its flowers a delicate blend of pink and white. "Take care, Lawrence. Please don't get yourself into trouble. I don't know what I would do without you," pleaded Jessica, her eyes shining with tears that she was struggling to hold back.

"I'll be careful. Goodbye, honey-bunch. You take care too," and with that he jumped into the car and was gone leaving behind a cloud of dust. Jessica stood watching the car go up the drive and then stayed where she was for a long time after he had disappeared from sight. She turned slowly back to the house and shut herself in her room where she threw herself and her fear onto the bed, hugging the pillow where Lawrence's head had rested so as to breathe in his scent.

"I suppose she'll be alright," speculated Georgina. "I'll leave her alone till lunchtime and then try to talk to her. Who knows? Maybe Lawrence will be back by then."

John did not look hopeful.

Meanwhile Lawrence was speeding towards Wiley's farm. Called Shemba ya Mkonge, it was a vast spread of 3,000 acres producing sisal, more of a plantation than a farm. The fields were planted in dead straight rows, the plants were well spaced and looked for all the world like giant pineapples with their long, grey-green, spiky foliage. As he reached the perimeter of the farm with his scarf tied tightly round his face, sunglasses firmly placed on his nose, his phone rang. It was Buckley wanting to set up the planning meeting with all the operatives for Saturday night. Lawrence quickly put him in the picture, telling him of Sylvie's kidnap, the arrival of Jacques and exactly where he was and what he was doing. "The bastards, exclaimed Buckley. This could rot up our plans for Saturday."

"We have to find Sylvie," Lawrence said. "Her father can pay, but he shouldn't have to. We don't want to jeopardise what we are doing on Saturday night so we don't want the police involved at this stage if possible, although they are following me to give me back up if need be. But if this is connected to the poaching raid on Saturday we don't want the gang to think we are on to them."

"Don't worry, I am not far from you at the moment and I have some of my men with me. We will give you the back-up you need."

"OK. I am on the road leading through the farm to the main house and I have just spotted a hut, a round mud hut with a *makuti* roof. It stands all on its own not far in from the road. It looks deserted. I am going to have a look there first."

Lawrence stopped his car at the side of the road. He didn't want to look secretive, he had to look like a lost tourist. He strung the binoculars and camera round his neck and pulled his scarf up around his face. He strode across the field towards the hut with more confidence than he felt and walked around it. He felt as though his insides were twisted into knots. The scarf made the heat unbearable. Drops of sweat were trickling down his face, neck and back. The smell of the dry as dust earth filled his nostrils making him sneeze. Arriving at the hut, he listened intently but could hear nothing from inside. There was one small window quite high up on the far side from where he had parked the car. He went up to it and peered in. At first he could see nothing in the darkness but gradually his eyes adjusted to the gloom and there sitting cross-legged on the floor looking dusty and dishevelled was Sylvie. He called her name, no reaction. He called again a little louder, this time she looked up but didn't jump up the way he expected. Then he realised why. Sitting under the window was a minder, a *bibi* who had been instructed to watch over her and who had a mobile phone in her hand to call for help. "Sylvie," Lawrence shouted again, "Don't worry, we'll get you out of here." At that point he heard a noise behind him. He turned quickly, just in time to see a man raise an arm wielding a *rungu,* (a truncheon), he caught the arm just as it was coming down to land him a heavy blow. His other fist shot out and connected hard with the man's stomach causing him to crumple to the ground. Then he felt a heavy thwack on the back of his head and everything went black as blood trickled round his ears and down his neck. Sylvie looking out of the window and shouting for help, saw him fall to the ground but she was pulled back inside by the old lady guarding her. Then she heard an engine, a car driving over the rough field. Oh my god, thought Sylvie they are coming after him. They will kill us both. But the car she heard was Colonel Buckley riding across the furrows like a knight in shining armour. He was on the passenger side hanging out of the window brandishing an AK47. As his jeep neared the hut the two men who had attacked Lawrence took out their guns and began firing at him. He returned their fire and when one of them was wounded in the shoulder they both ran off. "Bastards," Buckley yelled after them. Then he ordered his men to break down the door of the hut and get Sylvie and Lawrence into the truck. Lawrence came round with his head pillowed on Sylvie's lap just as the truck was accelerating hard to get out before the *bibi's* phone call could produce any reaction from Wiley. One of Buckley's men jumped into Lawrence's car to drive it back onto the main road. Only when they were clear, away from the plantation did they dare to stop.

"Are you hurt? Are you sure you can drive? Where do you want to go?" asked Buckley stopping the car behind Lawrence's. "My head feels like a lead balloon with the bumping over the fields and the heavy blow with a thick stick but I think it has stopped bleeding, I'll be OK. I'll drive straight to Georgina's. My grandfather and Jessica are probably worried sick about me. I need to get patched up. What about you Sylvie? You can come with me or one of us can take you to Hugo," said Lawrence sitting up.

"Lawrence, please, if you can, take me to Hugo. I need to clean up and have something to eat. I have clothes at his house and Cora will be there to help me too. They did not hurt me except for the bruises where they held me by my arms but it was very dirty in the hut and I had no food, only water and you know we French, we need our food," she smiled weakly.

"Yes, I can. Colonel Buckley, just let us out. We'll go in my car. You must have been very frightened," said Lawrence to Sylvie.

"Yes, I was frightened, especially knowing what happened to Jessica and her mother but I thought they wouldn't want to spoil their chance of making a lot of money. If they had hurt me or killed me my father would not pay."

"Well, before we go, Colonel, when do you want us to meet to plan our counter-attack on Saturday?"

"Tomorrow morning alright for you? Should have all the men gathered by then and it leaves us a day to organise supplies."

"Fine, I'll let Hugo know."

168

Sylvie and Lawrence arrived at Zinj Safari Camp just after lunch. Lawrence walked onto the veranda where the family was having their postprandial coffee announcing "Special delivery for Hugo." Sylvie was just behind him and she and Hugo rushed into each other's arms. It was left to Cora and her parents, Jenny and Robert, to thank Lawrence. Jenny was very concerned when she saw the blood on Lawrence's ear, neck and shirt collar. "Let me clean it up for you," she offered but he refused explaining that he really just wanted to go home, back to Jessica.

Lawrence hadn't wanted to admit it to the others but he was having trouble with his vision. His sight was blurred and every so often he saw double so the drive home was a struggle. He went slowly and cautiously not wanting to risk damage to himself or the car which after all belonged to Jessica. He finally arrived at teatime. Jessica ran to him and threw her arms around him. "Oh, Lawrence where have you been? We had a call from Cora to say that you had taken Sylvie there after rescuing her but that was ages ago. I've been so worried; my God look at your poor head. Come on upstairs so I can clean it up for you." Lawrence and she went up the stairs holding hands and he told her what had happened while she gently cleaned his head and washed the skin around his ears and neck. "There, now get into the shower." Afterwards she found him fresh clothes and asked how he was feeling. He told her about his blurred, double vision and how he hadn't wanted to damage her car so had driven really slowly which was why it had taken him so long to get home. "I've got a splitting headache now." Jessica bustled off to fetch him some paracetamol "I don't think you should go to bed. You must stay awake in case of concussion, so come downstairs and just sit quietly."

"So what have you been doing today, Jessica my love?"

"Nothing heroic like you. I'm afraid I hid in my room for a while. I was so frightened for you. But then I went to help Georgina look after Jacques. He was so thrilled to hear that you had found his daughter. He went straightaway to Zinj to see her. He will be back tonight."

"Did he get the money?"

"No, that kind of money is too much for our local banks. I don't suppose they have that much cash through their hands in a month never mind overnight. He was going to have to negotiate with her kidnappers for an extension."

"Just as well I found her then. She looked very distressed when I first saw her. I don't think they had fed her and she certainly hadn't been able to wash. It was dark in the hut, no toilet and only a little old lady who spoke no English or French to watch over her. A few more days like that could have driven her over the edge."

Over dinner that night Jacques expressed his gratitude to Lawrence, "You were so brave, *mon brave*," he grinned, pleased with his silly bi-lingual pun and relaxed now that his daughter was safe. He had lost the haunted look around his eyes and had obviously spent some time shaving before the meal. "I would like to do something for you, to say thank you." Lawrence shook his head and brushed it aside. "No need, I just did what any decent man would have done."

During the meal, conversation turned to plans for the counter-attack against the poachers and Lawrence explained that there was a meeting the following morning for all those involved. Jacques pricked up his ears and said, "But I can help you. I have money to buy weapons and I can call for my helicopter. You can use my helicopter; won't that be good?"

Lawrence thanked him and said that he would pass his offer on to Colonel Buckley.

Friday morning was like many others full of sunshine, sea breezes and birdsong. Georgina and John went down to the creek for their early morning swim while Lawrence and Jessica enjoyed the warmth of togetherness in their bed until hunger drove them to get up and go in search of breakfast. Jacques was already at the table when they arrived on the veranda. They sat down with him and helped themselves to some of the fresh fruit that had been put out for everyone. Jessica poured out coffee and they began discussing the meeting that Lawrence was going to that morning. Jessica was keen to know who would be there, for as she pointed out it was part of her story. "I think I should be with you. I know I can't come with you on the attack but I feel I have a right to know what is going on. Remember these people aren't just poachers, they are also the killers of my parents and their people, and the men who raped my mother. I would like to know what's going on. I might even be able to contribute some ideas."

"OK," agreed Lawrence. "You're probably right. You should come but we are mostly going to be talking about a strategic and very physical campaign."

"Perhaps I could come too," interrupted Jacques. "If I am to help with money and my helicopter I should be in on the planning, deciding how you are going to use them. I may not have any military training but I am used to strategy in the board room." And with a nod to Jessica, "I have some emotional involvement too. These are probably the men who kidnapped my daughter."

"Absolutely," agreed Lawrence with alacrity. "I am sure you could be very helpful."

Georgina and John came in from their swim looking refreshed but damp. John was keen to help but didn't see how he could given his age and his Parkinson's. "I was a lawyer, so perhaps I could help afterwards or even advise the police on security matters, you know, and how far they can go into someone's bank account to find their source of income."

"Now that would be helpful, Gramps. I'll tell Inspector Wanjiku that. For now, we had better get going. Come on Jacques, come on Jessica, we'll leave these two to enjoy their breakfast in peace."

The meeting was again at Denton's house with plenty of coffee and biscuits. Colonel Buckley arrived with his gang of ten anti-poaching rangers already dressed in combat fatigues. Hugo and his father Robert were there with several copies of the detailed map that they had of their safari park. Lawrence and Jacques walked in shaking hands all round. Jessica had to admit to herself that she felt out of place. Not only was she the only woman present but also the only person not going on operations on Saturday night.

Hugo and Robert were able to show the others all the possible access points to the reservation and all the areas where they might find cover from which to launch an attack on the poachers. They handed out photocopies of their map so that everyone had something to refer to. "We suggest placing people here on the west fence and here on the south side to watch for the poachers getting in. Then the elephants, the most likely target, are probably going to be here by the river, and the rhinos will be at their watering hole here, so some of us could watch over them. We must keep our mobile phones loaded so we can give a shout when we know where the poachers are coming in and where they are heading and everyone can get after them. We can only take the vehicles so far if we are to maintain secrecy. The rest of the way we must go on foot. The poachers will no doubt also be on foot, they will want to stay hidden."

Lawrence with his knowledge of navigation and seafaring was able to advise on the state of the moon that night. A night of no moon meant good cover for the poachers but equally hid their own group too. "Whatever it is, we have no choice since we didn't decide on which day to do this, we are driven by their decisions. But if we know in advance what conditions to expect we can adjust our strategy to take account of them. Looking up all the data, it seems there will be a moon, a waxing gibbous moon, so not too bright and visible early on. The weather forecast gives us a certain amount of cloud too. That means we have darkness to give us cover to begin with followed by a certain amount of light to help with visibility. They always say that a night of no moon is a friend to the hunted. It seems we have a good halfway situation."

Colonel Buckley then gave the lowdown on the number of men he had with him and the weaponry he had available. He also mentioned the one helicopter he had at his disposal. At that point Lawrence introduced Jacques saying that he was keen to help.

Jacques stood up and explained the he was ready to put his own helicopter at their disposal and that he was prepared to put money towards ammunition or other weaponry or equipment that might be needed. His offer was welcomed by everyone. But Hugo pointed out that the problem with helicopters was the noise they made which could alert the poachers that they were being tracked down. Buckley agreed saying that the plan was to use them to bring extra men in for the kill at the last minute. "Once we've found the bastards and we are going in to attack we call up the helicopters to bring in the extra men, they can come in very low and downwind so as to minimise the noise then they will use their heat seeking lights."

Buckley then turned to Inspector Wanjiku, "What have you planned to bring to the party?"

Wanjiku was a little confused by the question, "Party, what Party?" Denton rushed to explain, "Not a real party, he means the attack we are planning to launch."

"OK. Well I have four men available, so we have fourteen altogether. We have our guns too. But I have also applied to take a look at Wiley's bank details which could give us definite proof of his involvement when – if – we arrest them and get them into court."

"Good man," said Buckley. "That's fourteen men, you, myself, Lawrence, Jacques, Hugo and Robert. Twenty of us altogether. I think we should have half of us on the ground, the other half on standby to come in in the helicopters. Make sure you bring plenty of handcuffs, Inspector. We want to make sure we get the bastards."

Lawrence turned to Jessica to ask her if she had anything to add. "Only that I will be at Zinj to help Cora, Sylvie and Jenny in case any of you men are hurt. Perhaps some of what you buy could include good first aid equipment."

"Well, I think that about wraps it up for now. Come on Denton, let's crack out some beer," concluded Buckley.

After the meeting Jacques went with Hugo and Robert to see his daughter but Lawrence suggested to Jessica that they go down to the boatyard for lunch. "We could ask Jonathan to join us, I haven't seen him since the party. He might have noticed something when Sylvie was kidnapped."

As they kicked their way through the sand to the bar Jessica's heart sank. Annabelle was there with Jonathan. I should have anticipated that, she thought, I'll just have to make the best of it. The two men were obviously pleased to see each other and immediately began to plan their next sailing trip. Jessica greeted Annabelle with a warmth that she didn't really feel and tried to make conversation. Annabelle responded by being very distant and constantly fiddling with her mobile phone. She made it very clear that friendship was not on the agenda. Conversation turned to the night of the party and the kidnapping. Where was Paul in all this, Lawrence wanted to know. according to Jonathan, Paul was on the dance floor at the time of the kidnap, with his new girlfriend. "He didn't lose much time," said Lawrence. "No, well it was on the cards for some time that's why he and Sylvie split up. How is she, by the way?"

"She has had a bad fright but she wasn't hurt apart from bruises where they man-handled her. Did you see or hear anything that night?"

"No, nothing. I was too busy with the party and as for hearing anything, the noise from the music was deafening."

"What about you, Annabelle? She was your friend, after all."

"Not really," drawled Annabelle. "I didn't like her. She was French and smoked too much."

"Annabelle doesn't like anyone... except for me of course," grinned Jonathan. "Do you, my sweet?"

Annabelle scowled.

"Do you have a list of the party guests?" asked Jessica.

"I do. You can see it if you like. It's the same one that I gave to Inspector Wanjiku, I'll fetch it."

173

Lawrence and Jessica both scanned the list for anyone suspicious. The only name they recognised on there was Kahinde. Jonathan pointed to the two other names with his. "They are trouble. They deal drugs."

"So why did you let them in?"

"In an open air place like this it is impossible to stop them. I certainly didn't anticipate anything like this happening."

"We are pretty sure they are connected to the poaching gang that attacked Jessica's family and more recently Jessica herself. They have big money behind them, a man called Rod Wiley. Do you know him?"

"I do, he is a regular at the bar here but no sailor. He goes out sometimes on the big game fishing boats. Well, well so that's how he makes his money, what a piece of shit. But if they have all this money behind them why would Kahinde need to kidnap Sylvie to get money out of her old man. It could be that they need extra money for drugs, to break into the big time so it is nothing to do with Wiley and poaching. Or in order to get into the poaching game he needs money to buy his way in. Either way I don't think the kidnapping is anything to do with Wiley."

"So you think Sylvie and Jessica's family are just collateral damage. You see I think that the poaching is the reason behind all of it and Wiley is behind the poaching. That makes him as guilty as hell, in my book. We know he is planning a raid on Hugo's place on Saturday but we will be waiting for him," declared Lawrence.

At that point Annabelle suddenly stood up and walked away talking busily on her phone all the while.

Friday was the day for handing out weapons. Friday was also a day of anxiety. In Georgina's household everyone tried to stick to their usual routine but everything they did had an edge to it. Will I still be doing this so calmly after tomorrow? By the evening all were exhausted at the effort of keeping up a façade of normality. Conversation became desultory and faded away altogether. Georgina and John picked up their books to read, escaping into other worlds. Lawrence and Jessica watched a film but soon all were in bed where they slept only fitfully, tossing and turning and listening to the creatures of the night.

Saturday morning dawned; the night dwellers had given way to the creatures of the light. Monkeys were chattering, playing through the trees. Birds sang and the cicadas whirred to greet the day. In the house nerves were still on edge. Every time Jessica tried to speak to Lawrence he shouted "What?" at her. He was too absorbed in what might happen that night to think about anything else. For the first time they spent the day barely speaking to each other. Georgina and John were also sunk in their own thoughts, worried about Lawrence. Jessica spoke to Georgina, saying, "I haven't seen Lawrence like this before. He is so hard and distant. He doesn't seem to hear what I say to him."

"Don't worry, he is just very preoccupied with tonight. He must be very tense about it, probably frightened actually. It is a perilous mission they are going on. You know yourself how dangerous these men are."

"Yes, I do understand that. I'm frightened for him too. And worried that any one of them might get hurt badly and we won't be able to cope."

"I think you have to let him focus on the plans for tonight and not distract him. There will be time enough for talking afterwards."

There might not be an afterwards, thought Jessica. To Georgina she said, "I guess I feel guilty that I have landed on your family and am putting John's grandson into such a dangerous situation especially just now when John is unwell."

"My dear, we have been happy to help you and we too want to see these poachers brought to justice. I am sure Lawrence believes in what he is doing."

Jessica found herself one minute wishing the time away to get the mission over and done with and the next wanting to hold back time so that the moment would never come.

For his part Lawrence was also dreading the moment but part of him was relishing the challenge and being able to put his military training into practice.

That day, that Saturday, time crawled by, time flew by. Jessica had a knot in her stomach that would only unravel when it was all over.

Lawrence spent the day pacing up and down, flexing his fingers, stretching his arms, he was like a leopard baring its teeth, extending and retracting its claws.

Jessica and Lawrence left the house mid-afternoon to go to Zinj. As they walked up to Zinj house, they saw the two helicopters already standing by on the lawn. Cora, Hugo and their parents were waiting to welcome them at the front door. Jessica ran to Cora and Jenny and they hugged each other, an embrace that spoke of fear, tension and anticipation. The men all shook hands and with a brief 'OK?' 'Fine'. They went to study the maps that Hugo had laid out on the dining-room table. Jacques joined them and soon Buckley, Wanjiku and their men arrived.

Jessica could feel that knot tightening in her stomach as she, Cora, Jenny and Sylvie made sure all the men had coffee and snacks. The sun was setting, the men would be setting off soon.

By 7pm it was twilight, the in-between light when the sun has sunk into the horizon but the moon and stars are not yet marking the sky. With a great clattering of heavy military boots Buckley got his men into their jeeps and scrambled his pilot and men for the helicopter. Wanjiku's men also headed for their 4x4s, finishing cigarettes and spitting the butts on the ground as they went.

The others all said goodbye to their women folk. Jacques was going in his helicopter so he left first kissing Sylvie a fond farewell. Sylvie then rushed over to Hugo – take care, take care was all she said as she kissed him passionately so that he felt quite dazed as he left.

Jessica clung to Lawrence, "Come back to me, I love you."

"I love you too," He replied as he gently detached her arms from around his neck.

And they were gone. All those men going into a night that for any one of them could be an endless night of no return. The four women, Jenny, Cora, Sylvie and Jessica sat down to wait as women have done for centuries, waiting for their men to come home from that hunting expedition, that sea voyage, that spying mission, that war.

Out in the darkness of a night that so far had no moon, the men took up their positions, guns cocked and ready. Keeping in touch by mobile phone, helicopters hovering over the horizon, they waited. Hugo, Robert and Lawrence were together watching over the elephants, listening to their nocturnal rumblings and snorting as they soft-footed it across the savannah. They heard the cry of the hyena, a harbinger of death, the occasional snort of a zebra and the growl of a lion. Others were heading for the rhinos' watering place. But there was no sign of poachers. Nothing disturbed the tranquillity of that African night. Hugo's phone vibrated against his leg. It was Buckley calling from his position on the southern perimeter. "Anything to report?"

"Nothing." It was the same when Wanjiku rang from the west side and several hours later there was still nothing. By now the moon was up and bright enough to show the shapes of bushes, flat topped acacia trees silhouetted

176

against the dark sky, and animals, the hefty humps of the elephants and the light shapes of gazelles as they strolled by. Then about half past midnight Wanjiku rang to say they had caught someone. Hugo, Robert and Lawrence went to see. The poacher was a solitary man from a nearby village. He was carrying a couple of rock hares that he had snared. "Good meat, I need to feed my family. I sell in the market to buy things for family too. Please, sir, *tafadhali,* let me go. I have wife and four children and no money." At this point he grimaced widely in what he thought was an ingratiating smile.

"For God's sake," said Lawrence, "This isn't what we're after. Let the poor devil go."

But Wanjiku questioned the man first. "Name?"

"Jephat, sir." It seemed Jephat knew the men they were after and knew that they had planned a raid that night. It was aborted because they were tipped off that the police were after them.

"How the fuck could they have known?" asked Hugo.

"I don't know but maybe we should ask this Jephat man if he knows when they might try again."

Jephat didn't know but Wanjiku told him, "You will go to prison or you can help us. You tell us when the next raid is and we will let you go free. So go and find out, feed your family but give us the information we need." The man took off as if all the jackals in Zinj were snapping at his heels.

Lawrence rang Buckley to tell him the bad news. "The bastards," yelled Buckley predictably.

The men came back to find the women asleep in various chairs around the main room. Robert looked at them with a grin on his face and misquoted, "What, could you not watch with us a couple of hours? At which moment the women woke up."

"Oh thank God, you're back," echoed around the house. But they soon saw that the news was not good. Lawrence told Jessica, "I'm sorry, my darling. it was a non-event."

Buckley put it more cogently, "The bastards knew we were coming for them."

The women were enormously relieved that the men had come back safe and sound for the time being. "I suppose you are going to have to try again," said Jenny knowing how Hugo and Robert would want to protect their reservation. "Yup," Hugo answered. "We did catch one little *mutu.* A fellow called Jephat.

He was only out after red rock hares to feed his family. Not the kind of thing that counts. They're hardly an endangered species but Wanjiku has twisted his arm so he will tell us when the next raid might be."

"OK," said Lawrence looking tired and fed up, "I think we are all up for giving it another go. Just now I think it's time to go home and go to bed."

The following morning Lawrence's phone rang early. It was Jonathan asking him to go to the boatyard. He needed to talk to him. "Come alone," he said. So after calling up the water taxi Lawrence kissed Jessica goodbye, waved to his grandfather and Georgina who were in the garden and went down the cliff onto the beach to go across the creek in the tatty old boat. It was already hot, though the sun was nowhere near its zenith but a cool breeze created by the boat's motion stroked Lawrence's face. He went ashore to find his friend.

Jonathan was under one of the boats that had been propped up to have its bottom scraped and to be repainted, supervising the work.

"Hiya, glad you could make it. How did it go last night?"

"It didn't. It seems someone tipped them off that we were going after them. We're all pretty cheesed off about it I can tell you. But you don't look so happy yourself. What's up?"

"Come and have a Tusker while we talk."

The two friends headed over to the bar where Jonathan helped them both to a beer.

"OK, man. Now tell me what the problem is."

"She's left me. Annabelle has gone, walked out yesterday."

"But why? What did she say?"

"Oh, she said plenty. It seems I'm a loser and only have losers for friends. The boatyard doesn't make any money and she needs more out of life. She even brought Paul into it, apparently hanging out with a couple of sea gypsies is fun for a while but soon gets boring, not enough money it seems. No flash cars, no private jets, well you get the picture. Have another beer, keep me company."

"Thanks. I'm really sorry. You were quite serious about her weren't you?"

"I was, and I thought she was too. Shows how wrong you can be about someone, even someone you've lived with for four years."

"So where has she gone?"

"She's left me for that smarmy bastard Rod Wiley."

Lawrence was shocked, "But he's old."

"Not that old. Late forties maybe. Anyway it doesn't matter. He was always buying her drinks but I thought nothing of it. He was just one of those regular Sunday lunchtime cowboys. You know 'the usual suspects'. If it's money she's after I guess he has plenty. Have another beer."

"No thanks, I have to get back. Where's Paul, is he around?"

"Yes, he's just gone into town to get some supplies, food and booze. He'll be back soon."

"I just don't want to leave you on your own. You could come back with me, have lunch with Jessica and the others."

"Look no offence but I'd rather not. I don't want to sit and watch you and Jessica billing and cooing over each other."

"Well OK, but don't drink any more beer."

"I won't, if I want to get drunk, which I do, I'll move on to the hard stuff. I want to get there quickly not take all afternoon over it."

"You seem to be taking this really badly."

"What do you expect? Four years together and I thought this was it, we were a couple forever."

"Your forever girl?" murmured Lawrence in an echo of what he'd said to his grandfather.

"I'm not like Paul," continued Jonathan, "he changes his girl like most people change their socks. He's already replaced Sylvie and it's only a week since he chucked her. I see she's moved on pretty quickly too. Tucked in with Hugo, it seems. I was in it for the long haul. I know Annabelle and you were an item to start with but when you went back to the UK we got together. So that's why she doesn't like your Jessica, a touch of the green-eyed monster even though she's had no romantic connection with you for ages. She likes to think she is the one that matters for everyone."

"To be truthful, Jonno, she doesn't like anyone. Maybe she'll come back when she finds out just what a shit Rod Wiley is."

"Maybe, but I doubt it. He's got pots of money and it seems that's what she wants, not a struggling sea gypsy whose boatyard is permanently on the brink of insolvency. Goddammit," he swore as he started on the whiskey.

All the while they were talking, Lawrence was remembering the last time he had seen Jonathan. He saw with great clarity himself and Jessica talking to Jonathan about their plans to catch the poachers and Annabelle suddenly walking off and talking excitedly into her phone. Could she be the one who alerted the gang to their plans? Best not to mention it to Jonathan, he thought, it could upset him even more. He noticed Paul coming back just then so he turned to Jonathan saying, "OK, man. I'm off now. Maybe we'll come and see you tomorrow. Or we could go for a sail, just the two of us. Give me a ring in the morning. Take care."

He took one last look at Jonathan as he climbed into the boat to go home. He felt very worried for his friend as he saw him huddled over the bar helping himself to another whiskey.

As Lawrence arrived at the top of the cliff in the garden he saw Jessica helping Georgina with some planting. She dropped her trowel and ran to him. He felt his heart beat faster and ripples of fire ran through him as he watched her fly across the garden towards him…

"Hello you," Jessica greeted him, putting her arms round his neck and smothering him with kisses. "What did Jonathan want?"

"Oh, Jessica, Annabelle has left him. He is devastated, I'm worried about him I left him drowning his sorrows in a whiskey bottle. Paul is there but he is such a different character. He is more of a 'always another fish in the sea' type of man so `I don't know how sympathetic he will be."

"Perhaps that is just what Jonathan needs. Someone to shake him out of his mood. I didn't like that Annabelle, thought too much of herself and not enough of others."

"You'll like her even less when I tell you why she went and who she has gone with."

"Spill the beans then." And Lawrence told her about Annabelle going off with Rod Wiley and how he suspected that she was the one who had given them away. "Remember when we were there the other day, we were all talking about our plans for Saturday to catch the poachers? Annabelle suddenly got up and walked away from us talking long and urgently on her phone."

"Yes, I remember but she was always on her phone, talking or texting. I never gave it a second thought. Now you come to mention it she didn't even say goodbye to us when we left."

Lawrence was as good as his word, he set off at the crack of dawn to go sailing with Jonathan on *Mkwazi*. They took some Tuskers and sandwiches provided by Paul and sailed out the reef. They took one of the boys from the boatyard with them so that he could take care of the boat while they enjoyed some snorkelling. Being out on the water, riding the waves and feeling the wind in their hair seemed to make Jonathan feel a lot better. "I will be OK. I will not let this get me down. My business may be on the brink of bankruptcy but it hasn't fallen off the cliff yet and I have responsibility to Paul and to our work force to keep going. I will be fine," he said as they came ashore and sat down to have a drink with Paul before Lawrence went home.

That afternoon Lawrence's phone rang. It was Jacques with the news that he had been going through his company papers and discovered that Rod Wiley was a shareholder in his company. He looked through his file because it was company policy to run checks on major share holders' financial backgrounds and keep a record. It seems there was something of a mystery about the source of his wealth. A lot of his money came in from banks registered in Kenya, but also Beijing and Shanghai. Money also goes out to known arms dealers and some strange individual accounts particularly in Colombia.

"Do you have any names?" asked Lawrence.

"No, just the names of the banks. But the reason why I started looking is partly because I received a strange phone call. A ship's agent rang me, would not give his name but he asked if all was ready for the shipment to be picked up next Monday, and he called me Mr Wiley. He must have known I was not Mr Wiley by my accent but my secretary said he particularly asked to speak to the director of Afripharm. Strange don't you think? And the other reason is that he is about to pull out a load of money. I would say he is planning some big operation. He is on a three way split, arms, drugs and wild animals. Each one feeding the other and all of it making huge profits for him."

"That confirms what we already know. Have you any idea what the big operation might be?"

"Not really but I would say that the poaching, and the money he is taking out of his shares together with drug money, maybe even the money for my Sylvie, is all to pay for arms which he will supply to the nearest or highest bidder, maybe Al Shebaab, maybe Isis."

"I think I will get on to Inspector Wanjiku to see if there is any news from that Jephat. We need to know if there is another attack planned soon."

Having finished his call with Jacques, Lawrence discussed with Jessica what they should do next. As she said, Jacques's information merely confirmed what they already knew. "Unless we can catch him red-handed, we will never bring him down. It's personal now that we know he is behind all these crimes. The *watu* working for him are mostly just cannon fodder trying to make their living in a world of few opportunities where they can see legitimate jobs closing down because of the embargo on travel to this country. And the more the westerners stop coming as tourists and putting money into the economy the more people are driven to illegal ways of earning a crust. I think we should talk to Hugo. He may have heard something from the villagers living near Zinj. Come on, let's go and get changed for the evening. You've been out on the boat and I've been gardening all day so I feel pretty manky."

Later, Jessica's phone rang. It was Inspector Wanjiku who had been out to see Jephat and ask him if he had any information for him. "He is not a bad man; he is a frightened man. He says, 'if I tell you nothing I go to jail, if I tell you what I have heard I am a dead man.' So for now he is in jail. I tell him that while he is in jail he is safe, so he can tell me what he knows. Give it a day or two and we will persuade him."

Jessica didn't like the sound of that phrase 'we will persuade him'. "It makes us as bad as they are," she explained to Lawrence. "We have to get that information somehow, end justifies the means and all that," he said shrugging his shoulders. "Do you want to catch them or don't you? It's like Buckley said, you have to hit the bastards hard here."

"Well, I'm going to go and see him and offer him money for his information. That seems to me a more decent way to do it."

"I thought you were going to talk to Hugo."

"I am. I can do both," she declared as she dialled Hugo's number. But he was not much help. "Look you don't seem to realise my father and I are now on the alert 24/7. We have to keep watch in case there is any sign of the poachers coming back. Our staff are helping us but they are not trained to take on armed men. Buckley is on standby but it would take time for him to mobilise and get here if the shit does hit the fan and we have just heard that there have been raids on other reserves in the area. I don't have time to question anyone. Let me know if you find out anything useful and can get here to help."

When Jessica relayed all this to Lawrence he said he could only sympathise with Hugo and that they must do their best to get more information. "Which is why I am going to see that man, Jephat now," replied Jessica.

Inspector Wanjiku was surprised to see her so soon. And was even more surprised when she told him why she had come. He was reluctant to allow her into the cells to speak to Jephat but eventually agreed that she could go and see him; so long as he went with her. Down in the cells Jephat was sitting on the hard bench that doubled as a bed, head in hands. Underneath it, was an overflowing pot giving off a nauseating smell. Jephat was small and skinny wearing a pair of ragged football shorts and a torn string vest. His feet were bare, they were wide and calloused with spreading toes. He looked up as she arrived and the whites of his eyes were yellowed and red rimmed with anxiety. He took in her long limbs and thick dark chestnut hair. He knew immediately who she was.

"*Jambo*," she greeted him trying to give a friendly smile but feeling very nervous. It was dark and airless down in the cells and the smell was overpowering. She had decided to try to appeal to his better nature, to persuade him to cooperate out of sympathy for her but now that she saw him for real she wasn't sure he had one. There was a hard bitter look on his face. She took a deep breath and gave it her best shot.

"You know who I am, Jessica Langley. And you know my parents were both murdered as well as our staff and our house, horses and cattle set on fire." She wondered at herself being able to say this so dispassionately, as if she were talking about someone else. The adrenalin of the moment perhaps, she thought. "We, that is my friends and I and Inspector Wanjiku believe that the poachers were behind the killings. You can help us catch them, help us make sure they are punished for what they did. Please help, tell us what you know. The police can keep you safe here till they are behind bars."

Jephat gave her a strange look, part appreciation, part weighing up any possible advantage he might get. "My family will not be behind bars. They could be killed, my four children, very young. I have to protect them."

Jessica could quite understand the logic of this and decided that the promise of protection for his family and an offer of money might make him less risk averse. She turned to Wanjiku and suggested that Jephat's family should be protected as well. He agreed that they could come into the cells too and Jessica offered 50,000 Kenyan shillings, to help Jephat with expenses she said. At which point he told her he was sorry for her troubles and that the poachers were planning a new raid on Zinj in five days' time, on Saturday.

Back in Wanjiku's office Jessica breathed a sigh of relief and inhaled the comparatively fresh air. "Before we mount a new attack on the poachers we need to be sure that he is telling the truth," and she told him what Jacques had said to Lawrence. "Perhaps," she suggested, "you could enquire among the shipping agents down at Mombasa? It must be next weekend if the goods are to be shipped out next Monday."

Once Wanjiku had agreed that he would do that, Jessica left for home. 'Home' she thought on her way there. I have become so used to living there especially now with Lawrence but it isn't home at all really. When all this is over I will look for somewhere of my own, I really can't presume on Georgina's kindness and hospitality any longer. And maybe Lawrence will move in with me. And she smiled as she thought about how happy she was with him and how much care he had shown. She arrived back at the house to find that Lawrence had once again been organising things on her behalf. But it no longer annoyed her. He phoned Buckley, Wanjiku, Hugo and Jacques to ensure that they were all able to take part in a second attempt at an attack on the poachers on Saturday. He did not fail to remind them that they should not talk to anyone about the plan.

Chapter 11

They were counting down the days now. Tuesday came and went. Jessica and Lawrence spent the day swimming the creek and relaxing with John and Georgina. Only the phone call from Wanjiku broke the quiet tension of that week. He had just come back from Mombasa where he had visited all the ship's agents he could find. Fortunately there were not so many, only about half a dozen. Amongst the names he mentioned was Henry Randall. "Oh," said Jessica, "he was a friend of my parents. I had forgotten that that was what he did. He lives down in Mombasa during the week and comes here to Jaribuni to relax at the weekends. He has a tiny house, a shack really on the beach near the point."

"I know it. Anyway it is he who spoke to Jacques. This Rod Wiley has a man who works for him and arranges shipping for the sisal grown on Wiley's farm. He has booked space on a ship going to Singapore but its final destination is Shanghai. Henry told me Wiley's man had booked a space two weeks ago and had to cancel. That must be when we got in his way. Shanghai is not where Wiley normally ships sisal. Also, the man was insistent that there should be no delay, 'the product needs to be kept fresh,' that is not sisal."

"No, it doesn't sound like it. Did he know when the merchandise was going to be ready to be picked up?"

"They are taking it from Wiley's place on Sunday. The ship leaves that night."

Jessica thanked Wanjiku for the information and passed it on to Lawrence, who immediately rang the others to confirm that it looked as if the raid on Zinj would be on Saturday.

Wednesday, and waking up Jessica couldn't think why she felt so anxious at first then as the fog of sleep cleared she remembered. She kissed Lawrence's shoulder, "Are you awake?"

"I've been awake for hours. I heard the call to prayer at 5am and I've just been lying here thinking about Saturday. We only have two days to go. I keep thinking about all the things that could go wrong. We don't even know how many men we will be up against. Then there is the moon."

"What about the moon?"

"It will be a gibbous moon again but this time it will be waning which means that it rises soon after sunset and doesn't set until just before sunrise. There will be no real darkness to hide in unless we have a cloudy night which is unlikely."

"Try not to worry too much. We have got some good guys coming to help us. Buckley seems to know what he is doing and his men are well trained. Wanjiku's crowd might not be as efficient but at least it means we have the law on our side. For whatever that's worth here. And we have two helicopters, what can possibly go wrong?"

"Plenty," said Lawrence, getting up and striding up and down the room.

"Come on, you know I love you very much and will do, whatever the outcome. We will have given it our best shot and we will still have each other."

"That's part of my problem. I got into this to look after you, to protect you and help find the killers of your family. The poaching angle was extra, if you like. I don't want to let you down."

"You won't be letting me down. I just want you to be safe. I didn't want you to put yourself in danger. I am so frightened for you. Part of me wants the time to go quickly so that it is all over and done with and we can get back to a normal life. Maybe even find somewhere for us to live. Then the other part of me wants to hold back time. Stop it slipping along in its sneaky way. Leave us to stay in this moment together and safe forever and ever."

"I know what you mean," said Lawrence with feeling. "My other problem is that I have done all this military training in the RNR but I have no actual experience of combat. I have never shot at anyone, only targets. Will I be of any use?"

"I am sure you will be. You keep yourself pretty fit with all the swimming you do and jogging." Jessica got up and went over to Lawrence. She held his hand up to her lips and kissed it looking up at him through her long, dark eyelashes. "Come on let's go back to bed." And for a little while they forgot all their troubles as they tumbled back into bed.

Later over breakfast Jessica suggested that they could spend the day visiting her Great Aunt Miriam. But this didn't appeal to Lawrence. He preferred to go sailing so he rang Jonathan to see if he was able to get away for a while. When he asked Jessica if she would like to go she sighed and said that she would let them go off and be boys together. She felt the need to go and see her aunt, her one remaining family member, to talk. She didn't admit it to Lawrence but she also felt the need to get away to a different atmosphere. The two of them together were too intense, each one's fear adding to the other's. With Aunt Miriam she would be able to relax and talk openly without any pressure. So they both set off in different directions to spend their day in different ways. Lawrence took the water taxi across the creek while Jessica set off in her car to go out along the Mombasa road towards Miriam's place.

As she drove along she was looking forward to seeing Aunt Miriam but her mind was racing, much occupied with her worries for Lawrence and what he would be facing on Saturday night. She was terrified of losing him as she had lost her parents. Once she saw Miriam and was able to talk about her fears she felt better. They had lunch out in the shade of the trees in Miriam's garden. The garden was one of the greenest that Jessica had ever seen. There were few flowers except in pots near the house and on the veranda. The rest was grass and lines of trees giving a lovely, soft green, shady canopy. They chatted happily over several glasses of wine. Jessica enjoyed telling Miriam all about Lawrence and how they were now a couple and Miriam was only too pleased to listen. "I told you so when you first brought him here," she said, "I could see straight away that you were meant to be together. I'm very happy for you. Such a handsome man."

It was only on her way home that Jessica noticed that she was being followed again. They must have followed her that morning to know where she was. It was when she got to the top of Miriam's drive and turned on to the main road that she saw in her rear view mirror a car had pulled out, seemingly from nowhere, behind her. She couldn't think for the life of her why they would still be following her. She assumed that 'they' were part of the group of poachers working for Wiley but what could they possibly want from her. They must know that everything had been destroyed in the fire. They must know that Wanjiku and Buckley were after them anyway, not at her instigation only. It was late afternoon and there was little traffic on the road. The car behind seemed to be getting nearer and nearer. Jessica put her foot down to speed away from it, faster than she felt safe with, but it was a more powerful car and it came up behind her again then drew level and swerved at her forcing her to swerve off the road. At that speed her car jumped and skewed over the rough ground as she fought to bring it under control eventually hitting a fallen tree branch and turning over.

It was Inspector Wanjiku who turned up at Georgina's house to let them know that Jessica was in hospital. He had had a phone call from Henry Randall. Henry was driving back from Mombasa when he saw the car tumble over at the side of the road and had stopped to help. He had found Jessica unconscious and slumped against the side window. He opened the door with difficulty since it had been bent out of shape and then managed to drag her out of the car onto the side of the road. Aïsha was with him and between them they lifted her into his car and took her straight to the hospital. "Where is Lawrence?" Wanjiku asked. "I thought he would be here," he added as he dialled Lawrence's number. Lawrence was already on his way back across the creek so he arrived at the house within minutes. "Oh my God, is she alright? Gramps can I use your car? I must go and see her right away."

"She is not badly hurt," Wanjiku reassured him. "I spoke to the doctor; he thinks she can probably come home tomorrow."

But Lawrence had already left.

When he arrived at the hospital he found Jessica lying in a bed with her head wrapped in bandages and her arm in a sling. She was fast asleep so he spoke to the doctor who told him that she had some minor head injuries from being thrown against the steering wheel and the windscreen, just cuts and bruises, he said. Her arm was in a sling because her shoulder had been dislocated by the force with which the steering wheel had wrenched itself out of her control. He also explained that Jessica had been given a sedative as she seemed so distressed. Lawrence thanked the doctor and sat by her bed to wait for her to wake up. He looked around the room where there were ten beds. Narrow iron beds with thin mattresses and no pillows. The public works department had painted it in their usual tasteful way. Cream paint on the upper half of the walls and dark green below. Flies buzzed about and the fan which circled lazily above made little difference to the heat in that low-ceilinged space. I've got to get her out of here as soon as possible thought Lawrence. We can look after her at home. Then like Jessica he paused over the word home.

It's not really home, comfortable and welcoming though it may be. Perhaps Jessica and I could find somewhere just for us when all this is over. Then he thought about the day and cursed himself for not having gone with her. We all believed that they had stopped following her since the men who shot at Hugo and tried to rape her were arrested. She must have something that they want very badly, but what? After the fire there were only ashes left. None of her father's documents or the family possessions survived except what was stolen and she doesn't have those items except for the ring. His thoughts continued to buzz around inside his head and soon the hypnotic effect of the fan and his day out sailing got the better of him and he nodded off to sleep. When he woke up Jessica was awake and watching him. "Hello, you," she said smiling with the pleasure of seeing him again.

"Jessica, you're awake."

"Obviously," she replied.

"How are you feeling?"

"Weak and woozy."

"That'll be the sedatives they've given you. Are you in pain?"

"A bit but I think they stuffed me full of painkillers."

"Do you think you could manage to get to the car, I'll bring it right up to the front and I'm sure they would let us use a wheelchair to get you to the door. I think it would be better if you came home, cleaner, fewer germs and quieter," he said as the patient at the end of the ward began hawking and spitting loudly.

"Poor devil," said Jessica looking at her.

"I don't know what all these people have wrong with them but it doesn't matter, infectious or not, I would like to go home." Lawrence kissed her on the forehead.

"You just stay there I'll go and speak to the doctor." He came back a while later with a nurse who brought her clothes for her. Yet again her dress, one of her new ones was ruined by blood stains but she would have to wear it for now. The nurse shooed Lawrence away and pulled a screen round so that she could help Jessica dress. Lawrence waited patiently but every time he heard Jessica cry out in pain as she moved her arm to get her dress on, it was as though a knife were being twisted in his stomach. Soon she was ready and thanking the nurse for her help she levered herself slowly and gingerly into the wheelchair. Lawrence pushed her as far as the door and left her there to wait while he fetched the car.

Getting out of the wheelchair and into the car was also a slow and painful procedure, Lawrence did his best but it seemed everywhere he touched her it hurt. Georgina was horrified when she saw Jessica. Her eyes were beginning to go all kinds of exotic colours and her shoulder looked lopsided. "Whatever happened?" she cried out, all concern. She told the cook to make some soup and hustled Jessica up to bed immediately. Lawrence was left to have a restorative drink with his grandfather. "Well. you two do get yourselves into a pickle. I'm not sure you're safe to be let out on your own."

"Thanks, Gramps," said Lawrence as he was handed a generous glass of whiskey. "Come on tell me all about it."

"She hasn't said much yet. From what the doctors tell me and the snippets I have picked up from her, she was driving home and was followed again only this time they attacked her. They forced her off the road. These guys really do mean business don't they?"

"I'm afraid they do. The sooner you and your gang get them under lock and key, the better. Jessica obviously has something they want very badly, or some incriminating evidence that they want to get hold of and destroy."

"I can't imagine what. After all, everything at her parent's house was completely destroyed." "Just then Georgina came into the room to tell Lawrence that Jessica was now in bed and he could go up to her." Strange, he thought, how I know her body so intimately and yet the minute she is sick I am treated like a stranger who shouldn't see her naked. He walked into their bedroom and was shocked to see how pale she looked lying back against the pillows. He kissed her gently on the forehead again, feeling that he hardly dare touch her. Suddenly she was porcelain and alabaster. "Would you like me to sleep back in my old room tonight? I wouldn't want to cause you pain by accidentally lying on your bad arm."

"No, no," she replied alarmed. "I want you near me, I don't want to be alone. You can sleep on the other side, away from my bad arm."

He promised her that he would do that. "I'm just going to have something to eat then I will be back. I have some work to do. Figures to look at for my business in London, remember that? I've been neglecting it somewhat lately so I'll come back and sit here with you while I work till it's bedtime. You just rest and sleep if you can." But when he did come back upstairs he soon got into bed beside her and wrapped his arms around her holding her as if to never let her go.

190

Thursday morning Jessica woke in pain. Lawrence, worried and anxious, fetched her the painkillers prescribed by the doctor. Her head was spinning and aching so she got up slowly despite Lawrence trying to persuade her to stay in bed for the day. She preferred to get up and start moving, going downstairs to lie in the shade of the veranda where she could at least see life around her. Georgina was kind and solicitous as ever while John did his best to find reassuring things to say. Once the painkillers kicked in and Jessica had drunk some reviving coffee she felt a good deal better. She began thinking about what her attackers were after. The solicitor had sorted her financial affairs so that the money left by her parents was now hers but there were still papers, documents that she hadn't looked at properly. Could there be something among those papers that would incriminate Wiley? She asked Lawrence to fetch her file with all the documents in it from upstairs. As he handed it to her a key fell out. Jessica began to regret that she hadn't examined the file in detail. She had listened to the solicitor through a fog of misery, taking in only half of what he said. She had then come back to Georgina's and put the file away not wanting to rub salt into her own mental wounds.

Lawrence picked up the key and handed it to her. She recognised it as belonging to a post office box. Damn it, she thought, I've spent too long in the UK, I'd forgotten there's no postal service here. You have to rent a box at the post office and collect your mail from it. This key must be for my parent's mail box, but what is the number? I can hardly go along to the post office and try the key in every box there. She started to look through all the paperwork. Was she still paying for this box? If not, where had any mail languishing in it ended up? Lawrence helped her to shuffle through all the papers and suddenly shouted "Eureka! There is a note from Mr Gupta telling you that he has arranged for the standing order on your father's account that paid for the post box to be switched to you. So that's good news. You are still paying for it and own it. He has very helpfully put the number on the letter as part of his reference. It is PO Box 1348."

Jessica was excited to hear that "I can't believe that I didn't think of looking for a mailbox before," she said.

"You've become too anglicised and besides you have had a lot on your mind – me for one," he finished with a grin.

"Just for that you can drive me to the post office to open the box."

"Oh," she paused, "I've just remembered. I have no car."

John assured them that he was happy to lend his and Lawrence told her that her car had been taken to Jaribuni Motors. The car papers were also in the folder since it had been her father's, so taking John's car, the key and the car's documents they set off for Jaribuni to decide what to do about the car and to hire another one so that they had wheels to get about with for the time being.

At Jaribuni Motors they were told that Jessica's car was a write off. The repairs would cost more than the car was worth. Lawrence hired a car there and then saying they would come back next week to buy some suitable replacement.

When they arrived at the Post Office it was surrounded by a huge crowd. A lot of people were shouting, waving their fists pushing and shoving. Jessica asked in her best Swahili what was happening, "*Nini kinachoendelea hapa?*" She was told there had been a raid on the Post Office and all those with mail boxes and safety deposit boxes had come to check that theirs was intact. Jessica's heart sank and she felt a tightening in her stomach, had her mail box been raided? Could hers have been the main target of the raid? Having not known of its existence before, she now felt strangely possessive and protective of it. But they had to wait their turn, there was no parting of the waves to let them through first, in spite of Jessica's bandages and dramatic eye colouring marking her out as injured. It was by now nearly noon and very hot. Not a cloud drifted by to give even the tiniest bit of respite from the burning sun. After twenty minutes Jessica was feeling faint and her pain had come back. Lawrence sent her back to the car which he had managed to park in the shade of a neem tree. "I'll bring the contents of the box to you as soon as I can," he promised.

Left on his own, Lawrence was able to slip between all the bodies and manoeuvre his way forward so that half an hour later he was at the front of the mêlée. Waving the key at the officials who were struggling to ensure a calm entry and exit for everyone, he was eventually able to walk into the room where the boxes were. Some of the boxes had been broken into but the thieves, if that was what they were must have been disturbed. They had got as far as Box 1200 from then on, all was untouched. He slipped the key into the lock of Box 1348. It fitted perfectly and turned smoothly. He grabbed the stack of papers and pushed his way back through the crowd.

Out on the pavement he came face to face with Kahinde and two of his henchmen, wild-eyed and loose-limbed, they were moving purposefully towards him. "Come on, man, you just hand over them papers," demanded Kahinde, gold teeth flashing to match his heavy chain necklace. Lawrence tried to play dumb, "What these? They are mostly rubbish – bills, junk mail, you know catalogues and advertising leaflets." Kahinde was unimpressed, "Just hand them over, we decide what is junk." At a nod from him the two muscle men approached even closer, so close that Lawrence could smell their sweat. One of them held out his hand to take the papers. Lawrence grabbed his extended arm and swung him hard into his friend so that the two of them were flung into the road in a heap and were narrowly missed by a passing lorry. As they were scrambling around on the ground, Lawrence legged it to the car, jumped in and gunning the accelerator roared away back to the motor company to pick up the hire car.

Jessica couldn't believe her eyes. She had seen the whole thing so she asked no questions as Lawrence drove like a lunatic to Jaribuni Motors, pedestrians, cyclists, tuk-tuks all scuttling out of his way.

Once back at the house Lawrence handed John his car keys and Georgina offered to drive him to town to fetch his hire car. Jessica and Lawrence went out to the veranda to have a much needed drink. Later over lunch they told John and Georgina what had happened in town. Lawrence told how he had been attacked and how he had fought the two men off. "He was so brave," interrupted Jessica. He also told how the men had nearly been crushed by a passing lorry. "'God will Save' was the legend at the top of the windscreen but I think it should have been 'The Devil Looks after his Own'. Anyway we got away."

"Thank goodness," said Georgina filling up their glasses again. "Here's to you. Let's hope you stay safe."

"Thanks, Georgina," said Jessica. "Well. I guess we had better go in and take a look at those papers."

As Lawrence had said there was a great deal of junk mail. Advertisements, catalogues, subscription renewal forms but in amongst them were serious bank letters, letters from friends, letters from insurance companies and from the district governor's office. Then they saw it, a fat envelope with her father's handwriting on it. Jessica fought back the tears as she showed it to Lawrence. "Look, Lawrence, Dad's handwriting. Why would he be sending a letter to himself?" She ran her hand lightly over the envelope as though there might be some faint trace of his touch left on it. Then she held it up to her nose and sniffed. The ghost of an odour that she recognised as the smell of her parent's home, a mixture of dust and polish, still lingered. She closed her eyes and breathed in deeply as though she could never get enough of it.

Watching her Lawrence asked, "Are you OK?" Keeping her eyes shut, Jessica shook her head. She didn't want to speak, to lose the moment and she was afraid she might start to cry.

"Come on, Jessica, open it up," urged Lawrence. He put a sympathetic arm round her, "I know you're finding this difficult but I reckon your father must have sent this to his own post box for safekeeping and only one person could have told Wiley where 'it', whatever it is, is hidden. And that is Jaba. He's the only person from the household left, apart from you. It must be important and might have useful info for Saturday night's operations."

"OK, OK. Just give me a minute." Jessica could feel her heart pounding, her head and her injured shoulder were both throbbing. This could be the truth, the proof of who had killed her parents and why. Taking a deep breath she slid her thumb under the envelope flap and pushed along its length to tear it open.

Inside were several sheets of A4 paper folded in three. When she pulled them out Jessica saw a letter stapled to them, also in her father's handwriting. Emotion overcame her and she threw herself sobbing into Lawrence's arms. He held her close but gently for fear of hurting her, "Come on, now. Be brave. We're nearly there. The nightmare will soon be over. Dry your eyes and let's have a look at what he says."

"I don't think I can read it, you read it for me."

"Right," said Lawrence as he took the papers from her.

"The letter starts 'To whoever may be reading this, I sent the enclosed report to my own post box so that those who are named in it cannot get hold of it and prevent it from being made public. If you are reading this, something terrible has happened to my wife and me, our household and possibly Jessica."

At this point Lawrence hugged Jessica even closer as her tears fell unchecked. "Shall I carry on?" he asked. She nodded in silent agreement. "The enclosed document is a report that I wrote for KAP, Kenya Against Poaching, after many months of investigation. In this I was helped by Inspector Mona of the Jaribuni Police and members of the KAP committee."

The investigation showed that there is a syndicate operating in our area with a three-fold interest. Drugs and poaching are being used to finance purchasing weapons that are then sold on at a profit to countries with régimes whose humanitarian policies are atrocious and to terrorist groups such as Al Shebaab and Isis. Initial organisation and investment in this enterprise has come from Europeans. My report names and shows the links and communication lines of these three trades.

Inspector Mona is aware that I am writing this report. I promised to ensure that he would have a copy. After receiving several threats by email and telephone I wanted to ensure that this report would get to the right people. So, I made a second copy. The one that you have in your hand right now. By putting it in the post, I ensured that it could not be stolen from the house or destroyed in any other way.

Please make sure that Inspector Mona gets this report. Make several copies to be certain that at least one gets to him. Thank you.' Then he signs it Donald Langley with a date 4th December this year. So, just before Christmas.

"I arrived on the 6th. Oh, Lawrence, if only I had known."

"You couldn't have done anything."

"I don't know. Me arriving for Christmas, wanting to party and all that probably meant he stopped looking at what was happening. He took his eye off the ball as they say."

"Perhaps, but you can't blame yourself. If he had wanted you to be involved, he would have spoken to you about it. He probably preferred you not to know, wanted to keep you out of harm's way."

"OK. Maybe you're right. We'd better look at his report."

The report itself did indeed name names. Prominent among them were Rod Wiley, Derek Foster and Kahinde with Wiley being the principal. It also went on to list the equipment that they had at their disposal which included a helicopter, numerous 4 x 4 trucks, cars and jeeps and a stockpile of weaponry. It also enumerated the number of men that Wiley could deploy. All of this was practical information that Lawrence could relay to the others to better prepare for their operations on Saturday night. In addition the report highlighted links to big money men in Europe, the kind who own vast yachts and villas in the Caribbean or Mediterranean. Wiley may be the principal on the ground in Kenya but he was being run by men in Europe, big banks and finance companies hiding behind their security screens. There was the Legend Corp, a hedge fund owned by Sir Patrick Willoughby, Brooks Bank, one of the oldest on Threadneedle Street in the City, Ingrams Bank and also Medlar Venture Capital Group.

The report went on to detail the Chinese connections where the animal parts were sold which dovetailed neatly with the information that Lawrence had found. Shanghai and Hong Kong were the central hub of the trade there. The goods were advertised quite openly on the Chinese internet by Li Wei Wang. She had her own site advertising both live animals and animal parts for sale especially rhinoceros horn and elephant tusks. Chang Zhou in Shanghai offering horn and tusks as well as skins, was also named.

"Wow," said Lawrence when they had finished reading. "No wonder Wiley and his crowd were so keen to get hold of this. But what made them think you had it?"

"Perhaps they assumed I would have a copy as I was the only survivor of their attack and the fire at the house. Now we need to tell all the others what we are up against on Saturday and get a copy of the report to Inspector Wanjiku, Colonel Buckley and James Denton."

"It's going to take us some time to scan and print all these pages especially as we need them three times over."

"I can make a start on that. You could phone round everybody to tell them. Perhaps we need another meeting tomorrow?"

"I think we should email a copy to Denton and Buckley this evening. Has it occurred to you that Wiley and his men must know by now that we have this report. That makes us even more of a target."

Later, as Jessica was still busy with the scanning and printing Lawrence came to tell her that he had spoken to Buckley and promised to email a copy of the document to him. He had then phoned Wanjiku but the news there was not good. It seemed a terrorist threat had been received; someone was threatening to blow up the bridge. All police officers were on high alert, leave cancelled and all men, including the ones detailed to watch Georgina's house, expected to patrol the bridge and the town centre.

Jessica looked terrified. "I never imagined those men guarding us would be very effective in a crisis but they were at least some sort of deterrent. Do you think it is more than a coincidence that this is happening now?"

"I do. I am sure this is a put up job to reduce the numbers we have on our side on Saturday. Wanjiku says he can spare us one man, Mwangi, who was working on the investigation with Inspector Mona, your father and the KAP."

"Oh, yes. I know Mwangi. He is a good man; you probably saw him at the funeral. He was very close to Mona. I think Mona was encouraging and tutoring him."

"Well then, for tonight we are on our own. No protection other than Georgina's *askari*."

"And the dogs," added Jessica but Lawrence looked sceptical about that.

They told Georgina and John what the situation was and they immediately made sure that the house was securely locked. They suggested having the evening meal upstairs where it would be more difficult to break in and locking Donald's report and the copies in the safe.

The night was full of the usual sounds, the rustling of palm leaves, the screeches of owls and bush babies together with the tweeting whirr of the crickets, and the croaking of frogs. All four of the people sitting on the upstairs balcony were stretching their ears to hear anything unusual, anything that didn't fit the pattern of the night sounds. They peered through the light given by a pale moon that allowed them to see dimly, darkly across the garden. At nine o'clock they heard the final call to prayer from the muezzin but no other human sound disturbed the night. No-one wanted to go to bed, all felt the need to stay awake and alert. John had his pistol out on the table ready and waiting. Lawrence had armed himself with a heavy *panga* that he had found earlier in one of the sheds. Georgina and Jessica crossed their fingers and prayed silently. Then the dogs started barking madly. Lawrence and John leapt up to look down into the garden. They could see someone moving through the trees. John cocked his pistol and Lawrence picked up the panga. As the person drew nearer they could see it was Mwangi. "*Jambo, jambo*," he called out. "It's me, Mwangi. I thought you might need some help. I know that Wanjiku has taken most of the officers to keep watch at the bridge but I told him I would come here to keep watch with your *askari*." Lawrence and Jessica heaved huge sighs of relief. They thanked Mwangi and finally felt able to go to bed and get some sleep so as to be prepared for the next day which was to start with an important meeting.

Friday, only 24 hours to go.

Jessica was already feeling better although her arm was still in a sling and her eye sockets were now yellow. She and Lawrence left promptly for the meeting at 10am. As they went through the town and across the bridge there was no evidence of any terrorist threat but there were half a dozen policemen milling around, stopping cars, interrogating people, which tended to confirm their theory that it was a false alarm devised to take police away from any attempt to prevent the poachers shooting their prey.

Denton, Buckley and Wanjiku had been very excited by the news that Lawrence had relayed to them. Jessica had also rung Hugo and his father to put them in the picture.

Arriving at Denton's house with all the copies of the report they realised that the meeting might be a long one as the others needed time to read and absorb its implications. Denton had something of an advantage as he had worked on the investigation with Donald Langley but he had never seen the completed document. He was all concern for Jessica wondering if she would be able to help at all on the night with her arm bandaged up as it was. She soon put him straight pointing out that she might not be able to help much with anything heavy but if Cora and Jenny were doing first aid she could be fetching and carrying, liaising on the phone and providing cups of tea or coffee.

The others soon arrived too and as Jessica expected some time was spent on studying the report. James Denton was the first to speak and express his relief that they now had all the facts and figures they needed to put the poachers in prison for a very long time. "So this is what they mean when they talk about the white gold of jihad and warlords of ivory. They could get the maximum, life or a fine of $200,000. Hopefully, life. That would hurt the likes of Wiley and Foster more than a fine. With a fine either you can pay it or you can't, if you can't they take it off you slowly, no problem. A life sentence in a Kenyan jail would hurt them more. But none of these guys is the Mr Big that we need to catch. We've only really got the foot soldiers here, the small fry."

"Better that than nothing. It's a start and puts a stop to poaching raids even if only temporarily. Maybe the top guys will be caught next time but some co-operation from European governments would be needed and if they are important financiers and bankers the governments won't want to lose their goodwill. Next time they run out of money they would have no-one to turn to," said Jessica.

"True," replied Lawrence, "but for now we need to focus on the task in hand."

"Yes, we've just got to get on and nab the bastards we've got," added Buckley. "A bastard in the hand is worth two in the bush. We have to make sure that when we catch them we keep every scrap of evidence clean and safe as well as accurately labelled."

The meeting then focused on how to organise everything for Saturday night but that part didn't take long as they decided to re-run the plan they had before.

The remainder of the day was spent in a fever of anticipation as before but with the added worry that Georgina's house could still be attacked. The previous night had passed uneventfully but Jessica and Lawrence still felt vulnerable. They wondered whether Wiley and his gang would be too busy preparing their raid to be bothered harassing them but that wasn't a reassuring thought. Mwangi came up trumps again though and offered to watch through the night with the *askari*. When they asked how he would manage to stay awake all night again and still be able to help out against the poachers he told them he would sleep in the day. So that was settled but even so no-one had a restful night. Lawrence and Jessica in particular slept only fitfully.

Jessica woke up first. She was in pain because she had rolled over onto her injured shoulder. Lawrence soon woke up when he felt her moving. "Are you OK?" he asked noticing the tense expression and the way she was holding her arm. "I'll be fine. Just need another pain-killer, I slept on my bad shoulder. How about you, did you sleep well, are you nervous about tonight."

"I certainly am. I keep wondering, are we the hunted or the hunter?"

"I suggest we ring Cora and Hugo to see if we can go over there earlier this time. We could spend the afternoon there instead of staying here chewing our fingernails to the quick. We need some distraction but not to be taken too far from tonight's plan. What do you think?"

Immediately after breakfast they rang Cora who agreed that their plan was a good one. She felt that she and Hugo didn't want to be just hanging around either.

As they drove through the town, life seemed to be carrying on as normal but everything had an edge to it. Jessica's nerves were taut like piano wire and she found that she and Lawrence couldn't speak without snapping. This time it didn't upset her so much, she remembered how irritable his nerves had made him last time. She looked at him as he steered the car through the streets that were littered with bicycles, pedestrians, children and all the other vehicles, *tuk-tuks* and *matatus* that veered alarmingly into their path. Lumbering lorries threw up choking dust and sharp stones that threatened the windscreen. Lawrence's jaw was set rigid with tension and concentration. Not for the first time Jessica sent up a silent prayer for his safety to whoever might be listening. Once through the town he relaxed a little as the driving became easier.

Cora and Hugo together with their parents were waiting to welcome them and had prepared a good lunch. The four friends went swimming first, enjoying the physical activity that distracted them from their worries. But once they sat down together to eat and drink, conversation was all about the evening's operation. Hugo and Robert had been tracking the elephants carefully over the last two weeks and were confident that they knew exactly where they would be. They also warned that the poachers must have been tracking them too so that they would know where best to attack them. Lawrence asked about rhinoceros and Hugo told him that they had very few in the reservation now as they had already lost two to poachers several months ago. Lawrence remembered Cora telling him about caring for an orphaned baby rhinoceros. It seemed that the rhinos were mostly nocturnal and always went to the same watering hole making it easy to keep track of them for game wardens and poachers alike. Fortunately the watering hole favoured by Zinj's rhinos was not far from where the elephants were expected to be. They then discussed the pangolins who are also wanted by the same traffickers who want rhino horn and elephant tusks. Their meat is eaten, it is a delicacy it seemed, and the scales used in traditional medicines, folk remedies. They are even believed to protect against witchcraft and evil spirits. It seemed that they too were nocturnal and trundled around on their own at random and so were more difficult to protect. Jessica was amazed to find out that they are the most poached mammal in the world. "Their natural defence mechanism doesn't help them when faced with humans, if that is the right word for these monsters who prey on defenceless animals. The other predators are leopards and hyenas, when approached by these the pangolin rolls itself into a ball, rather like a hedgehog does and also emits a nasty smelling odour just as skunks do. That is enough to deter all but the most famished of leopards or hyenas but men can just pick them up and put them in a cage," explained Hugo.

"I never thought I would be protecting pangolins," said Jessica. "By the way where is Sylvie?"

"She is spending the day with Jacques, her father, but she'll be back here this evening. They are in Nairobi but plan to return by helicopter this afternoon."

Hugo turned to Lawrence, "You're a money man. Are you sure none of your investment companies is involved in this trade?" Lawrence was surprised at the question which felt quite aggressive, He thought that hostilities had been abandoned once and for all now that Hugo had Sylvie but it seems there was still a residue of jealousy. Was poor Sylvie second best, he wondered. He assured Hugo that as far as he knew his own company and those he traded for had no money in the banks and finance groups mentioned in Donald's report. Still, I had better double check he thought.

By now the sun was sinking and the men all began to think about getting geared up for the battle ahead. Lawrence had even brought the very useful *panga* he had found the other night. Hugo looked alarmed when Lawrence brought it out, "Not sure about that one, man. I think a gun might be more useful, especially as the poachers come armed with chain saws."

"Chain saws?" questioned Lawrence. "Yes, you know to cut the horns or tusks away as quickly as possible."

"Ugh, that sounds so gruesome," declared Jessica.

Robert took charge at that point telling Hugo and Lawrence to begin loading the guns into the car. Just then they heard the sound of helicopter blades whirring as Colonel Buckley's pilot brought his machine down on the lawn. This was quickly followed by Jacques's helicopter which landed a little way off. Sylvie and Jacques ran to the house to join the others. Buckley arrived in a 4 x 4 with several of his men, the rest came in another vehicle. The troops are gathering thought Jessica but where was Wanjiku and his men? They will be going in short-handed. The same thought had occurred to Robert and Colonel Buckley. Now they only had two groups to cover three important areas of attack. A third was needed. Just as they were re-organising some of Buckley's men to go in a separate group, Inspector Wanjiku turned up with Mwangi apologising and explaining that owing to the supposed terrorist threat they were the only two who could be spared from normal police duties. Colonel Buckley detailed them to join the party going to the south perimeter access. He also handed round black balaclavas. "I know it's stinking hot but you don't want to be too visible. I see you bastards are all in dark clothes and boots which is good. Here are some night vision glasses to help you as well. You might not want to be seen but you do want to see as much as possible. Once we leave the cars we should walk in silence and tread as softly as we can. If we spook the bastard animals, the gazelles or zebras or any others we come across, that will alert the poachers to our presence. Remember the helicopters can only come in close when we tell them to and come from downwind so that the noise of the engines doesn't give the game away. Finally, turn off the ring tone on your mobile phones. We will operate them by vibration so keep them close to your leg or chest where you will feel it and the light from them will be hidden." Turning to the women who were standing by watching all the preparations he handed Jenny a gun saying, "You had better have this pistol ready. If they get away from us, they might come here and attack. You need to be able to protect yourselves. We have no idea when we will be back, you will just have to wait like last time. If we are successful in catching these bastards we will be very late because we will have to get the bastards rounded up and put in prison before coming back here, especially now we have so little help from the bastard police. OK, men, let's go." And with that all the men trooped out to the cars and helicopters.

To Jessica the house suddenly felt hollow, empty and she had a sinking feeling in her stomach, terrified as to what the night might hold. Sylvie was now chain smoking, pulling on her cigarette as if it were her last breath while Cora and Jenny busied themselves with kettles and cups, never once looking at each other or speaking. The room was thick with nervous tension.

Chapter 12

Just as the house had been full of nervous tension so the cars were full of nervous energy. Now that they were finally on the move Lawrence was feeling his adrenalin levels rising and the conversation in the car with Hugo and Robert was upbeat, all excitement and anticipation. They were happy that they were at last doing something positive and not just talking about it. Lawrence thought back to his days of training in the RNR. Would he still be able to run for hours with a 30 kg pack on his back or climb a net at top speed or wriggle on his belly through mud. How useful would he find these skills in the dry as dust savannah country, singularly free of nets and carrying only a gun. Equally unhelpful was his training as a gunner or in ship handling and navigation. Hugo and Robert at least knew the terrain intimately, like the veins on the backs of their hands but he was following blindly.

Soon Robert pulled the car over and parked it in a clump of low, scrubby trees. From here on they were on foot. They got out of the car closing the doors softly and hefting their guns onto their shoulders. The night was just setting in and the sky was graphite dark, paler than the deep blackness of night and the moon was already rising giving an eerie pearly quality to the twilight. With Hugo leading the way the three of them walked silently through the reserve putting their feet down carefully and quietly. The occasional owl hooted and the cry of the bush baby floated out from the trees. The ceaseless whirr of crickets and cicadas sounded from the straw-dry grass and every so often a monkey chattered or a hyena howled. As they neared the waterhole where Hugo had said the elephants would be they could also hear the croaking of frogs. There was also a great shuffling and grunting noise from the elephants who suddenly came into view. Hugo counted them; the whole herd was there from big bull elephants to the smallest babies trotting alongside their mothers. Their great grey humps like distant hills, looked soft in the weird light of the night vision goggles as they shuffled about swinging their trunks, occasionally taking a drink of water, while their tusks were white and luminescent. Lawrence was thrilled by the sight of them. He had never been so close to an elephant without there being cage bars or without being in a car on a game drive. He suddenly felt very small and feeble compared to them. Strange to think that they were the ones who were vulnerable and needed protection. Robert whispered in his ear that they were not going any further as it might be dangerous to get any closer especially as they had young with them. He indicated some bushes where they could be hidden and from where they could keep watch over the elephants. They went and hunkered down under the bushes some of which were thorny with vicious spikes.

Hours went by. Lawrence lost interest in the elephants who weren't doing much. In his combat gear, heavy boots and balaclava, the heat was oppressive. Sweat trickled down his face making the balaclava damp and unpleasant. He shifted his position every few minutes so as not to get cramp taking care not to be speared by the thorns. He could see the others were feeling just as uncomfortable. He hadn't anticipated the hours of waiting and watching that might be involved. He was anxious to be doing something, anything. Bring it on he thought and then, no, don't, it could all go so horribly wrong. He fingered his gun worrying that he had had no practice at all in using it. It was an AK 47, the favourite gun of terrorists across the world not least because you could buy one for under £500. If they found it so easy to use so should he be able to manage it even though it was some time since he had been trained how to handle one. He remembered telling Jessica that he had never shot a person or animal. It was true, all his training had been target shooting. He couldn't imagine what it must feel like when you see a live being in front of you and then after you have fired your gun they drop to the ground and are stilled forever. He hoped that if or when the moment came he would be firing in self-defence and that in the adrenalin of the moment all squeamishness would evaporate. He could feel the sweat trickling down his back, was that from the heat of the night or was it due to nerves?

He looked at Hugo and thought about how he didn't seem to have any qualms. But then he was protecting his property and livelihood and had experience of shooting animals from when he had to put wounded creatures out of their misery. Strong motives. Useful practice. Robert was the same and in addition had years of experience behind him.

The moon was now fully up, a waning gibbous moon as Lawrence had predicted, it gave only just enough light to see shapes and outlines, an eerie silver, watery light. The three men were well hidden crouching in the darkness of the bushes.

Over on the western perimeter Colonel Buckley and some of his men were also watching and waiting. They too were tense and uncomfortable wondering what the outcome of the night would be. Colonel Buckley knew he couldn't go in to the fight, if there was one, because of his prosthetic leg but he could still shoot with his one good eye and could advise and encourage his men from the back. The men came from different parts of Kenya, drafted in through advertisements telling them what an exciting, important job they would be doing and guaranteeing an income that hopefully rivalled what the poachers made so that they would not be tempted to switch allegiance. The colonel knew he could trust his men. He had trained them and formed bonds with them, getting to know their families, taking an interest in their children. He was a man the rangers respected. He knew that those he had sent to the other access point to the south of the reserve could be trusted to stay with Inspector Wanjiku and support him.

Meanwhile Wanjiku and his group including Mwangi were watching beside another waterhole favoured by rhinoceroses. So far that night they hadn't seen any but still they watched and waited. Sure enough some hours later two rhinos lumbered up breathing heavily, snorting and grunting as they came. Their big prehistoric heads and horns were silhouetted against the moonlight. Buckley's men warned Wanjiku and Mwangi to stay very still. They were the ones with experience of wildlife and they knew that a rhinoceros can attack for no apparent reason. With poor eye sight rhinos rely on a sense of smell and of hearing so it was best to stay behind a tree or bush and make no sound at all. The two rhinos paddled in the shallows of the watering hole and bent down to drink after which they shuffled back up the bank and began grazing. They seemed very tranquil and untroubled. But Mwangi had his ears alert for any sounds that were not of the night and its creatures, all the while wondering how, if the rhinos had such poor eyesight they could find their way around in the dark.

Back at the house Sylvie was feeling sad. She had hardly seen Hugo before he rushed away with the other men and he had scarcely stopped to say goodbye. He seemed to just disappear into a forest of dark, camouflage clad men. Cora re-assured her that Hugo did care for her and explained that he was often like that once he was focused on some mission or other especially if it was dangerous and involved guns. Jessica backed her up telling how Lawrence had been so tense the first time they had tried to track down the poachers that he could barely speak civilly. "I was very upset that time. I thought I had done something wrong. We hadn't quarrelled once since we've known each other and I felt hurt and confused when he snapped his replies at me. I spoke to Georgina about it who said pretty much what Cora has been telling you. Anyway, this time I kind of knew what to expect. We barely spoke to each other over the last two days."

Sylvie shrugged and lit another cigarette. Jenny bustled in at that moment with plates of sandwiches. "They rushed off like children on an adventure and they will be hungry when they come back. Then they'll appreciate us. Come on Sylvie, get some glasses out of the cupboard over there. They'll be thirsty too."

Like her mother Cora was all practicality. It was she that had sorted out the First Aid box and set Jessica to putting all the items they might need together in the study which was furnished with couches and had a bathroom right beside it. It also had the advantage of being close to the front door making it easier to carry in anyone wounded who couldn't walk... Now she went and fetched some plates and a bottle of wine. "Come on," she said holding up the bottle, "we may as well have a drink or two while we wait. It could be a long, long wait."

"The longer, the better," said Jessica, "if they come back too soon it will mean it has been another abortive attempt."

After filling their glasses they all went to sit on the veranda hoping to pass the time as pleasantly as possible, sipping the evening away and keeping their worries at bay. But they couldn't pretend for long that this was a normal social occasion. They were too well aware of the dangers the men were facing. Sylvie and Jessica especially, since they had first-hand experience of the brutality and callousness of the poachers.

Conversation waxed and waned like the moon and as the evening wore on they became convinced that tonight, unlike the last time, was no abortive attempt. Now they were beset by fears. At frequent intervals one or other of them would say "I wish we knew what was happening." Sylvie suggested phoning the men but the others told her they mustn't do that. Either it could alert the poachers if they heard a mobile ring or saw it light up, or if the men were already engaged in fighting or stalking, it could be a dangerous distraction. Waiting was the only option. "We will all have to be patient like Penelope," said Jessica.

"As long as you don't expect me to do any weaving," retorted Cora.

Jessica kept looking at the clock on her phone, hours seemed to have gone by, but every time she looked the digital display showed a difference of only ten minutes or so. There were times when she thought it might be going backwards. When she wasn't looking at the time, she was twisting the ring on her finger, the one that had been her mother's. Her finger was getting sore and red. "Oh, my God, when will we hear something? All of us sitting here food ready, beer in the fridge, plasters at the ready and our phones mute."

No-one answered. They were all thinking the same thing. And there was no answer. Jessica began to wish that she smoked, envying Sylvie who was constantly playing with her lighter and her packet of Gauloises, chain-smoking and pacing up and down the veranda. Cora was staring blankly into the darkness beyond the reach of the house lights as though expecting her brother, her father or one of the others to appear there. From time to time she squeezed her mother's hand. No-one wanted to drink any more, they were all sunk into their own nightmares. Jessica stood up and joining Sylvie began pacing like a caged lion. She looked for the hundredth time at the clock, it was nearly midnight. They went inside to the sitting room in an attempt to change the mood. Surely they should hear something soon.

Meanwhile out on the reserve squatting in their hideouts the men tried to move as little as possible for fear of making a noise that might spook the animals and give away their whereabouts to the poachers. Lawrence kept flexing his fingers and toes to try and ward off cramp. The shadows had shifted as the moon continued its journey across the gunpowder black sky. Now a noise was heard. There was an engine and men shouting. It seemed the poachers were not worried about being seen or heard. Lawrence looked at Hugo and Robert for the signal to start moving. They were both speaking quietly into their phones to tell Wanjiku and Buckley what the situation was.

Wanjiku and his team were to stay put in case there was a second group of the poachers going after the rhinos. Buckley and his men were to come directly to the elephants' water hole. Robert gave them the exact co-ordinates so that they could find their way. The poachers were still some distance away but seemed to be moving fast. Lawrence hoped that Buckley and his crew would reach them before the poachers did.

The engine noise was thrumming louder as the vehicles came closer. Then suddenly all was silent. The cars had stopped, engines switched off with one final throb. They could now hear the sound of heavy boots crashing through the bush, foliage rustling and twigs breaking. They could hear voices both English and Swahili. "Take it easy now. Go slowly. *Pole, pole.* You don't want to spook them."

Crouching in the scrubby bushes where they were hiding, Robert was waiting until he knew the poachers were within firing distance of the elephants. He knew they wouldn't want to get too close for fear of being trampled if the elephants charged. They would approach just close enough to be able to pepper them with bullets. He also knew exactly which elephant they would target. There was one big bull elephant who had huge, magnificent tusks that seemed to gleam in the moonlight and pierce the stars every time he raised his mighty head to look around. That would be the one they would want and once they had shot him and moved in to steal his tusks the rest of the herd would turn away and move off back to the open plains or they could trample everything, including them, in their path as they made a wild dash for safety. The trick was to catch the poachers just before they began shooting and to be out of the way of the herd when they moved off.

The voices were louder still. Robert reckoned the poachers were about one hundred yards away. In fifty yards he would have to give the signal to Hugo and Lawrence to attack. Where the hell is Buckley, he thought. It looks as though we will be completely outnumbered. Now he and Hugo and Lawrence could make out shadowy shapes moving towards them. They all three shifted their positions so as to be ready to spring up when the poachers reached the spot that Robert reckoned was fifty yards away. The moment came and Robert gave the signal to Hugo and Lawrence. "Now," he said in a loud, urgent whisper and all of them leapt up to confront the poachers. "Stop right there," shouted Robert as the man in front of the group lifted his gun to fire. Robert followed by Hugo and Lawrence all held their guns at the ready aiming at the group ahead of them. "Eh, meh, what you doing, *unafanya nini?*" shouted back the front man of the poachers. Before Robert could answer a voice from the back which Hugo and Lawrence recognised as Wiley's shouted "What the fuck are you doing? Shoot the buggers." At that moment another voice bellowed out into the night. "Oh no you don't. We've got you bastards covered." It was Buckley and his group of men much to the relief of Lawrence and the two with him. By now, with all the crashing about and shouting the elephants were nervous. The big bull lifted his trunk and trumpeted a great clarion call at which the whole herd turned and headed away from the watering hole crashing through the bush to safety out onto the dry starlit, moonlit plain. At that moment Wiley recognised Buckley. "Oh shit, it's you, Buckley! It seems we're on opposite sides here."

"You bet we are, you bastard. We always were. You may have changed your name, you bastard but you are as much of a bastard as you ever were Colin Simpson. Get over there with the rest of your bastard crowd."

"I guess you're going to screw me over once again."

"I hope you'll get what you deserve, you bastard piece of shit."

"Well, fuck you," replied Wiley as he was handcuffed.

Buckley's helicopter which he had called as he walked towards the watering hole arrived at that moment whirring, thrumming, throwing up a dust storm and ruffling the water. It also frightened away the animals for several miles around. It landed near where Buckley and the others had herded the poachers together to be taken into custody. The pilot jumped out and walked over to the group hitching up his trousers as he went and wanting to know 'who was for the chopper', "No pun intended, mate," he laughed as he spoke in a strong Australian accent. The two who were to go in the helicopter with one of the anti-poaching rangers standing guard were Rod Wiley and Kahinde, both now in handcuffs; Buckley considered them to be the most dangerous and so the first to be 'sent packing'. "They are the real bastards, these others are cannon fodder, bastard minnows in a pond too big for them."

Among the men, the minnows, that were waiting to be taken in one of the trucks was Jaba. He stood looking at his captors with a sneering look on his face and when told to get into the waiting vehicle he spat a great ball of spittle onto the ground right by Buckley's foot. Buckley laughed at him, "It's OK, That is my prosthetic leg. That foot doesn't feel a thing."

The minnows were hand-cuffed and packed into one of Buckley's vehicles and taken to Jaribuni Jail under the watchful eye of two more rangers. Buckley himself stayed with Robert, Hugo and Lawrence. "We'd better check up on

Wanjiku and Mwangi." Lawrence pulled out his mobile to ring them. There was no answer.

"This could mean they're in trouble," declared Buckley. "We'd better get over there as soon as possible. Where is your car?"

"About a mile away," replied Hugo. "We didn't want to scare off either the elephants or the poachers with our engine noise."

"Quite right, quite right. Obviously, I can't run with this bastard leg of mine. You two must run and fetch the car, pick up us two as quick as you can." Robert handed over the car keys and Lawrence and Hugo set off running, their breath coming in great painful spurts. The ground was rough with clumps of plants, tussocks of grass, trailing vines and snake holes as well as dry ravines or small water channels, the *mitaro midogo,* formed by rain running off the hard earth, all ready to trip a person up and there was very little light to see the hazards. The two men also worried that there could be animals who would see them as a threat and attack to defend themselves. After a few trips and bumps they made it to the car and were back with Buckley and Robert in no time. Buckley had tried several times to contact Wanjiku and Mwangi while he was waiting but there was still no answer. He and Robert quickly clambered into the car followed by the rest of the men who all piled into the car as best they could some of them clinging on to the outside. They headed straight for the other watering hole where the rhinos went. "Rhinos like to be alone," Hugo explained to Lawrence.

"Slow down as we get close," Robert told Hugo, "we don't know what situation we might find there." Hugo eased off on the throttle as all four men peered into the grey darkness for signs of activity.

"I thought I heard something," said Lawrence.

"Listen." Hugo switched the engine off and they all listened intently. Suddenly shots rang out.

"That's it, go in fast!" yelled Buckley. Hugo stamped on the gas pedal making the car leap forward with such force that they were all thrown back in their seats. "OK, OK, steady on, man," said Buckley. Within minutes they were at the waterhole where they could see Wanjiku and his men confronting the poachers. "At least we can even the numbers up, let's go guys. Let's get the bastards. Go round behind them, then we've got them covered on both sides." Lawrence, Hugo and Robert leapt out of the car and ran to get behind the poachers while Buckley limped after them.

Wanjiku and Mwangi with the rest of Buckley's men were between the poachers and the rhinos. As the poachers fired again at them, one man went down wounded in the leg. Mwangi ran in under a fresh hail of bullets to drag him to safety out of the line of fire and away from the rhinos. Lawrence was unnerved by the screams of the injured man but soon began firing alongside the others to attack the poachers from the rear. They now had to fight on two fronts. Soon one of them was wounded too, he took a bullet in his chest. As Buckley and the others closed in on the poachers from behind, the rhinos were snorting in anger and pawing at the ground. Lawrence began to manoeuvre to the side to try and take the poachers unawares while they were focused on Wanjiku in front of them and Buckley behind. One of the poachers nearest to him saw him approach. He tried to fire but for some reason the gun failed, he threw it to one side impatiently and rushed at Lawrence pulling a panga from his belt. Lawrence managed to stop the raised arm, knocking the panga out of his hand but the man now threw a punch to Lawrence's jaw which knocked him sideways briefly. Kicking the panga away, Lawrence punched back in the man's solar plexus. As he doubled over struggling for breath, Lawrence caught hold of his arm and twisted it behind his back. The man fell to his knees and Buckley threw Lawrence some handcuffs. Just as he secured the man to a nearby tree the rhinos had finally had enough and charged thundering across the ground towards Wanjiku's group. Lawrence suddenly noticed that Mwangi, all unawares was right in their path. It was as though a tank was roaring towards him out of control. Lawrence made a dive for Mwangi and succeeded in knocking him down, and rolling him out of the way of several tons of rhino. The remaining poachers seeing the rhinos charging and realising that they were losing their fight, were now trying to make a run for it. Mwangi, Lawrence and Hugo gave chase. Crashing through the bush again they gave no thought to the dangers under foot of trailing vines, snake holes and other trip hazards. The lead man caught his foot in a rabbit hole and fell headlong. The others ran straight over the top of him. Mwangi stopped to arrest him while Lawrence and Hugo carried on in hot pursuit of the others. And it was very hot. Both men could feel the sweat pouring down their backs as they ran, jumping over low bushes and holes in the ground. They very soon caught up with the poachers and stopped them at gunpoint. One of the men fired at Lawrence and Lawrence fired back, a knee-jerk reaction. The man dropped dead in front of them. Hugo, Lawrence and the remaining poachers all stopped still in shock. To Lawrence it was as if time stood still. Suddenly the African night was silent, it was as if nature herself held her breath. He felt hollowed out, as if part of his soul had gone with the dead man. But he had no time to think as Hugo urged him on and they organised the men they had captured to carry their dead friend back to the waterhole to be arrested along with their fellow minnows.

Hugo and Lawrence with the two poachers that they had captured and the dead man arrived back at the rhino's water hole where Buckley, Wanjiku and Mwangi were checking on the two wounded men. Mwangi took off his shirt and tore it up to make a bandage of sorts for his friend's leg. Buckley had already called up Jacques who now arrived in his helicopter amid a loud whirring of blades. With the arrival of the 'copter they now had some first aid equipment so they used some of the wadding to staunch the blood pouring from the poacher's chest wound. Buckley's main concern was to get the poachers into custody as quickly as possible. Jacques helped him get them into the helicopter. There was no room for any more. Buckley and the others were shocked when Lawrence and Hugo arrived with two men arrested and one dead. It was decided that the dead man should go in the back of one of the cars going to Zinj House.

"I'll come back to Zinj House with you. Mwangi can go in the helicopter to keep *ces connards* under control," suggested Jacques. "What about the two wounded men?" asked Buckley concerned for his man rather than for the poacher who was bleeding profusely from his chest. Robert immediately suggested they should go in the cars back to his house where they would be given First Aid by Jenny and Cora and made as comfortable as possible before being driven to hospital by Wanjiku.

Back at Zinj House the women had moved indoors and were increasingly anxious. By now it was one o'clock in the morning. The sandwiches were drying and curling at the corners. They were also extremely tired with waiting and wondering. Jessica yawned and stretched for the hundredth time saying, "It's amazing how you can stay up all night partying without any problem at all but sitting up like this with nothing to do but fret, I struggle to keep my eyes open." Sylvie, the party girl par excellence, agreed. "Me, I have passed whole nights without going to bed many times, but always laughing, dancing, drinking. It's OK," she finished with a shrug of her shoulders. "And smoking," added Jessica with a smile. "Don't forget the smoking." Sylvie merely smiled, gave another gallic shrug and lit yet another Gauloise.

Cora said, "Well, I'm no party girl like you two but I have sat up all night caring for sick or orphaned animals. It's true, while you have something positive to focus on, you can do it. Just sitting around like this it's very hard to stay awake."

"Shush," said Jenny. "I think I can hear a car." They all fell silent and sure enough a car engine could be heard increasing in volume as it approached the house. It was followed by two more all cutting their engines just outside. Jessica picked up the pistol that Buckley had given them for protection in case they came under attack. She undid the safety catch, very afraid that the cars might not be the ones they hoped for. Seconds later they recognised the voices of their menfolk. Lawrence was first across the threshold but he stopped hard when he saw that Jessica had a gun pointing at him. She laughed at the look on his face and reassured him that she had put the safety catch back on explaining that when they heard the cars they weren't sure who it was.

"Well, it's us, as you see all safe and sound," Lawrence said as he approached her and gently took the pistol away to put it down in a safe place. Only then did they embrace and Jessica was able to tell him how glad she was that he was safe. They held each other close for a long time though Lawrence flinched with the pain from his bruises and his battered jaw. The others were also greeting their loved ones. Cora and Jenny were quite conflicted between hugging Hugo and hugging Robert while Sylvie also wanted to hug and kiss Hugo. Wanjiku and Buckley stood back grinning while all the osculation was going on, pleased to see the love and happiness that was now palpable in the room and flushed with the success of their mission.

They soon reminded the others about the two wounded men. With the help of Hugo and Lawrence they brought the casualties into the house. Cora and Jenny leapt into action showing the men into the study where the two couches were prepared and first aid equipment ranged in the adjacent bathroom making everything ready for cleaning the wounds and bandaging the men up prior to sending them to hospital. Leaving the wounded to the women to care for, the men all went to tuck into the sandwiches and much needed glasses of beer. Sylvie and Jessica stayed close to Hugo and Lawrence and made it their business to see that all the glasses were kept topped up. Buckley raised his glass in a toast, "Here's to you guys. Well done. A good job. Brilliant." Robert and Hugo thanked everyone for saving the Zinj elephants and rhinos. "Even if it is only one or two animals on one occasion that are saved it is worth doing. Today at least two magnificent beasts were saved from slaughter."

"And," added Jessica with a catch in her voice, "it may be that we have found the rest of the men who burnt down my home and raped my mother." Lawrence moved close to her and put his arm round her waist, "Let's hope so. Let's hope this will bring your ordeal to an end."

Wanjiku went to see how the first aid was going. He was anxious to return to Jaribuni, deliver the men to the hospital and go home to his family who he knew would be worried about him. Jessica went with him to see if any help was needed. Cora and Jenny between them had cleaned the wounds and put fresh bandages on so the two men were ready to be taken to hospital. The two men were talking, the poacher whose name was Manda was telling the injured policeman that he had had nothing to do with the attack on Jessica's family. "I know nothing about that," he asserted. "I am poacher, not murderer."

Once Wanjiku had left with the two men it was time for everyone to go home. Before he left Buckley suggested that they should meet the next day to talk through the operation and to find out from the police what proceedings they were going to take. Lawrence and Jessica had left their car outside the house so they set off promptly. Lawrence couldn't wait to get in the shower to wash away all the sweat and dirt of the night's exertions and slip into cool, clean sheets with Jessica beside him. Jessica too was desperate to get home and for the two of them to be alone without the nervous tension of the last few days.

They crept quietly into the house, or at least that was the plan but the dogs thought otherwise. A volley of barking fit to wake the dead greeted them as they opened the front door. Lawrence and Jessica froze in their tracks and sure enough John soon appeared at the top of the stairs looking tousled and sleepy and toting a gun, "Just in case," he told them. They soon reassured him that all was well and he went straight back to bed. Lawrence and Jessica went into their room where Jennifer treated Lawrence with arnica for his bruises after his shower. And they were soon in bed. "I was so frightened that I would lose you, like I lost my parents," Jessica admitted as they lay holding each other tightly. "Don't worry, I'm here now and I still love you," murmured Lawrence. "I love you too," replied Jessica as they both fell fast asleep.

People wake early in Africa to enjoy the day when it is at its coolest and freshest seeming to promise so much. Jessica woke soon after sunrise as usual that morning, stretching and luxuriating in the knowledge that she and Lawrence no longer had anything to fear. The sun was already up and creeping across the room, strands of light threaded through the slats of the shutters. She lay for a while watching Lawrence as he slept. He must be exhausted she thought looking at his classical features, his roman nose, the curve of his lips, his fine dark eyebrows and long black eyelashes, longing to kiss him. Soon he woke up too, his deep blue eyes clearing of sleep, he kissed her tenderly then leapt out of bed saying "God, I'm famished. A few measly sandwiches is not very sustaining when you have such a hard night. Let's go down to breakfast. I expect Georgina's staff have it all laid out ready." But Jessica wasn't ready to go downstairs just yet. "Come back to bed," she urged, "I want to enjoy the morning with you now that we seem to be without a care in the world for the first time in weeks." Sometime later the two of them finally went downstairs to have breakfast on the veranda where Georgina and John were still sitting over their tea enjoying the view of the creek with the boats slowly going about their business, the fish eagle soaring and the blue flash of kingfishers darting into the water on fishing expeditions. Jessica sank back onto the sofa with all its colourful cushions reflecting the vivid hues of the many flowers, hibiscus, geraniums, bougainvillea in pink, purple, orange and white breathing in the sweet yet spicy scent of frangipani whose creamy, waxy blossoms showed delicate against their leathery dark green leaves. For the first time she was able to truly concentrate on the beauty of the flowers, the view of the water and the antics of the creatures that made their home in the garden and around the creek.

John and Georgina were keen to hear all about the operation against the poachers and Lawrence was happy to tell them. It all seemed to have gone so smoothly. Georgina and John congratulated him on his part in the successful arrest of the poachers. "So what's next?" asked John. "What will you do for entertainment now that all the excitement is over?"

"It's not quite over yet. We have a meeting with the others again today to talk about the operation, in particular why it ended with one man dead. Also we need to find out from Inspector Wanjiku what he is going to do next. Will they be able to prosecute the poachers especially Wiley?"

"Also," added Jessica, "we may have caught them for poaching but we still have to find out who torched my family home and murdered my parents, not to mention their staff."

"Who died and who killed him?" asked John and Georgina in shocked unison. Lawrence began to look uncomfortable. "I'm afraid I was the one that fired the shot. The man was one of the poachers."

"So I don't feel at all sorry," said Jessica. "He could have been among those who attacked my home and family, especially my mother."

"How do you feel Lawrence?" asked John.

Lawrence shrugged and looked away but while the two women were talking together about how it felt to be waiting all that time knowing the danger the men were in, John, anxious about his grandson, repeated his question.

"I have to admit it is playing on my mind," explained Lawrence. "I have never shot at a live target before. He shot at me first, so it was an instant reaction, a moment of retaliation, revenge, if you like. It didn't feel good. All those cowboy film images of smoking guns, all those Bond films where he kills and moves on without blinking an eye – the reality isn't like that. Or maybe it is after you have killed several victims. I just feel I left something of myself behind on the savannah last night. You must have experienced something similar in the war?"

"I was a very young soldier in the second world war. I don't know if I killed anyone, it was all too remote. In the Korean war I came face to face with a young Korean soldier who fired at me. Like you, I automatically fired back. He crumpled to the ground, then lay lifeless in a spreading pool of blood. I was horrified. Soldiers from my company pulled me away otherwise I think I would have been standing there, transfixed, staring till this day. I left part of me on that field, as you put it. It doesn't make you any less of a man to feel that way, quite the reverse. Just as fear doesn't make you a coward, horror of death doesn't make you a wimp. Just a human being."

"Wise words," said Jessica coming over and putting her arms around Lawrence. "In any case, he is my hero. Has he told you how he saved Mwangi from being trampled by a rhino?"

After that story had been told it was time to head for Denton's place and the 'wash-up' meeting as Buckley called it.

Hugo and Cora, together with Jacques and Sylvie arrived at the same time as Lawrence and Jessica. Buckley was already there. For the meeting, instead of the usual coffee, Denton laid on champagne, the best he could find in Jaribuni's only booze shop, run by an Indian named Sampat, it was dark and dingy and had a dry spicy smell like wood chippings but the champagne was as good as anywhere. Glasses raised, James Denton gave the toast to the rangers and all those helping them before telling them that the news of their successful raid against the poachers was already in the papers and on websites. While he was talking the phone rang and everyone fell silent while he listened and responded with many polite expressions of thanks to the speaker at the other end. Everyone wanted to know who it was and he announced there and then that it was none other than Uhuru Kenyatta wanting to congratulate them and thank them. After that they all got down to the business of what had worked well and what could they have done better in the middle of which Wanjiku and Mwangi arrived. A glass of champagne was pressed into their hands and everyone hurried to tell them about the phone call from the president. "Ah, yes," said Wanjiku. "I too have had a call from the president to congratulate us. It is important that we keep this news in the papers and websites so that people don't forget what is happening out here." Now innumerable questions burst on his ears. Everyone wanted to know what had happened since last night. He told them that the men who had been arrested were all being questioned and he had no further news until that process had been completed and charges brought.

"I hope you fix the bastards good and proper," declared Buckley.

"We will do our best to get a fair result," was Wanjiku's diplomatic reply. Then turning to Jessica he told her that all the men would have to undergo a DNA test to see if any of them had been involved in the attack on her parents.

"What have they been saying? Are they admitting anything?" Wanjiku sighed, he too was anxious to find the culprits.

"So far they are admitting nothing. All of them say they had nothing to do with it. But I am sure we will find them out when we get the DNA test results. Also the two whom we arrested when your friend Hugo was shot and Jessica attacked – we already know they are friends of Jaba so they are highly suspect."

"It will be good to have answers, to have closure as the cliché goes," replied Jessica.

"I will call you to let you know what has been discovered," promised Wanjiku.

"But you seemed to know this Rod Wiley," interposed Hugo turning to Buckley. "You had quite an exchange of insults I seem to remember,"

"That's right. I did. I hadn't seen him here and the bastard has obviously changed his identity so I thought nothing of it until last night when we came face to face out there on the reservation. We have history as people say. His name was Colin Simpson. We were in the same regiment in Iraq and Afghanistan but I discovered that he was secretly trading drugs and girls. I didn't report him immediately, I investigated to make sure I could nail him with the right evidence. As soon as I had the information I needed I went to the Colonel and put it all in front of him. There was a court-martial and he was stripped of his rank and sent packing from the army."

"That would explain it. So he's always been a piece of shit," said Lawrence.

"Yup, a complete bastard," replied Buckley. "Well, that's it time to go, I think."

After saying their goodbyes they all went their separate ways. James Denton went back to his quiet social life and planning his next sailing trip, Buckley was looking out for another anti-poacher operation; there had been news of poachers taking game on the Somali border. Jacques was heading back to Nairobi to continue his business meetings while Hugo and Sylvie were returning to Zinj Safari Camp.

As they were leaving Lawrence suggested that they should go to the boatyard for a drink with Jessica and himself. He felt they needed to let Jonathan know the outcome of the night's activities.

At the boatyard they found Jonathan deep in conversation at the bar with none other than Annabelle. Jessica was disgusted, "I hope she isn't trying to weasel her way back to him," she whispered to Lawrence. "I hope so too," he replied, "she has behaved pretty badly but we had better be polite to begin with in case she is coming back to him."

As they approached quietly through the soft sand they soon became aware that the conversation was not going well but they couldn't quite work out what was happening. Hugo, Cora and Sylvie caught up with them. "What's going on?" they wanted to know. Jessica shrugged. She and Lawrence said hello to Jonathan and then to Annabelle who turned up her nose and walked away. Good riddance thought Jessica but Jonathan seemed upset.

"Hello Jonathan, remember me," said Sylvie greeting him with an enthusiastic kiss.

"Course I do," he replied hugging her tight. Then he greeted Cora and Jessica with a kiss too.

"Drinks all round?" asked Lawrence, trying to lighten the mood. Once they were all settled with their drinks he asked Jonathan what was happening.

"That bloody woman. She came to see if I would forgive her, if she could come back. I just sent her packing. I could forgive her ordinarily if she had simply strayed, you know, fancied someone else for a bit, after all we weren't married or anything. I can't forgive her for going with that man, a poacher and for all we know a murderer and even worse from what you have told me it sounds as though she informed on you to him when you had your first raid. That is too much, man, too much, trouble is I still love her," he said shaking his head. "I suppose she should be arrested as an accessory, or is that handbags and shoes? Whatever the word is she helped a bunch of criminals but I can't find it in me to shop her to the police."

"So where has she gone now? She seemed to be heading for your house," asked Jessica. "Oh, she's picking up the remainder of her stuff."

"Well, good riddance, I say," declared Lawrence.

"But you guys should be celebrating," said Jonathan suddenly. "I hear that last night was a great success." Turning to the barman he called "Hey Jaali, bring some champagne and glasses. We'll have a toast. So how are you all doing now? Are you happy Sylvie?"

"Oh yes, I think I have found my man," she smiled and put her arm around Hugo who kissed her forehead.

"Good, great. Paul seems to be quite happy too with his new girlfriend though I haven't met her properly yet." "What about you Cora? I liked that guy you brought here, Daniel somebody or other."

"Daniel Parker," corrected Cora, "he's back in London but promises me he will come to visit soon."

Jessica snorted loudly, "Don't hold your breath," she blurted out.

Sylvie suddenly said, "It reminds me of a rhyme I learned as an enfant. My grandfather taught it me. He loved Juliette Gréco and I think she sang it. Let me see, it goes like this.

219

Un petit poisson et un petit oiseau,
S'aimaient d'amour tendre,
Mais comment s'y prendre,
Quand on est dans l'eau.
Un petit poisson et un petit oiseau,
S'aimaient d'amour tendre,
Mais comment s'y prendre,
Quand on est là-haut,
Voilà.

"What does that mean?" asked Jonathan.

Jessica quickly translated – "A little fish and a little bird were in love, but how could that be when one lives in the water, the other in the sky."

"It is a problem for us," admitted Cora. "He is in London and wants to stay there, I am here and want to stay here. It looks like long-distance love for us."

"I suppose it's no worse than for people in the forces or in the merchant navy. There are many couples who cannot be together all the time," said Lawrence trying to be reassuring.

"What about you two?" enquired Cora. "How will you work things out?"

"I intend to stay here in Kenya," declared Jessica. "It has been the scene of my greatest tragedy but also of my happiest times. It's up to Lawrence what he decides to do but it would make me very happy if we could be together forever."

Lawrence reached out and took Jessica's hand. "I am thinking I could make this my home. I have been coming here every year since I was a teenager and once you know Africa it takes a hold of you. I would have to keep travelling back to UK for business reasons but so much can be done on line that I don't need to live there permanently."

"So it's Africa that you are in love with, not Jessica." Jonathan laughed.

Lawrence shrugged and laughed too. "Of course it's staying with Jessica that is most important. She has stolen not only my heart but also my soul."

"Wow, very romantic!" exclaimed Cora.

"You mean she's got hold of you by the *cojones*," said Hugo, lowering the tone but making everyone laugh.

Epilogue

Now that all danger seemed to have passed Jessica was starting to look for somewhere of her own to live, somewhere that Lawrence would also feel happy to settle. Georgina was very helpful as she knew so many people; some of whom had properties to let. It felt good to be focusing on something positive, a move towards a future for herself and Lawrence. All the while however she was also fretting about getting a resolution to the tragic events. Had Wanjiku found out who was responsible for the attack on her parent's? What would happen to the people he had arrested? Would she have to give evidence in a court of law? Would Lawrence and the others have to give evidence? All these questions spun around in the back of her mind while she went about house hunting.

Even so, she had come to a decision. She was determined to build another house on the farm and to set up businesses. She was sure that Zarifa and Durah would be glad to work with her and earn themselves some money. Her business plans included a honey farm, a leather workshop and, knowing that Durah could sew, a textile shop, not clothes but cushion covers and table cloths and other such things for the house.

At last Wanjiku contacted her. He arranged to come to the house and wanted to make sure that Lawrence or Georgina would be with her. He remembered how distressed she became last time he told her that they had caught two of the men involved in the death of her parents. He was sure that she would need support when she heard the news this time.

On being asked to have Lawrence or Georgina with her when Wanjiku came to talk to her Jessica's heart was full of fear, lurching and pounding against her ribs, leaving her like a piece of rag snagged on barbed wire twisting and turning in the wind. She had to endure a whole day and a night of waiting and agonising. Lawrence promised he would stay with her when Wanjiku came which reassured her a little but nothing could stop the whirling of her mind with its nagging questions.

The day that Wanjiku came was grey and cloudy. Everyone was talking hopefully about rain. Everywhere was bone dry and brittle from weeks of hot weather. Lawns were parched and water tanks empty. Some families had had to resort to getting bowsers to deliver water. Rain was needed. Wanjiku arrived amid the usual cacophony created by the dogs. He was sweating profusely in the oppressive heat, mopping his brow with a large colourful handkerchief. *"Jambo Bwana."* Lawrence met him at the door and led him into the sitting room where Jessica was waiting, twisting her ring round and round her finger which seemed to have become a habit with her when she was nervous or anxious, just as her mother used to do. Lawrence offered to get them both a drink and then he and Jessica settled down on the sofa to hear what Wanjiku had to say.

Wanjiku took a large slurping sip of his lemonade before he began. Then with a deep sigh explained that he was going to begin with the easy part. He told Jessica first that he had questioned Rod Wiley and the poachers extensively and all had denied any knowledge of the attack on her parents. He had also arrested Derek Foster on suspicion of being involved with the poaching but it seemed that his only connection with Rod was friendship. However, his connection with Kahinde was more interesting. Kahinde and he had been dealing drugs, in his case covering-up by use of his gold dealing business. Then he had not been able to extricate himself when he no longer needed the money from drugs. His gold dealing business was going well but Kahinde now had a hold over him threatening to make public their association and business dealings. It would have ruined him. Kahinde needed to keep the partnership going so that he had some way of laundering his drugs cash. His reason for kidnapping Sylvie had been that he needed extra money to buy into the poaching cartel as a partner, not a mere gofer. Meanwhile he was being paid by Rod Wiley to follow you to try and recover any evidence your father may have had about his poaching activities and Jaba, a heavy user of cocaine, heroin, ecstasy, anything he could get hold of, was one of Kahinde's 'clients' who told him about the file that your father had.

"So what about the attack on me at the farm? Was it Rod Wiley who ordered that?"

"No, he did want you to be followed and to retrieve the documents he believed you had but Ali was acting alone in attacking you. It was an opportunistic attack."

"Oh, that's awful," shuddered Jessica.

"If Rod Wiley and Kahinde weren't involved in the murder of my parents, who was?"

"I thought you were going to test them all for DNA?" she queried.

"I'm just coming to that," replied Wanjiku. "That is the hard part to explain and to hear."

Jessica listened with every nerve and sinew, leaning forward so as not to miss a word. At last she was getting answers, getting close to the truth. She tensed herself for what was coming next and Lawrence took hold of her hand to reassure her but she shrugged him off impatiently wanting to focus entirely on what the inspector had to say.

"We tested all the men for DNA as I told you we would. There is no trace of Rod Wiley, Kahinde or Derek Foster at the scene of your parent's death. There are no DNA matches and no footprints."

Jessica breathed in deeply. "OK, did you find anything at all?"

"Yes, we know of course that the man arrested when your friend was shot and the one that attacked you were matches for the DNA found on your mother's body…" Jessica breathed in again and held her breath, clenching her jaw… "that left three men unaccounted for." This time it was Jessica who grabbed hold of Lawrence's hand and held on tight. "I believe we now have those three men in custody. One of them is Jaba, the other two are friends of his from the poaching gang. He had promised them that there would be plenty of valuable things to steal and that they would make a fortune from selling it all. Jaba wanted revenge against your father for dismissing him but also against white people in general because his grandfather had passed his own obsessive hatred on to him." Jessica fell back against the cushions and leaned on Lawrence's shoulder, her eyes shut, as she took in this new information. The vision of the scene that she had stumbled into all those weeks ago came back to her in all its vivid horror, the burnt out house, the poor dogs, horses and cattle and above all, the mutilated and wretched bodies of her people. Lawrence held her tight as Wanjiku continued his story.

"So, we talked to the man at the shop in Mombasa where you found the ring. We showed him photographs of the three men and he identified Jaba as being the one who sold him your mother's ring. He did not recognise the other two but they may have sold things elsewhere or in the case of the guns, kept them. We have been out to search their homes and found some guns that we need you to identify."

Jessica nodded her agreement but added, "I know very little about guns. You might find that James Denton or Robert Patterson-Smythe would recognise them more readily. They were friends of my father's and went shooting with him occasionally."

"What about Inspector Mona? Have you found his killer?"

"Ah, yes, sorry, I forgot. It hasn't been easy coming to tell you all this knowing how much distress it would cause you. Now the man who killed Inspector Mona was Ali, Kahinde's man, the one who attacked you at your farm. The Inspector had found out about their drug dealing."

"I am so sad about him and sorry for his family. He was so very kind to me and I think he worked hard too," said Jessica.

"He was a good man," agreed the Inspector. "Now you know everything, I will leave you to comfort each other."

"What happens next? Will we be witnesses?"

"Next we charge these monsters with what they've done. The lawyers will build their case and yes, you will be asked to give witness statements both to the murders and to the poaching."

"What will happen to them all after that?"

"If the prosecution lawyers do their job well and they are all convicted they will all go to prison for a very long time. Although Rod Wiley, or rather Colin Simpson as he is actually may have clever lawyers who will make sure he pays a fine rather than going to prison."

"Now that I know he wasn't implicated in any way with my parent's death I don't feel he is deserving of any extra punishment."

"I will try to make sure he is treated with the full power of the law," Wanjiku promised.

After Wanjiku left Jessica said in a quiet voice, "I can't believe that I worried so much about Jaba and felt sad that he might have been kidnapped or caught and killed somewhere when all along he was one of the murderers. And how is James Denton going to feel when he knows that it was the man that he introduced to my father who was behind the horrific attack?"

"You couldn't possibly have known about Jaba back then. It's not something you should beat yourself up about," Lawrence told her.

"But when you think that my father took him on to try and help him in life, it's all so wrong, pure evil."

"They say time heals all yet when you look at the world you see how hatred and resentment is passed down the generations. I think that Jaba was made to feel the way he did from living with his grandfather's obsession. No-one can deny that some terrible things were done in the colonial era but there were good things too. Education, decent medicine, roads and railways, communication."

Jessica laughed. "You sound like that Monty Python thing, you know, 'What did the Romans ever do for us?'"

"Well, Ok, maybe, but life has moved on and we all need to – not forget but – forgive, to reconcile and come together as human beings."

"Ancestral memories– very powerful. Perhaps not on the same level, but I know my pupils when I started teaching French used to say 'oh, Miss, the French ran way in the war'. Their grandfathers were too young to have fought in the war, in some cases their great-grandfathers, but the myth carries on."

"There seems to be no answer, perhaps we should follow Voltaire's advice and simply cultivate our own gardens."

"E.B.White, do you know him, he wrote *Charlotte's Web*, a book I often read with the children, well, he wrote a letter to someone who was despairing of the human race saying roughly 'Tomorrow is another day and I shall wind the clock as my contribution to order and steadfastness'. I think that's what we all need, order and steadfastness. And now that I have some kind of closure, as they call it, I can move on. I will wind the clock. I am moving on."